Boy Gone

OTHER BOOKS BY MWM

Scrapyard Ship Series
Scrapyard Ship (Book 1)
HAB 12 (Book 2)
Space Vengeance (Book 3)
Realms of Time (Book 4)
Craing Dominion (Book 5)
The Great Space (Book 6)
Call To Battle (Book 7)

Tapped In Series
Mad Powers (Book 1)
Deadly Powers (Book 2)

Lone Star Renegades Series
Lone Star Renegades (also called 'Jacked') (Book 1)

Star Watch Series
Star Watch (Book 1)
Ricket (Book 2)
Boomer (Book 3)
Glory for Space Sea and Space (Book 4)
Space Chase (Book 5)
Scrapyard LEGACY (Book 6)

The Simpleton Series
The Simpleton (Book 1)
The Simpleton Quest (Book 2)

Galaxy Man Series
Galaxy Man (Book 1)

Ship Wrecked Series
Ship Wrecked (Book 1)

BOY GONE

Mark Wayne McGinnis

Published by:
Avenstar Productions

ISBN: 978-0-9992147-6-3

To join Mark's mailing list, jump to:
http://eepurl.com/bs7M9r

Visit Mark Wayne McGinnis at:
http://www.markwaynemcginnis.com

PART I
Ways Of The Human

chapter 1

Sixteen years ago ... Nantucket, Mass.

The silver G-Class Mercedes Benz SUV glided up the driveway and came to a gentle rolling stop, directly in front of the sprawling, colonial-style, beachfront home. It was a surprisingly warm Memorial Day weekend and the family of five, along with their dog, clamored out of the Mercedes. Even at nine years old, Scotty knew the drill—no one goes into the house empty-handed. All five lugged their suitcases into the front foyer, dropped them there, then hurried back to retrieve what seemed like an endless supply of filled plastic Stop and Shop bags.

Ten minutes later, wearing a grape juice-stained tank top—and, with the assistance of his mom, who'd rolled up the cuffs of his jeans—Scotty Sullivan was back outside. An unruly towheaded boy, with bright blue, mischievous eyes, he stormed toward the beach—excited to be out of the house, away from his cranky little sister and bossy older brother. Scotty glanced up at the darkening sky. A warm sea breeze was blowing onshore from the southeast. Choppy ocean wavelets, dancing in the distant Atlantic, were a magnificent glimmering spectacle, but one that soon would be ignored by the exuberant boy, now storming toward the distant surf.

Scotty and his siblings visited their family vacation home every year since he could remember, sometimes twice, maybe even three times, each year. He figured today there would be fewer crowds on the beach—the typical Nantucket Island vacationers—since officially it wasn't even summertime yet. So, for the most part, their late afternoon beachside frolicking belonged to the two of them.

"Come on, boy!" Scotty yelled over his shoulder without looking back. He knew Larry would follow him. The three-year-old golden retriever mix, named after Larry Fine, from The Three Stooges, never strayed too far off. Never left his side for more than a few minutes before lumbering back to check on him.

Scotty crested the tallest of the sandy dunes, squinting against the wind- blowing sand. He surveyed the beach for any sign of others but found the seashore completely deserted. Fast-running strides, along with the heavy sound of panting behind him, brought the boy's attention back to his lumbering dog. A stick—twisted and smoothed from years of floating adrift at sea—protruded from both sides of Larry's open, gaping muzzle.

"Hey, give me that!" Scotty demanded, tugging the three-foot-long piece of driftwood from the dog's reluctant jaws.

Taking ahold of it at one end, he held it tightly within two clenched fists and he made the accompanying sounds, "*Voop, voop, voooop!*" The makeshift light saber moved smoothly within his well practiced—left to right, then right to left—arcing sweeps.

Now, with the intergalactic weapon held high overhead, both boy and dog were off—charging through bunched tufts of beach grass, then down the slope of another sandy bluff toward the calling surf, some fifty yards away.

Scotty hadn't remembered how strange it felt for the cool wet sand to slosh beneath his sneakers from his visit there the summer before. Nine months' time seemed an immense span of time for one as young as nine. He ran right into the chilly surf then let out a scream, surprised when a somewhat higher wave crashed into him, nearly bowling him over. Scotty flung the stick toward the next approaching high swell, laughing aloud for no particular reason.

It occurred to Scotty that Larry had been barking pretty much non-stop for a while now. Typically, he didn't mind his dog's incessant barking. The silly animal barked at just about anything—the dorky paperboy, riding his old Schwinn bike too close to the house, a high-pitched sound that only a dog could hear, or at a big rock that looked, perhaps, something like a rodent.

"Geez . . . what's wrong with you? Knock it off, Larry!"

Scotty saw that the thrown stick, bobbing now in the surf up ahead, was farther out than he figured he should go to retrieve it. Neither advancing nor receding, it appeared stuck within battling currents. A dark shadow above was suddenly upon them—a cloud passing overhead. Larry's barks turned to more of a constant howl.

Glancing overhead again, Scotty noticed the cloud was not a cloud at all, and he heard a faint *humming* noise. Larry, also staring upward, ceased howling. Together, they watched as the object hovered above them. Eyes wide, his mouth agape, Scotty took in the impossible—that which only occurred on TV, or in the movies. Nope, there was zero doubt about what he was seeing. It was a real spaceship, he was sure of that. But it didn't have a definitive, geometric shape, like those he'd learned about in school. Neither chevron nor hexagon in shape, nor triangular, like a rocket, it slowly and steadily descended downward. Then, some fifteen feet above him, the strange vessel began maneuvering—its flight becoming more horizontal, more circular.

Excited, Scotty began waving his arms up high. "Hey ... do you see me up there?"

The spaceship suddenly descended, came all the way down to eye-level—where it hovered—almost close enough to touch. Ocean waves lapped against its underside. Scotty now could make out more of the craft's intricate detail—its odd design, with various parts of its exterior protruding out in furrows and ridges like the worn-tanned surface of an old man's face. A sudden movement caught his eye when a series of articulating arms began twisting outward from a recessed little nook on the side of the craft closest to them. Then each claw snapped open and remained that way. Reaching further and further outward, Scotty realized they were coming toward him and Larry.

Only then did Scotty's thrilled expression switch to something that suggested concern, realizing now he might be in real danger. That he should not be there—alone—with this now not so friendly-looking spacecraft. He felt cold and began to shiver. He shot a backward glance toward the large beach house, partially obscured by distant dunes. His home now seemed so very far away. The next series of waves, crashing loudly onto the sandy shore, drowned out Scotty's voice as he frantically shouted out for someone to please come help him.

chapter 2

Present day ...

Officer Donald Platt stared at the ancient police mobile radio, hanging a little off-kilter just below the dashboard. "You have to be fucking kidding me," he said aloud, through a mouthful of egg salad sandwich. He brushed the most recent avalanche of crumbs away from his gargantuan midsection. Reaching for the mic, he hesitated, chewing a bit more and then swallowing. He snatched up the mic and keyed the talk button.

"Yeah, Joan ... I can take that call," he said, listening to the hiss of prolonged dead air. He rolled his eyes, *Christ.* "Officer Platt, going 10-8 ... that any better?"

Dispatch came back with, "Possible 10-91A, reported by resident homeowners in the vicinity of Dover and Pritchett Drive."

Platt glared at the radio. *Come on, Joan, you stupid bitch.* Who the fuck would remember what a 10-91A was? Prowler? No ... maybe it indicated an intoxicated asshole. Then he remembered it had something to do with animals. He cursed under his breath. Added to that, Pritchett Drive was way the hell over on the far side of the island. "10-4, rolling now ... be there in about ten." Replacing the mic, he leaned back and continued to devour the rest of his egg salad sandwich.

At thirty-four years of age, Officer Donald Platt was the latest addition to the Nantucket Police Department. More accurately, his employment would be limited to this summer only—a hiring contract extension possible only after a three-month evaluation by his direct superiors. It was his fourth transfer position within five years and his first stint above the Mason Dixon line. Pratt, a good ol' country boy from Louisiana, tended to be a handful. He already knew that— was fine being considered as such. He was also something else too—*a change agent.* Hearing that term used recently on TV, he'd adopted it for himself. He was a change agent, for things that needed changing. Fortunately, an out-and-out firing of a police officer wasn't all that common these days. That entailed far too much paperwork. The risk of litigation, in today's sue-happy climate, was way too high. Better to just make him some other precinct's problem. Again, he was fine with that. Sure, he had his own way of dealing with the lowlifes who broke the law. But he got results—his own kind of results.

How Platt ended up amongst the prissy-rich island home-owners, and the hordes of affluent pre-summer vacationers, wasn't all that complicated. The Nantucket station was in dire need of able-bodied officers. They'd lost another two cops already this year. Apparently, crime-stopping duties of finding stolen bicycles, tracking down the jerkoff who'd keyed someone's new Mercedes, or rousting the growing homeless community, weren't nearly exciting enough for burgeoning Nantucket Academy graduates. So Nantucket had become a constant revolving door—good cops off to other, far more crime-stricken precincts, like those in Boston, or even Manhattan. And then a brew of perhaps not so qualified, maybe even problematic, cops coming in. But desperate times called for desperate decision-making. Thus, Officer Donald Platt's somewhat colorful, and highly edited, past employment history passed muster. To that point, he'd landed what was sure to be, in his opinion, a piece of cake summer gig. Hell, he could have done a whole lot worse for himself.

Getting a bit turned around en route to the scene, it took Platt close to twenty minutes to arrive at Dover and Pritchet Drive. Prior to opening the cruiser's driver-side door, he turned on the overhead dome light and checked his reflection in the rearview mirror. Making a sucking sound, he used his tongue to evict hanger-on globs of egg and bread still snagged between his oversized incisors, canines, and premolars.

Hefting his two-hundred-sixty-pound bulk up and out of the car, he repositioned his duty belt so his service weapon hung down properly by his side. As an afterthought, he leaned back in and retrieved his Streamlight PolyStinger flashlight from the passenger seat. A cop with a PolyStinger had no need for a baton. These things were heavy—practically indestructible.

Standing tall to his full height of six-foot-three, Platt took in the cool salty air. Squinting into the near total darkness, the sound of distant crashing waves gave him an indication of his proximity to the vast ocean beyond.

Platt spun around, hearing another sound—the *squeak, squeak, squeak* of a Stop & Shop shopping cart. One of its wheels obviously out of alignment, it wobbled as it rolled along. Platt instantly recognized the scraggly, bearded man, pushing the filled-to-the-brim grocery cart, holding an assortment of only God knew what. It was Dr. Klaus, one of the growing number of seaside bums taking up residence recently on Nantucket Island. Platt had no idea if Klaus was an actual physician, or anything else, regarding his back history. And he didn't care to find out either. The recent arrivals were little more than vermin. Little more than disgusting animals with their bad hygiene and constant rummaging through curbside trash bins. But Dr. Klaus had apparently stepped up his game since the last time Platt had seen him. Sure, his long hair was still a tangled, matted mess, and his scraggly beard could be harboring all sorts of crawly things, but today he was better dressed, wearing clean, pristine in fact, khaki overalls that almost looked like some kind of uniform. Typically, he was barefooted, but tonight he wore shoes, or maybe boots—hard to tell in the night's near-total darkness. Officer Platt was tempted to arrest the man, but just the thought of the foul-smelling bum sitting within the confines of his cruiser—all those lingering odors . . .

"Officer! Over here," came a woman's gravelly croak, clearly someone who'd been a long-time smoker.

Platt looked around—noticing no corner streetlights anywhere. Moving toward the lady with the scratchy voice, he could just barely make out several shapes in the near distance. Looked like at least five, maybe six folks huddled together.

Switching on his flashlight, pointing it directly at their faces, their hands came up to block out the high-powered beam. "What's the problem here, folks?" Platt queried in his friendliest Southern drawl. He kept the light shining in their faces, figuring nary a one of the old geezers was younger than seventy-five or eighty.

"Can you please lower your torch?" a woman asked, her British accent heavy with indignant irritation.

Platt ignored her. Instead, he redirected the beam straight into her face and held it there. He repeated himself, now in a louder voice—like she might be hard of hearing or something: "Exactly what's the problem here? It's a busy night, so what do you say we bypass the idle chit-chat."

One of the two elderly men, this one tall and mostly bald, pointed a crooked finger out into the darkness. "There's a dog right over there. If you listen, you can hear it panting. Been barking for over an hour now. You know, we have strict leash laws around here."

One of the three women broke in, "The dog's quiet now . . . but I assure you, the barking's been non-stop."

Platt redirected the beam of his flashlight to follow in the direction of the man's still outstretched pointed finger. Sure enough, something was scurrying around over there—around something lying on the ground.

"Dog like that could be wild . . . rabid, even. Lucky none of us got bitten," the old lady continued.

"Yeah . . . uh huh," Platt replied dryly. "You people need to stay back. Better yet, let's get yourselves back inside your homes. Let the police take it from here . . . okay?" Platt waited for them to move. "Come on . . . get . . . your presence here is a form of obstruction of justice," he lied.

He waited for them to move off—ancient hunched-over couples now going in opposite directions. Only then did he approach *whatever* was nestled in the dunes just ahead.

At ten paces out, Platt held up. The dog's eyes, eerily reflecting back into his own, were glowing like hot-white embers, were beginning to freak him out. The dog, now squatting on his haunches, was lying next to *something,* or someone, on the sand. Platt slowly moved his free hand down to his duty belt. Finding the canister of mace secured there, he repositioned his hand further back, onto the butt of his service weapon. "Easy boy . . . no need to make this difficult."

Platt panned the beam of his light over what was obviously a man. A totally nude man, his eyes were closed, his lips purple-bluish in tone. *God, the guy's dead.* Platt never liked being around dead people. Went to great lengths over the years to avoid any such encounters. He reached for his shoulder mic then remembered he wasn't wearing one. *Of course not!* Issued the oldest cruiser in the department—the crappiest, most worn-out equipment—he was still on the waiting list for a repaired mobile radio unit. *God forbid they'd ever buy the new guy anything new.*

The dog now had his head resting on the chest of the dead guy. Ready to call it in when back in his car, Platt took a step backwards. Then the naked 'dead' man moved an arm.

chapter 3

Base Ship Communications: Protocols Initiated . . .

Absolute Command: Searching Broad Spectrum Spatial Coordinates . . .
Absolute Command: Intermediary Organism Identified . . .
Absolute Command: Synchronizing To Intermediary Orand-Pall 052333 . . .
Absolute Command: Initiating Direct Contact With Host . . .
Absolute Command: Communications Not Established . . . Timeout / Abort . . .

* * *

He awoke feeling cold. He remembered that was the word for it, *cold*. Immediately, he regretted being here. The loss of freedom hit him first, coupled with a nearly overpowering sense of isolation—that and despair. He had to fight back emotions not to weep. *God . . . how do others handle this?* Survive the minutes, let alone hours or days, feeling like this? Being Human again. That and the result of something referred to as a *Projected Transport.* Truly a horrible way to travel.

His eyes fluttered open but found only darkness. *Did something go wrong? Am I both miserable and blind?* Something was in his mouth—something gritty and salty. Sand. He tried to spit.

He touched his face, feeling scruffy stubble on his cheeks and chin, then ran a hand up his bare abdomen onto his chest. *That's strange . . . didn't expect to be naked.* Where are my clothes? My boots? *Terrific . . . someone has stolen my clothes.*

Something wet touched his hand. Startled, his breath caught in his chest and he ceased his moving about. Then he recalled what it felt like to be licked just like this. The licking tongue, more vigorously now, moved up onto to his face. He felt his heart leap, remembering a friend he'd neither seen, nor been licked by, in many years.

"Is that you, Larry? Hey, boy. Yeah . . . I missed you too." His words came out slurred—he wasn't accustomed to talking while embodied in a physical form. *How unexpected!* No way was Larry part of the plan. Although an added complication, for sure, he was a most welcome one. Moving somewhat erratically, he put his arms around the dog's thick furry neck, pulling him closer. "It's okay, boy . . ."

Evidently, Larry had also awakened here on the beach—totally unaware that so much time had passed. Sixteen years. Pushing the dog away, he said, "Okay . . . let me get up, boy."

The man was becoming more and more conscious of his body's reaction to the chilled environment—uncontrollable shivering set in. *What a strange sensation.* Pondering the cause of such a thing occurring, he instantly knew it was a reflex reaction—one triggered to maintain homeostasis. His Human skeletal muscles had begun to exhibit the telltale jittery movements.

As his other sensory faculties began to reanimate, he felt his breathing begin to slow, his heart rate settle down into what would be considered normal for a typical Human subject. He mentally chastised himself, *I should have spent more time in this physical form.*

Best I get started. There was an objective with a limited timeframe. He dreaded what lay ahead. Knowing these people as he uniquely did, it just might be impossible. Earth was not nearly ready for this . . . *not ready for him.*

He lifted his head and concentrated. Earlier he'd heard murmurs—a woman and a man talking in hushed tones, not so far away. He now turned his head to better listen. Another recognizable sound was coming back to him from years past—the soft, not so distant, padding of feet walking across a sandy beach. *Good . . . perhaps someone's come to help me.* The dog began barking again—louder than before. The man felt a familiar, albeit slightly uncomfortable, tingling sensation. It was akin to a small electrical charge, taking place within the interior of his right forearm. It was his *Orand-Pall*: An implanted, living organism, which was imbedded in there. One that he'd relied upon for his very survival more times than he cared to remember. It was his one connection to the others—and, of course, to the spaceship. Instinctively, he ran his fingertips over the half-dollar-sized protrusion, wondering how long they'd been trying to reach him? Hell, how long had he been unconscious—lying there in only his birthday suit on the sandy beach? He'd give it a moment before answering their call—let his motor skills return some . . .

chapter 4

Keeping a wary eye on the dog he said, "Mister, my name is Officer Donald Platt . . . can you hear me?"

The prone individual said something back unintelligible.

"Look, buddy . . . you're already in a whole lot of trouble. Best you listen up and do exactly what I tell you to do. To start, I want you to place your hands behind your head and intertwine your fingers. Do it now!" Platt watched as the man slowly raised one hand then the other. He didn't seem to have the right coordination to bring them together, let alone inter-twine his fingers. *A drunken asshole—a 10-56.*

Officer Platt wasn't averse to having the occasional drink, preferably something amber, on tap, but he found it hard to tolerate a man who couldn't handle his liquor. Only a pussy got himself into this kind of predicament. He ran the beam of his flashlight up and down the man's body. Lying on his back, he looked to be in his mid-twenties. Longish blonde hair covered half his face. He seemed to be in fairly good shape; no tats—at least none that he could see.

The dog, rising to his feet, was growling now. Platt, in no mood to put up with both a homeless naked fool, *and* a vicious dog, decided this was the kind of situation mace was intended for. He fumbled at his belt until he had the slender canister clutched within his thick fingers. Directing the spray nozzle away from himself, holding it out in his outstretched arm, he moved purposely forward. The dog's growls intensified, then the barking resumed. The man lying on the beach shifted about, seemed to be getting agitated. Platt, approaching the dog, yelled, "Get back! Back, mutt!" The animal nervously skittered backward.

Still trying to move around him, Platt blocked the dog's way as he skirted left then right, trying to get back to the nude man, lying on the beach. Platt depressed the spray valve atop the mace canister, while simultaneously closing his eyes. This shit, he knew, stung to high heaven—no way was he going to inflict that kind of pain on himself. Apparently, his aim was true, because the dog yelped in apparent agony. Smiling, Platt opened his eyes, just in time to see the dog, tail tucked between his legs, running off into the dunes—into the near-total darkness. He heard a scream behind him.

Swinging back around to face the naked man—the drunken fool—it was evident he would be in no condition to cause much of a ruckus. Platt cast one last glance toward the dunes before kneeling down beside him. Shining the flashlight's beam into the man's face, he ordered, "Get yourself up . . . we're going for a little ride."

"Larry . . . where's Larry?"

"Yeah ... Larry's not here, whoever that is."

The man grumbled something else. Eyes fluttering open, he made three attempts to rise, finally getting onto his elbows. It was then he flailed out with his right arm, all spastic-like, knocking Platt's Streamlight PolyStinger flashlight from his hand. Blinking several times, the flashlight turned off then came back on. Platt stared down at the long, black, cylindrical object as if it had personally insulted him. And, in a way, perhaps it had. Leaving it where it now lay, the big cop slapped the man's face—slapped it hard. Platt was well aware there wasn't anything much more humiliating for a full-grown man than to be bitch slapped—even better when it can be done in public. "Now you get yourself up onto your feet. You hear me, mister?"

The prone man shook his head, abruptly inhaling a deep breath. Once again, he tried to rise but his limbs just didn't seem to be working properly. Momentarily, Platt wondered if the guy wasn't so much drunk but maybe a cripple.

"Don't ... hit me ... asshole." The words had come out somewhat slurred.

Platt stared at the man, hardly believing what he'd just heard. "That's the wrong thing to say to an officer of the law ..." Now, reaching a meaty hand down and wrapping it around the man's neck, Platt tightened his grip. In a move surprisingly athletic for such a robust man, Platt manhandled the man up to his feet. Now, in the dim light of his half-buried flashlight, he stared at him face-to-face—was looking into the man's unfocused blue eyes. "Stay on your feet or I'll really fuck you up ...

hear me?" When he let go of him, he stood back and watched as the man teetered and swayed about unsteadily. As quickly as he could, Platt bent over to retrieve his flashlight then straightened up. That was when the motherfucker spewed vomit onto his face and into his open mouth.

Gagging, spitting, and swearing—and clearly unable to contain his now out-of-control rage—Officer Platt first used his sleeve to wipe the dripping mess from his cheeks and chin. Then he swung his three-and-a-half-pound Streamlight PolyStinger flashlight hard against the back of the man's head. He watched the man's eyes go vacant before he toppled to the ground. Then Platt bent over and, putting his substantial weight behind it, whacked him again—then whacked him one more time for good measure.

* * *

Oh God it hurt. Slumped against the cruiser's bloodied and smeared inside window, he silently cursed the all too inHumane Human race. He blinked and even that brought forth further excruciating pain. Visually, everything was a blur—the landscape rushing by outside; the interior of the vehicle, with its cage-like partition; and the monumentally large head and shoulders, there, protruding above the front seat.

His thoughts were all a-jumble. He knew he had only just begun the acclimation process—one required after a projected transport. It all began as he was informed it would. Several hours would be needed for the entire reintroduction process to be complete. A process where his memories would become fully jelled, lost recollections would be properly restored, and his bodily functions would acclimatate within the new environment. None of that had happened. Not completely. He tried to think through the fog—the pain. No. The re-acclimation process, he now feared, had been irreversibly circumvented.

I'm going to live the rest of my life like this: brain-damage, a simpleton. I know there's something important that I'm here to do, to accomplish. What is that? Why am I here?

His mind flashed back to what had just happened. At the time, he remembered enough to say *something* to the police officer. Told him to stop. *Stop hitting me, asshole.* But who's *me? Who am I?*

Trying to move his arms, he was quickly reminded he'd been restrained. *They're called handcuffs.* So I'm a badly beaten, brain-damaged simpleton, and I'm being transported to . . . ?

"Hey . . . you still alive back there, mister?"

He didn't answer him.

"The morgue's the same distance as to the station, either way. Makes no difference to me."

The policeman shot a quick glance back at him over his shoulder. "Nah . . . I can see . . . you're still breathing."

He felt that familiar tingling on his inside forearm. *That means something . . . I'm supposed to do something.*

Perhaps it was the constant drone of the engine, or the gentle back-and-forth swaying motion while sitting within the confines of the cruiser that seemed to help somewhat. His eyes closed as sleep enveloped him.

chapter 5

At that moment, passing overhead some two-hundred-forty miles straight up, the International Space Station was traveling at approximately 17,150 miles an hour, or roughly five miles per second, while orbiting around and around planet Earth below.

Typically housing a crew of five or six, or even seven, this was one of those rare occasions when only three crewmembers were actually manning the ISS. A serious flu strain had invaded the close-quarters space station just three weeks prior. Two men and two women had become deathly ill. A mission specialist that had recently arrived for a short timeframe had been the culprit. He was gone now, but had left a lingering virus behind within the ISS. With only one of the two toilets operational, the situation had become quite serious. Serious to the point a Russian Soyuz rocket had to be launched ahead of schedule to retrieve the sick astronauts/cosmonauts to get them the medical attention they sorely needed. Rampant diarrhea in space shouldn't be a laughing matter, but to US astronauts

Commander Jack Landon and Lt. Greg Fischer, and Russian cosmonaut Peter Mirkin, a bit of adolescent humor helped them pass the time and had kept this undermanned mission a bit more light-hearted.

All three men would be going home soon on the arrival of the next Space X Crew Dragon capsule. At that point, a full international transfer crew, one that included two Americans, two Russians, one Indian, and one Japanese, would replace them. Both of the Americans, Commander Landon and Lieutenant Fischer, were ready to get back down onto solid ground after completing six months in space. Initially, their relationship was tenuous. Both alpha males, they were far too similar to feel comfortable around one another. But that was months in the past. Now they were the best of friends—ones that made plans to go big game hunting together in Colorado, where Landon had a rickety old cabin, in the mountainous terrain of Grand County.

Typically, with each new influx of fresh ISS crewmembers, an accompanying assignment for zero gravity science experiments came with them. Some continued ongoing research, while other tests required mere days, or just hours, to complete. But with the abrupt departure of the two unwell premier NASA scientists, who'd headed up those endeavors, that left only Landon and Fischer—doing double duty—to at least partially complete several of those already initiated, time-sensitive, tasks. Between Mission Control and Commander Landon, they had divvied up the responsibility pretty much down the middle. Landon would resume work on experiments started by

Peggy Whitson, PhD. that had to do with identifying internal station microbes, while Lieutenant Fischer would complete the work started by Dr. M. Drango that had to do with tadpoles existing in a microgravity environment. Their intervention allowed the Russian cosmonaut Mirkin time to complete some necessary mechanical upgrades and make needed repairs to the ISS.

Commander Landon ran a hand over his thinning, salt-and-pepper buzz-cut, frustrated with his results of Peggy Whitson's ongoing experiments, especially those having to do with identifying, then sampling, DNA/genes in real-time while stationed onboard the ISS without having to send the samples back down to Earth for analysis. The ability to do that successfully would be a game changer and had far-reaching implications.

The muscularly built, broad faced, Slavic-looking Cosmonaut Mirkin, on the other hand, was happy—now freed from the confined, close quarters environment aboard ISS. Having less of a science background, his education primarily one of engineering, he was assigned several out-of-station duties. One had to do with adding a new experimental solar panel to one of the large array units. The new panel, with its hundreds of individual solar cells, had the potential capability to nearly double the conversion of light to electricity, a process called *photovoltaics*. It would require no fewer than three separate spacewalks to complete the task. Mirkin, completing the first spacewalk the previous day, was now halfway through his second, four-hour, assembly process.

Currently, both Commander Landon—inside the MLM module lab—and Mirkin, now strapped outside to the port-side solar array arm, were pretty much in constant contact with Mission Control, as well as with each other.

Landon was specifically conversing with a recovering Peggy Whitson, now down on Earth, at NASA's Marshall Space Flight Center, in Huntsville, Alabama, within the Payload Operations and Integration Center, typically called POIC. Here, experiments, and the various science projects pertaining to the ISS, were all coordinated. Peggy Whitson, plus a revolving door of other prominent scientists working in related fields, directed experiments in Combustion, Human Life Sciences, Physical Sciences, Biological Sciences, Space Product Development, Fluid Physics, and Educational Payloads. These scientists were the primary interface to ISS crewmembers and their associated onboard experiments.

Having screwed up his latest gene-splice experiment, he needed a little expert advice on how *not* to make the same damn mistake twice. It was then Commander Landon heard *something* in Peter Mirkin's typically cool, calm, and collected—yet heavily Russian-accented—voice.

"This is Houston Mission Control, ... can you repeat the last transmission, over?"

"Roger that, Houston. Need telemetry coordinates on possible sighting. Um.... I have a visual on a solar reflection ... approximately thirty degrees over the MBS."

"This is Houston, roger that, Peter. Know that external cameras are working nominally. Hang tight... telemetry verification may take several minutes."

"Roger that, Houston," Mirkin said.

Listening, Commander Landon stopped what he was doing. Pushing off from the lab table before him, he floated out through a connecting hatchway and into the recently added new NASA module, the Galaxy-1. With more workable space within the module, it was chock-full of vertical racks, holding high-speed computers on one side. No less than five mounted flat-screen monitors, along with numerous shelves—containing soft storage containers—were accessible on the other side. A myriad of stretched-taut blue bungee cords crisscrossed from deck to ceiling. Galaxy-1 also had several sets of thick-glassed, triangular portholes inset into both bulkheads. Peter Mirkin's bright-white spacesuit, visible to him even at forty yards away, was positioned halfway up the portside solar array support arm. Landon repositioned his line of sight and his angle of view in an attempt to discover what Mirkin was referring to. He then spotted it—a bright pinpoint of light. A pinpoint of light, growing brighter by the second. Whatever it was, it was definitely coming closer.

"Houston, I can verify that sighting, over," Landon said, knowing Mission Control always knew who it was speaking and where they were positioned—whether within, or outside of, the ISS.

"This is Houston Mission Control. Roger that, Commander. Please stand by."

Landon heard Greg Fischer, working on the other side of the ISS, within the Zvezda Service Module, join the conversation. "Houston, make that three sets of eyes confirming that same sighting, over."

"This is Houston Mission Control; roger that, Lieutenant Fischer. Still awaiting input from multiple sources. Give us a minute. Over."

Landon didn't like hearing that. For Houston not to see what they were viewing seemed, well, *impossible*. Every satellite, every errant, manmade space artifact—along with every sizable chunk of orbiting space debris—was already being meticulously tracked. And what the three astronauts were witnessing now certainly wasn't small. What the hell was their problem, anyway, not tracking—

The audio feed cracked to life, "This is Houston Mission Control; we have an update on the probable sighting, over."

"Roger that. Go ahead, Houston," Landon said.

"No detection. Repeat, no detection. Consider the sighting to be a visual anomaly. Both satellite and ground detection sources come up negative. Over."

Landon stared out the porthole, not believing what he was seeing. "Houston, that visual anomaly just changed course, over. And, clearly, it is an object of significant size. Repeat, Houston . . . it is an object of significant size. Over."

"This is Houston . . . Commander, we're in the process of reorienting two external ISS cameras. Will attempt getting a visual on the object."

Commander Landon continued to stare out the porthole window. "Peter—I want you back inside the ISS immediately!"

"This is Houston, Commander. The lieutenant still has another good hour of..."

Landon cut in, "It's a vessel, Houston! I can see it now. It's a damn UFO of some kind! Peter, I want you back in here. Now!"

chapter 6

He was startled awake as the police cruiser's side door he was cozied up against was abruptly jerked open. Nearly toppling out—big hands were there to grab him. Gazing up through half-opened eyelids, he caught sight of the portly man in blue. *Who is he, again?* Although his mind had definitely cleared up some, it still took a few beats to remember. It was the one who had attacked him—the policeman. The one called Officer Donald Platt.

At that moment, Platt was glaring down at him. Suddenly, he was yanked up, both hard and fast, out of the cruiser's rear seat. His head began to pound from the rough treatment, with hot bile burning the back of his throat. He felt nauseous.

Catching his breath, just above a whisper he asked, "Where are we going?"

"So now you want to talk? Little late for that, dirt bag," Platt shot back, as he half-shoved, half-dragged him in through automatic double-glass doors. They next continued down a narrow hallway and into a medium-sized room, with polished linoleum tiled floors and pale-blue painted walls. Platt plunked him down onto one of the three metal stools lined-up in front of a counter with a short Plexiglas partition. Platt un-cuffed his arms from behind his back then re-cuffed his right hand to a waist-high metal railing. He felt the cold metal stool beneath his bare buttocks—against his exposed testicles.

"To answer your question, dirt bag, I'm booking you into this here fine, five-star hotel establishment. Make sure you ring for the complimentary room service."

Blurry-eyed, he tracked Platt as he moved behind the Formica counter. Placing his hands on his wide hips, Platt looked around. "Yo, yo, yo... anyone working the desk tonight?"

A silver-haired man, with piercing blue eyes, peered out through a glass door on the opposite side of the room. Throwing out an annoyed glare as he pulled the door all the way open, he just stood there, garbed in a crisp, navy-blue uniform. Little gold stars decorated his shirt collars; his shiny badge reflected the overhead florescent lights. First glancing through the clear counter partition at him, then over to Platt, he asked, "Why is there a naked, bloodied man sitting in my booking room?"

"Hey, Cap."

"No! I'm Captain Brooks, not, 'Hey, Cap.'"

"Oh... yeah, sorry. No disrespect intended. Anyway, Captain Brooks, I answered a last-minute call tonight—a 10-56. Came right at the end of my shift. Guy over there was sprawled out, buck naked, lying off in the dunes. Neighbors all in a tizzy about it."

Captain Brooks stared back at Platt blank faced. He then came around the counter and looked down at him. With a creased brow, he leaned in a little closer. The captain touched the side of his bloodied face, probing it with his two extended fingers.

"Ahh!" the prisoner inhaled sharply, feeling renewed, searing pain.

"How did these injuries occur?"

Platt said, "Yes, sir. The perp needed to be restrained after he went for my gun. Had to give him a couple of whacks to settle him down."

"Officer Platt . . . please come with me," the police captain said, standing upright. He then purposely moved back behind the counter and disappeared through the still-open doorway.

Platt narrowed his eyes at the naked man. "Don't you go anywhere." He gave the man's secured wrist a few unnecessary tugs, then followed in the captain's steps out of the room.

The door remained open and the prisoner could still see Platt, but not the police captain, though he could still make out their hushed voices. "I think that man out there has a broken cheekbone! Could be his orbital bone. His lip is split in two places, and he very well could have a concussion. What the hell were you thinking?"

"He was a wild bull at the time . . . maybe hopped-up on something. Probably ecstacy. To be honest, I feared for my life," Platt said, adding a well-timed wince to emphasize his point.

"Goddammit, Platt! I'll deal with you later." Looking furious, the captain stormed back through the open door, then made his way over to the prisoner. Platt, almost leisurely, followed behind him.

Kneeling down, placing a hand on the prisoner's shoulder, the police captain asked, "Hey ... what's your name, mister?"

The prisoner thought about that. "I ... I don't ... remember." Then he did recall something, something from his distant past. He remembered a woman's voice, his mother calling to him, and then again, but much more recently. "Wait, it might be ... Scotty. I think I remember being called Scotty." He glanced up at the captain questioningly.

"Come on! Full-grown man like that and his name is Scotty?" Platt said, rolling his eyes.

"So, you've been drinking a bit tonight, that right, Scotty? Partying it up? Maybe you took some drugs, too? What exactly did you take?" the captain asked.

He thought about being called Scotty. It felt fine. *It felt right.* Almost imperceptibly, he shook his head. "No drugs. Nothing to drink."

The captain, standing all the way up, glanced over to Platt. "There's no nystagmus occurring with his eyes ... the jiggling back and forth of the eyes you see with ecstasy users. And although his breath is beyond foul, I smell no alcohol."

Officer Platt nodded then shrugged. "Must be something else, then."

"Did you think to cover him up—put a blanket over his shoulders? You know there's one in every cruiser's trunk."

"Nah, Cap ... um, Captain Brooks. With all the ruckus, I was lucky to even get him cuffed and secured inside the car."

The captain continued to stare at Platt, then down at Scotty again. "Here's what you're going to do. Take him through the booking process; print him and get pictures taken. Also, get a DNA swab of his cheek, then get him into a clean jumpsuit."

Officer Platt, already vigorously shaking his head, to the point his double chin was flapping from side-to-side, said, "Captain, I'm totally beat—my shift ended over an hour ago ..."

Captain Brooks continued, "After that, I want this man transported over to Nantucket Cottage Hospital for further evaluation. Have I made myself clear what is expected of you, officer?"

"I understand what you're saying, Captain, sure. But I don't understand why Ellis or Kaplan can't handle this now? They're on duty, I'm not."

"You're on duty as long as I say you're on duty. We have limited night-duty staffing here, as you well know. Ellis is already on patrol and Kaplan won't be in till his 5:00 a.m. shift starts later today. But, even more importantly, since you were the cop who beat this man so viciously into submission, you'll be the one to take him over to NCH for evaluation and treatment. I'll run his prints to see if anything shows up regarding his identity. Officer Platt, you will treat this prisoner with respect. Don't let me find out he's been any further abused."

"Yes, sir."

Platt came closer and began to unlock Scotty's cuffs. Scotty kept his eyes on the captain then turned his attention to the small rectangular device secured to Platt's chest. Scotty pointed at it with his free hand.

Captain Brooks pursed his lips. "One more thing, Platt . . . did you initialize your body cam upon arriving at the scene?"

Platt fumbled with the cuffs, eventually getting them ratcheted closed behind Scotty's back, then hefted him up to his feet before answering, "I'm just not used to the damn things, Captain. We didn't have much in the way of modern police technology at my last assignment. Sorry, sir"

"All right, I'm going to have to write you up, Platt. The problem is, you've already been skating on thin ice around here." The captain moved in closer, reaching out a hand to touch the middle of Platt's chest, and switched his body camera on. "That stays on till you've clocked out. Just know I'll be able to watch all your movements, in real-time, via the cloud. Now get going." Captain Brooks made momentary eye contact with Scotty, "We'll get things figured out, young man," giving him a quick, reassuring nod.

chapter 7

FBI Special Agent Alison McGuire sat in her car, located within the below- deck parking structure of the Hyannis to Nantucket ferry. Cool and dark here, but most of all, *thankfully* quiet. She momentarily closed her eyes and breathed in the smell of the sea.

She was using the ferry's one-hour crossing time to catch-up on seemingly endless interdepartmental emails. *How does anyone get anything done in this job?*

Glancing up from her iPhone, Alison caught sight of the distant, sandy-colored patch of land just coming into view through a narrow opening on the side of the ferry. She hadn't been back to Nantucket Island since she was fourteen and her feelings were mixed about coming back. Excited, because this was her first solo FBI bureau assignment, but somewhat saddened too. It was here, on that last mid-summer visit eleven years ago that her father—bodysurfing right beside her—suffered a massive heart attack. Dropped dead trying to make it to shore. But she didn't want to think about that, certainly not right now.

Alison reached for the manila file folder, laying on the passenger seat. Upon opening it, she leaned it up against the steering wheel, then placed the envelope with the subject's prelim DNA results at the very back of the folder. She'd already read the case file twice; had inserted a number of small notes within both margins. Scotty Sullivan, Caucasian male, was nine years of age when he went missing, late one afternoon while on a family vacation.

His disappearance, reportedly, took place close to the beachside vacation home of his parents, Andrew and Brianna Sullivan. Andrew was a financially well-off day-trader for Goldman Sachs, and she a stay-at-home mother to three children: Kyle, eleven, the oldest child; Scotty, nine, the middle child; and Sara, their three-year-old daughter. According to the mother, Scotty was wearing rolled-up jeans and a tank top. Also, their dog, Larry, was outside with him. Late in the afternoon, it was already starting to get dark outside. The mother had told Scotty to be back inside the house within a half-hour. She remembered seeing clouds and the wind picking up outside the kitchen window. Temperatures along the New England coast had cooled, but Scotty was insistent about wanting to play outside—if only for a little while. And that was the last time that anyone ever saw the young boy.

The police were called and within two hours, an extensive search had ensued. All available police officers, a number estimated to be around twenty-five, scoured acres of nearby dense scrub oak which bordered the exclusive neighborhood homes in the area, and also along the southeastern Nantucket shoreline. But nothing turned up. Scotty's footprints, as well as Larry's, the dog, were found, leading down to the beach, but found nowhere else.

Island authorities checked the small local airport, as well as the Steamship Authority, to see if a young child matching his description had accompanied anyone on a departing flight or aboard any of the leaving ferries. Personnel at Nantucket Cottage Hospital were also interviewed; on the chance someone had taken him there. They checked if a boy matching his description had been admitted, but still nothing showed up. The search expanded into the moors, to Polpis Road and Sankaty, and out to the cranberry bogs. By noon the following day, a Coast Guard helicopter was dispatched to assist the growing search team on the ground. It now included State Police troopers and Island firefighters. For close to a week, there was a non-stop search of Nantucket Island by up to sixty-five public safety personnel. They covered the entire island, much of it on foot, checking unoccupied houses, and even closed retail establishments. Numerous attempts to send dive teams into the frigid waters along the coast were hampered by the turbulent seas. By then, the FBI had assumed full control of the search and investigation. Investigators found no signs of foul play and, after three months, concluded that both dog and boy had been swept out to sea. The file would be kept open, just in case, but no one expected to hear anything further about the missing boy.

Paper-clipped to the folder was a snapshot of a smiling, nine-year-old Scotty Sullivan that looked to be a school picture. *Cute kid*, Alison thought. Another snapshot was paper-clipped right next to it. This one was of a bare-chested, full-grown man with unkempt blonde hair. The side of his face was swollen showing clear signs of recent trauma. Clearly, someone had beaten the shit out of the guy. Thumbing through the file pages, she stopped at a page holding multiple fingerprint images and leaned in closer. She studied one of the circled sections, which matched to an adjacent set of prints. The boy, Scotty, and the young man's prints seemed to be similar. But matching fingerprints of children with their potentially older selves had been known to be problematic. But still, this match up was compelling—at least to her it was. She flipped to the front of the folder again, looking back and forth between both of the snapshot faces. She said aloud, "You *could* be the same guy, I guess."

Prior to heading out that morning, making the four-hour drive from the Chelsea, Massachusetts FBI office where she worked, Alison's supervising agent, Donald Price, gave her one full day to get *all this bullshit kicked to the curb,* as he had off-handedly exclaimed. He was convinced that there was no possible way, after sixteen years, for a missing kid to just suddenly, *miraculously*, show up again in practically the same spot where he originally went missing. *No fucking way. I don't trust the prints on this ... and Quantico says preliminary DNA markers are inconclusive. Not definitive. It's all in the file. Anyway, try to clear it up ... and be back here tomorrow.*

Alison McGuire shrugged. She'd spent a year and a half of her life training with the FBI just for a day like today. As far as she was concerned, Donald, a patronizing closet misogynist, could go screw himself. She had a job to do—one that entailed collecting all available information, following up on any new pertinent clues, and then determining if the case required further investigation. She pursed her lips. The depressing thoughts of her long-departed father began diminishing back into the deep recesses of her mind. Anticipation of actually getting started on the case filled her with both nervousness and excitement. No matter what Donald might say, she knew this case was important—she just wasn't sure how. She was ambitious. *So what?* Nobody was going to hand her success—if she had to be a little aggressive, so be it. On the flipside, if she handled things wrong, she could bring undue attention—or even worse, bring unwarranted hope—to a small tightknit community, which even today, she was certain, hadn't fully recovered from what happened there sixteen years in the past. She could derail her career—even before it had gotten started.

chapter 8

There were only two ways to enter in and out of the International Space Station. One was through the newer US-constructed Quest airlock, which was large enough for astronauts to use with their bulky Extravehicular Mobility Units, or EMUs. There also was the smaller Russian segment airlock, located on the Pirs Module. Through the latter, Landon and Fischer assisted Peter Mirkin in re-entering the ISS. They worked quickly and in silence. The three men weren't discussing the UFO. Perhaps if they didn't discuss it, it wouldn't be real.

But Mirkin seemed no worse for wear—the one in closest proximity to *whatever* that thing out there really was—Landon thought. He watched as Fischer gave Peter a couple of pats on the shoulder before pushing out through the connecting hatchway. Landon stayed behind a few minutes, helping Mirkin shed his outer gear, then asked, "You got the rest of this?"

Mirkin nodded. "Yes, thanks. I'm good."

Landon left the way Fischer had, letting the cosmonaut complete the lengthy routine of properly stowing away his spacesuit.

Five minutes later, Landon was back. Staring out through the Galaxy-1's module porthole, he became transfixed at what he was observing. The UFO, at least from his current perspective, appeared to be oblong in shape. Dark gray, or maybe brownish in color, its uneven surface possessed a strange exterior of ridges and protrusions of indeterminate functionality. Now positioned close to the ISS— so close, in fact, he could no longer see Earth—its mass was blocking any line of sight downward. Thinking about it, the UFO's position also obscured the ISS from anyone viewing them from down on the surface. It was a long ten minutes before MCC was back on the line.

"This is Houston Mission Control, Commander. Our preliminary ground and satellite numbers are in. The latest telemetry indicates nothing aberrant being tracked. Repeat . . . nothing aberrant currently being tracked, over."

Landon forced himself to swallow hard. "And you're currently monitoring all ISS external video feeds?"

"Copy that, Commander."

"Seriously, you still don't see . . . this *thing*?" He thought about how to best describe what he was seeing. A spacecraft— plain as day—a mere stone's throw away from the ISS. "The . . . object," he inadequately clarified.

"That's a negative. Not picking up anything out of the ordinary, Commander. We just don't see it. Over "

Landon blinked in rapid succession—perhaps he shouldn't believe his own eyes. "Greg? Peter . . . ?"

"Copy that, Commander," Peter said, in his thick Russian accent. "Yeah, I see it too . . . a UFO. A very large UFO."

"Copy that here too, Commander" Greg said. "But hey . . . maybe I'm looking at a different object. One the size of a New York City block, sitting . . . right off our portside, over."

Landon appreciated Greg's ability to find humor, even in the most tense of situations. Maybe it was a stress relief mechanism. He could hear both men's accelerated breaths, coming over coms. All three of them were more than a little freaked out. The sighting was huge, a life-changing moment. No, more a *historical,* world-changing moment.

Landon continued to stare outward at the alien spacecraft: a spacecraft physically dwarfing the ISS in size by a factor of ten. Hell, maybe twenty. It hadn't maneuvered from its present position for close to an hour now. There had to be a valid explanation why mission control wasn't picking the sighting up—detecting the huge *spacecraft.* Aware there were numerous high-orbit US satellites in the vicinity, he said, "Houston, please double-check . . . all telemetry from our high-orbit birds."

"This is Houston Mission Control. Commander . . . we do not have tracking telemetry, or visuals of any kind, that confirm the presence of said object. Apparently, the three of you, stationed within the ISS, have a unique perspective. We'll need a detailed verbal description of what you are viewing."

Landon liked her. Margaret Haskell was their most frequent conduit down to Earth below—the friendly voice now speaking to them from Mission Control's CapCom. But right then he wanted to scream at her—to all of them below—to just look at what should be visible right before their *fucking* eyes. Glancing over his shoulder, he watched Greg Fischer weightlessly swoop into the Galaxy-1 module.

"I think it's best if I take a look out from in here—see if we're both seeing the same thing." Greg extended his hands out just in time as his body made contact with the module's nearby bulkhead. Sliding in closer to Landon, he peered through the porthole window. "Yep, pretty much the same object I viewed from the other end of the station."

Landon and Greg stared solemnly at each other, both wearing the same bewildered expression. "I guess we're on our own with this," Greg said.

Landon nodded. He heard Margaret Haskell's intense, growing ever more exasperated, voice in the background requesting further information. A much more detailed description of the alien vessel. But Greg was right. They were on their own in dealing with this UFO outside.

"Should we try to . . . I don't know . . . contact them?" Greg asked.

Landon looked out through the porthole. "I don't know. Damn. We make the wrong move, who knows how it will be interpreted."

"Or misinterpreted," Greg added, with brows raised.

chapter 9

Scotty Sullivan, awake for a while now, realized he was in a hospital. A window on his right showed the sun was up. Although his head still pounded from being beaten repeatedly with a heavy flashlight, it hurt slightly less than before. He reached up and touched a bandage secured to the left side of his face. Bringing his hand back down, he stared at it as if it belonged to someone else. Rubbing his fingers together, he felt the soft texture of flesh moving against flesh. The sensation still seemed unfamiliar. He felt strangely disconnected—to everything.

Only when he heard the sound of metal scraping against metal did he realize his right wrist was handcuffed to the hospital bed, an IV drip line attached to the same arm.

A man in a white coat, holding an electronic tablet, came around the suspended privacy curtain. Of medium height, he appeared to be of foreign descent. In accented English, he said, "Good morning, sir, I am Dr. Patel. Do you know where you are?"

"I am in a hospital."

"Correct. You were brought here, to Nantucket Cottage Hospital, very early in the morning . . . a day and a half ago."

"A day and a half?" Scotty asked, his voice filled with incredulity. He slowly nodded his head but immediately wished he hadn't.

"The pain will subside over time," Dr. Patel said, looking down at his tablet. "Can you tell me your name?"

"Scotty."

"And what is your last name, Scotty?"

Scotty searched through his memories, hoping some clue would be available. "I don't know. Guess that's kind of weird, huh?"

"No . . . not at all. Your body has withstood serious trauma. Above and beyond having a concussion, you have a hairline fracture of your left cheek. Above your lip, several sutures were necessary. Do you remember how you acquired these injuries?"

"Sure I do. A cop hit me with his flashlight."

Dr. Patel stared back at him. "Did you provoke him . . . perhaps?"

"I don't think so. Can't really remember ever provoking anyone."

The doctor looked momentarily baffled; unsure how to continue questioning. "There's also this," the doctor said, gesturing to the half-dollar-sized protrusion on Scotty's inside forearm. "Seems to be . . . maybe a growth of some kind. Let's not get overly concerned about it at this juncture, but it will need to be biopsied as soon as—"

Just then a woman peered around the curtain. "Excuse me, Dr. Patel?"

The doctor spun around to face her. "Yes, I am Dr. Patel. Can I help you?"

"Sorry to interrupt... I'm FBI Special Agent Alison McGuire. May I have a few words with you?" She was holding a leather satchel in one hand and an envelope in the other. He saw the words *DNA / Sullivan,* handwritten across the top.

Scotty watched her glance his way.

"In private, please." Her shoulder length hair was dark brown, and she wore an off-white buttoned blouse beneath a navy blue jacket with matching pants. All business, she appeared to be about his same age—mid-twenties—and pretty, with a strong air of confidence. Scotty watched as both the woman and the doctor disappeared behind the curtain, leaving him alone.

His mind was still a-jumble, but not like it was earlier, when he was on the beach. He glanced around at what he could see of the room. *Geez—why was everything so alien to him?* Not just being in a strange hospital room, but being here—among these people. As if he were a visitor: one who hadn't been present for a very long time.

He heard murmurs, probably coming from out in the hallway. He looked at the closed curtain as the woman and doctor continued to speak in low tones.

He thought hard; desperate to arrange the puzzle pieces in his disjointed mind into some semblance of order. *Who am I? And where was I ... before three days ago?* He turned his attention to the window. The sky was an intense blue, and the sun—high in the sky and out of sight—filled the room with both light and warmth. He scratched at the annoying tingle on his forearm. Then, studying the area, he noticed he'd pretty much scratched himself raw there.

And then he remembered. First, it came back in visual bits and pieces; then, like scenes taken from a movie, memories began unspooling into his consciousness—scenes unveiling a life in space, on another planet. He then remembered it all. Remembered he was both: Human and Vallic. And he remembered what he was here to accomplish. Something *impossible.* He couldn't wait to get started.

Scotty used his index finger to make two counter-clockwise circles within the round confines of the spherical protrusion on his right forearm. He then tapped at its center four times. He felt the small organism within do its excited, almost undetectable, little dance. *"I'm glad too, my little Orand-Pall friend,* Scotty conveyed back mentally. *And thank you for being so patient. Please relay to them that I am fine now; fully capable of completing the mission.* Scotty waited for the Orand-Pall, the intermediary, which had taken up residence within his arm so many years ago, to complete the other side of the conversation.

They are glad you are well . . . but you need to be conscious of the schedule, Scotty.

Scotty nodded. *Orand-Pall, ask her . . . how is she?"* He waited a full minute before receiving an answer back.

You need to hurry, Scotty. She will try to hold on.

Scotty felt the Orand-Pall relax, settle down within his arm, returning to a kind of slumber-like mode. The conversation was over.

chapter 10

D r. Patel, with the trim, brown-haired woman close on his heels, appeared around the curtain. The doctor, in his pleasant, singsong-accented voice, said, "Scotty, this is—"

Scotty cut in, "Sullivan. My name is Scotty Sullivan. I remember. I remember everything."

Momentarily mystified, the doctor glanced toward the woman, then back at Scotty. "Excellent! Very nice progress, young man." He began tapping something on to his tablet.

Scotty was excited, actually jubilant. He had much to do, starting with getting out of this bed—this hospital.

"So, he does remember," she said, looking and sounding skeptical.

"As I told you, Ms. McGuire, with serious head traumas such as his, a condition called retrograde amnesia, it would be impossible to predict either how or when a patient's memory would return."

"Hi there, I am FBI Special Agent Alison McGuire," she said, thrusting out a hand. "May I call you Scotty?"

Scotty, intending to shake her hand, the way he recalled doing it so many years ago, first felt, then heard, the handcuff jangle on his right wrist. Awkwardly, taking her right hand in his left instead, he fumbled, giving her an overly enthusiastic handshake—not accustomed yet on how to shake hands properly. "Yes, call me Scotty."

The corner of one side of her mouth crept up, as if pulled by an invisible thread.

"I would like to ask you a few questions, Scotty. Your doctor is concerned that it may be too soon. Are you feeling up to it?"

Glancing up, irritation flashed across the doctor's face. He, apparently, felt it should be him initiating any conversation regarding his patient's wellbeing.

"Um . . . I'm okay, I guess. But I need to leave," Scotty said. "I . . . I remember I have to be somewhere else."

Dr. Patel said, "You'll be here another twenty-four hours minimum, Scotty. We can't underestimate the seriousness of those blows to your head. As for being questioned right now, it might be best if you take another day."

"No, it's okay, Dr. Patel. I'll talk to her," Scotty replied, but concerned with the prospect of having to be hospitalized another day.

The doctor stood silently a moment before saying, "If you need anything, your call button is right here." He repositioned the cord on Scotty's bed, near his free left hand. Smiling, he nodded, then left without acknowledging the FBI woman further.

Alison, looking about the curtained room, spotted a lone chair in the far corner. Scotty watched as she retrieved it—pulled it around—shoving it in close to the left side of the bed. Sitting down, she refocused her attention fully on to him. She took in a controlled breath, as if quelling some growing inner excitement. Eyes sparkling, she smiled for the first time.

Scotty quickly turned his eyes away and cleared his throat. At that moment, changes were rapidly occurring within his body. Physiological deviations, he knew, that weren't the norm. His body's temperature had risen noticeably; his hands felt clammy and he had to fight against a strong physical urge to wipe them on the bed sheet. Moisture too was forming on his upper lip. *What the hell is happening to me?* He swallowed hard and, with reluctance, stared back into her sparkling brown eyes. *God, she's really lovely.*

"Scotty, there's quite a bit we need to go over. Do you mind if I show you something?" Alison looked around the floor, spotting the leather satchel she'd dropped when she went to fetch the chair. Pulling it now up onto her lap, she opened it and extracted several sheets of white paper. "Three days ago, all kinds of alarms went off at the FBI headquarters in Langley, Virginia. Apparently, you were taken into custody and booked at the local Nantucket police station here . . . do you remember that?"

Scotty, unconsciously reaching up a hand to touch the bandage still covering a portion of his face, nodded back.

"Like I said, all kinds of alarms went off. Folks have been searching for you," she glanced down at the papers in her hand,

"... for over sixteen years." She looked back up. "This is a print-out of fingerprints, taken when Scotty Sullivan was a child. It was a fairly common practice, even back then, for parents to have their kids fingerprinted, most often done at school. These sixteen-year-old prints are a match to your booking prints." Alison held up a page, featuring a series of oblong smudges—fingerprints—along with a number of circles and handwritten notes scribbled all over the sheet. "There are some ... discrepancies, that I've already discussed with your doctor, concerning your DNA test results."

Scotty nodded, his attention drawn to her lips as she spoke. He took in the tilt of her head, the way she used her slender fingers to secure back an errant lock of hair behind one ear. *How long had it been,* he wondered, *since anyone had this kind of effect on him?* A *long* time, he knew. His mind then flashed to another time—another planet. He thought of Tori and was immediately filled with sadness. Placing his hand on his heart, he tried not to remember.

Alison continued, "I've enlisted the doctor's help and he's checking with the hospital lab folks now. But getting back to these fingerprints, they're fairly definitive." She looked up, "Are you ... okay?"

"I'm fine," Scotty lied. "And yes, that's me. I am the same Scotty Sullivan. And you want to know where I've been all these years."

Alison shrugged in assent. "There was a massive ground search for you. Lives were torn apart—your parents, your siblings. In time, you were decreed dead. It was determined you'd been swept out to sea when at your vacation home while playing on the beach. Not everyone believed that . . ."

But Scotty had ceased listening, her comments still repeating—an endless loop inside his head. *Lives were torn apart . . . your parents . . . your siblings.* For many years he'd missed them terribly. Had to mentally train himself—force himself—not to think about them at all. But now those same mental safeguards, one after another, were slowly falling away. His mother's face, out of focus, undefined, came into view. Then, as if adjusting a camera lens, her features sharpened and he saw the way she used to look at him: with patience, amusement, and love. He remembered his father too—sitting on his knee as Scotty showed him something imprisoned in a capped jar, a bug of some sort. And then he thought of his baby sister and older brother. Questioning himself why, after three plus days back, he'd only then thought of them.

"Your mother. She never believed you were dead. Never stopped looking for you. Spent every cent she had on private detectives."

"Wait . . . where are they? Where's my family?"

"Your father works and lives in Boston. Your brother is married and lives in Los Angeles. Your sister is finishing up college in Boulder, Colorado."

"And my mother? Is she still . . ."

"She's here. Never left Nantucket. As I said before, she never stopped looking for you. I'm sorry to say, but your mother and father split up ten years back."

Scotty took it all in. The lives of his family members had, of course, moved on without him. Except for his mother, apparently. He felt sad and a bit guilty too—although he'd had no say in the matter, of course, all those years back.

"So now it's your turn, Scotty. Where were you all these years? What happened to you?" Alison asked.

"I was abducted . . ."

Alison nodded, lifting one brow. Her expression read *Okay, I already figured that much out.*"

". . . by aliens." He stared back at her expressionless.

chapter 11

US astronauts Commander Jack Landon and Lt. Greg Fischer, and Russian cosmonaut Peter Mirkin, were assembled within the ISS's dome-shaped observation cupola, with its seven individual windows.

"They're going to kill us, or, at the very least, take us prisoner. Do their experiments on us . . ."

Landon glared at Fischer, who was starting to get on his nerves. "Okay— enough of that kind of talk," Landon said. "So, you've checked the parabolics?" he asked, referring to the US Orbital Segment that utilizes two separate bowl-shaped radio antennas mounted to the Z1 truss structure.

Landon continued, "Doesn't take much to get either one of them pointed in the wrong direction. One unintended nudge, and there you have it—our coms are cut off."

Fischer said shaking his head, "But both antennas, at virtually the same time? Come on, how the hell does something like that happen?"

"I think we three know what really happened," Peter Mirkin said, "It was no *nudge*. The signals are purposely being blocked." The Russian's attention was focused on the alien craft, still positioned off the portside of the ISS. He turned away from watching the alien ship centered in the grouping of portholes. "What do we do now? I don't like just sitting here . . . being at their mercy, so to speak."

Greg Fischer shook his head. "What do you suggest? That maybe we should fire up the phasers, or the pulse cannons? Or maybe shift into warp drive, jump to light speed?"

Showing annoyance, Peter said, "First of all, you're inter-mixing your stupid American science fiction. Second, I'm simply saying we should be proactive, that's all."

"He's right," Landon said. "At the very least we must attempt to communicate with them."

"The parabolics are down. We just discussed that," Greg said.

"Let's try one of the Ericsson MP-X handhelds," Landon said, referring to the small commercial radios that were some-times used to communicate with amateur radio enthusiasts around the world.

Peter shook his head. "If the aliens were clever enough to block the parabolics . . ."

"Come on, can't we give it a try before we start overthinking things?" Landon asked, ready to throttle Greg.

At that precise moment everything within the observation module went dark. The constant hum of onboard computer server hard drives became silent. Equally important, if not more so, the station's environmental air circulation system ceased flowing. Almost immediately, the temperature within the compartment began to drop.

Nearly pitch-black, even with a minimal amount of light shining in through the cupola windows, for a moment no one moved or spoke.

"It was a dark and stormy night . . ."

"Hush, Greg!" Landon barked. "Let's get into our EMUs. We'll at least be prepared if . . ."

"They start firing on the ISS, blowing these tin cans apart, one by one," Greg added.

They had actually trained for just such a scenario. Not for the arrival of an alien vessel, but for the catastrophic failure of one, or more, internal ISS systems. Landon knew that getting into the EMUs—each a virtual, one person spacecraft unto itself—would give them time to think. Action instead of prolonged fruitless discussions dwelling on their worry of running out of air or being frozen by the ever-decreasing internal station temperatures.

They needed to split up. Typically, no more than two EVAs/spacewalks occurred at any one time. Landon and Fischer weightlessly pulled themselves along through the darkness in the direction of the Node 1 airlock. Through a combination of tight left and right turns they quickly made their way through the maze of interconnected passageways and modules. Golden swaths of sunlight suddenly streamed in through the Galaxy-1 portholes, making navigating somewhat easier. Since there were only two EMU NASA spacesuits, hanging within the Node 1 airlock, Peter Mirkin left them and headed for the Russian Pirs Module airlock. He would have to do his best to get suited-up on his own. Not an easy task—but doable.

Landon and Fischer entered the Node1 section—called Kitman's Lock. Both had earlier grabbed emergency flashlights along the way. Two EMU suits were hanging inside, secured on opposing bulkheads. First, though, came dressing into the accompanying undergarments: one a type of adult diaper, and the second, named a Liquid Cooling and Ventilation Garment, was similar in appearance to long underwear. Dressing for space was a long, tedious process. Since there were no portholes in this section of the ISS, dressing was much more difficult—only the limited illumination from their flashlights providing them with light.

Landon and Fischer continued assisting one another through the dressing process. The fact that an EMU had only a limited oxygen supply—about eight hours—wasn't lost on Landon. *Then what?* He considered what Mission Control might do to help them. How long before they sent up an emergency rescue rocket? Truth was, the alien ship hadn't been detected by any of their ground sensors, or by any of their orbiting satellites. Did Houston believe, fully accept their report of a UFO nearby? Did the sudden cut off of all contact get the ball rolling? Initiate rescue protocols? Of course, virtu-ally all emergency scenarios were well rehearsed, trained for, even anticipated, but as Landon stepped one leg at a time into the bottom portion of his EMU, he couldn't remember what those protocols specifically called for. At the moment, Houston didn't know their key ISS environmental systems were also down. Unaware, unless the systems came back online, that in eight hours they would be running out of air. Houston prepping a rocket for liftoff, even fast tracking the entire process for an emergency such as theirs, would take a hell of a lot longer than eight hours.

"Did you feel that?" Greg asked.

Grasping the oversized D-ring opening, Landon pulled the pants-like lower section garment up. "Feel what?" But then he saw, more than felt, what Greg was referring to. The Node 1 module had moved. They stared at each other then simultaneously said, "Hurry!" Together, they quickened the pace, fully inserting their bodies into their EMUs.

Landon felt more repetitive jarring—something making abrupt contact with the ISS. It took all his willpower to finish what he was doing, not head over to the view station cupola to see what the hell was going on out there.

* * *

On the other side of the ISS, within the Pirs module airlock, Peter Mirkin was not nearly as far along climbing into his EMU. He'd taken a short detour first, relieving his bladder within the lone ISS toilet facility. When he noticed the jarring motion going on around him, his first inclination was to use the station's inter-module communications system. Of course, that was no longer an option. Weightless, he only knew some sort of collision was taking place outside the ISS. Massive vibrations occurring around him, everything was shuddering.

Maybe Greg's comments about being attacked weren't that far off the mark. Moving now with haste, he hurried to climb into his EMU.

Suddenly much louder now, forcing Peter to put his hands over his ears, the sound of metal grating hard against metal telegraphed throughout the International Space Station. He reached for his helmet, muttering, *Какая трахается! (What the fuck is happening!)*

chapter 12

" Oh... aliens?" Alison said smiling at his juvenile-like humor. "Ha-ha. Well, I guess that explains why you're about as pasty-white as any person I've ever met. Tell me, those aliens keep you buried under a rock somewhere?"

Scotty stared back at her, not returning her smile.

"Seriously... tell me. Where have you been for nearly two decades?" It then occurred to her that the subject of his disappearance, his memories of the abduction, might be painful. Perhaps even embarrassing, or humiliating to speak about to a woman. She felt guilty for making light of that fact. "You're actually the victim here, Scotty, I'm not here to judge you in any way," Alison said, her FBI training kicking in. *When questioning a subject, you need to give them enough space to feel comfortable. Let them talk—don't dominate the discussion.*

Alison sat back and observed him as he took in what she'd said. What hadn't gone unnoticed on her was that the patient, sitting up in bed, was both ruggedly handsome and uniquely humble. In her past experiences with attractive men, humility wasn't a trait typically associated with good looks.

She heard a noise behind her. Dr. Patel, poking his head in from around the curtain, said, "Excuse me." He was holding the envelope with the DNA report she'd given him earlier; the same report provided to both her supervisor and herself by the FBI lab in Quantico. They had been adamant that the test results appeared wonky—due perhaps to compromised swab sampling at the police station. The techs were going to process his sample again, but they'd provided her this preliminary readout, anyway. She figured by letting Dr. Patel take a look at the report, she just might get the genetic confirmation match she was looking for—even if the readings were somewhat flawed.

Alison stood and smiled. "Excuse me, just need to speak with the good doctor for a moment." She patted his covered leg, "Don't go anywhere, Scotty, I'm not through with you yet."

She followed behind Dr. Patel, passing the one other patient in the room—a thin-as-a-rail elderly man. He was staring up at the TV, mounted high on the adjacent wall.

They moved out into the corridor. From his dour expression, she figured he'd had no luck getting an exact match.

"Ms. McGuire . . ."

"That's Special Agent, McGuire," Alison said, correcting him. Just because she might look a little young to be an FBI agent didn't mean she didn't deserve to be recognized by her title. She'd worked hard for it. She was damn certain the good doctor wouldn't care to be called *Mr.* Patel.

"I apologize, Special Agent McGuire. Let me explain what I've done . . . to give you a clear perspective of what was involved."

Involved? Alison nodded.

"Nantucket Cottage Hospital is right next door to where we send our blood work specimens out for analyses. DNA testing, if requested, can be included. So even before you provided me with the genetic test results from your FBI lab, I gave a vial of Mr. Sullivan's blood to the folks next door and requested the testing process be expedited." Patel held up the envelope she'd given him earlier in his left hand and several sheets of paper in his right. "Agent McGuire, the results are basically identical. Rest assured, there were no sampling mistakes made, as your FBI lab feared. And I feel comfortable telling you that the patient sitting up in Room 289, is, in fact, Mr. Scotty Sullivan."

"That's great!" she exclaimed, then noticed the doctor wasn't sharing her enthusiasm. "So, why so glum?"

"There are other . . . concerns."

"What kind of concerns?"

He exhaled a stale, coffee-scented breath. "Without Mr. Sullivan's explicit consent, I am not at liberty to reveal a patient's medical information."

"You're talking about HIPAA," she said.

"Yes. So, before we proceed further, I'd like to ask Mr. Sullivan if it would be all right if I share this with you."

"Okay, let's do that."

Together, they marched back into Scotty's and the elderly man's shared hospital room. A news bulletin was flashing up on the TV—something about NASA losing contact with the orbiting International Space Station—and they stopped to watch. The news correspondent, standing in front of NASA Mission Control, in Houston, Texas, reported:

"Things, sadly, are not looking good for the three-man crew— two Americans and one Russian—onboard. Since no part of the ISS is currently being detected, or is trackable, there is strong speculation the space station has met with disaster."

Continuing on ahead, Dr. Patel shook his head. "So terrible . . . such a tragic loss."

Alison held back a moment longer to watch. She'd actually considered becoming an astronaut as a teenager. The faces of the crew were now up on the screen. Feeling sick about it, she glanced back to see the elderly man's face streaked with tears. She said, "Well, let's hope for the best."

Coming back around the curtain separating both beds, she found Scotty staring out the window, wearing a dreamy, contemplative, expression. She briefly wondered what he was thinking about.

"Mr. Sullivan?" Dr. Patel prompted.

Scotty, blinking away distant thoughts, nodded at them.

"Would it be all right if I share your medical information? It pertains to your genetic test findings. Share it with Ms. . . . um, Agent McGuire?" The doctor held up the sheets of paper in one hand.

Scotty, seeming to consider his request, nodded. "Sure. I have no secrets."

"Very good. First of all, I have no reason to believe that you are not, indeed, Scotty Sullivan. Included in the report, provided by Agent McGuire, I have the DNA sample—taken from the toothbrush of the missing boy—as well as your own recent DNA tests. I see no sufficient discrepancies to conclude otherwise: you both are one and the same person."

Alison watched Scotty slowly nod—their findings didn't seem new to him.

The doctor continued, "What I would like to talk to you about though, are other aspects of the test findings."

"The erroneous markers," Scotty said.

Both Alison and Dr. Patel exchanged a puzzled glance.

"Well, that's correct. So, you already know about them?" the doctor asked, seeming bewildered.

Scotty nodded again.

"Excuse me if I get a little technical here," the doctor said. "Huntington's Disease and Fragile X Syndrome have been found to be associated with certain patterns in mini and micro-satellite DNA. Regarding Huntington's Disease, the number of CAG, cytosine-adenine-guanine, differ between normal individuals and those where the disease is present. In other words, the loci, the specific locations on the DNA strand that we look at, are not only used for individual identification purposes, but can also be used for determining certain physiological, and pathological, conditions.

Alison watched Scotty as he pondered the medical gobble-dygook the doctor was spewing out.

Scotty nodded. "I assure you, I have neither of the two diseases you just mentioned, Doctor."

"Well, more tests need to be run first, but the indications are . . ."

Scotty smiling, said, "If you will allow me to interject, I may be able to better explain to you what you are viewing on your printout." He reached his free hand out and took the sheets. Placing them on his lap, he positioned them so both Alison and the doctor could better see them. The printout, filled with several rows, contained numerous spikes, similar to the results seen on a lie detector test. He looked at Alison. "Here, see these peaks with the numbers below them? That is my DNA profile from sixteen years ago. That matches the profile from the toothbrush, I assume?"

Dr. Patel hesitantly nodded.

Alison wondered how Scotty could possibly know that without actually comparing the two.

"Now, if you look closely, you'll notice extra peaks that shouldn't be there, right? Extra peaks, showing at each of the loci—or locations—on the DNA. But the difference is, the extra peaks don't have numbers assigned to them. That's because the machine couldn't recognize them—what is called the ladder—as being real alleles."

Dr. Patel stared at the pages on Scotty's lap and slowly nodded. Alison, glancing at both, felt more than a little lost, but mostly curious. *How did Scotty know* about any of this stuff?

"Thus, what you thought were shadow markers really are not." Scotty said.

Alison held up both hands, as if attempting to stop traffic. "Excuse me. Sorry, but you've totally lost me here. Beside the impressive fact you know so much about the workings of genetics and DNA profiles, can you repeat it again...in a way I can comprehend its meaning too?"

The doctor interjected, "Well, assuming Scotty is correct, that the erroneous markers are not indicative of some kind of genetic disorder, like a disease, I suppose having one or two erroneous peaks could be attributed to certain artifacts, usually the result of machine error, or a high background noise." The doctor hesitated, as if considering his own words, then said, "But they wouldn't be reproducible, especially when two separate labs ran the test." He shook his head. "So having a whole extra "profile" of these shadow markers is unexplainable." The doctor appeared even more perplexed.

Scotty said, "Ah...but it *is* explainable. There are not one, but two, complete DNA profile markers here. Your instrumentation threw-out the second set, having nothing to compare them to within its limited database. Only one of those sets was determined to actually be of Human origin."

"What? You're saying the other set is from what, another species entirely? I assure you, Mr. Sullivan, that is not possible," the doctor said, with an uneasy smile.

"Sorry, Doctor, not only another species, but a species from another world. Scotty shrugged. "In time, you will come to understand this to be true."

Alison, reminded of Scotty's previous joke, of being abducted by aliens, thought, *Crap, this guy really is bat-shit-crazy.*

Too bad, too. She'd sort of hoped things would have gone differently. Perhaps it was past trauma, his abduction, or . . .

Scotty chuckled. Gazing at Alison, he said, "I assure you, I am not crazy. In time you'll believe me." He then turned to the doctor. "If it is important to you, you can run the tests again."

"I suppose, but considering the lab results at hand match those of the FBI's, I don't see much benefit in doing so."

"I'd like to provide you with a new regimen with far more detailed test parameters to run. As well as an expanded genetics database to draw from."

Only then did Alison realize Scotty's right wrist was no longer tethered to the bed. Abruptly standing, she moved around to the bed's far side and stared down at the now-empty handcuffs, dangling from the metal railing.

Looking sheepish, he said, "Oh . . . sorry. The cuff was becoming rather uncomfortable. I can put it back on if you want."

chapter 13

An exhausted-looking Brianna Sullivan, age forty-five—
her hair now lusterless, roots sprouting gray, used her key
to open the door into her second-story, one-room flat. Tossing
her keys onto a side table, she used the heel of her shoe to kick
the door shut behind her.

Her commute to work each day consisted merely of walking
the single flight of stairs either up or down at *Stillworth's Skiff*—a
dimly lit bar and grill in existence for well over one hundred
years. As a server there, she had no idea who Stillworth was, or
why the seedy pub was even named after him in the first place.
All she knew was she wanted to get out of her foul-scented
clothing—smelling of on-tap beer and cooked clams—then
take an extremely hot shower.

She fumbled with the knot in her apron strings, tied
behind her back. Almost ready to find a pair a scissors and
cut the *fucking* things off, she felt her left butt cheek vibrate.
Giving up on the knot, she retrieved the cell-phone out from

her jeans back pocket. She peered down at the caller: *Nantucket Safe Harbor Animal Shelter.*

Brianna let the phone ring in her hand. Someone requesting a donation from her undoubtedly, she almost laughed. She'd be lucky to make the rent this month. Even this shithole of an apartment was ridiculously expensive. Everything in Nantucket was ridiculously expensive. The small pittance of alimony she still received from Andrew hadn't covered her bare-bones expenses for years. Not with what she'd paid out to Tony over the last sixteen years. She thought about Tony Rizzo, the barrel-chested, sixty-five-year-old Boston PI who'd been searching for her son for over sixteen years now. Maybe it was time. Time to put an end to the search. She answered the phone on the fifth ring, "Hello?"

Sounding like a young male teenager, he responded, "Yeah ... hi there ... this is the Nantucket Safe Harbor Animal Shelter."

"Uh huh, I gathered that from the Caller ID. What ..."

He cut her off. "We have a dog here, came in a few days ago. The imbedded microchip's an old one; points to a Massachusetts registry. Long story short, we tracked the owner to this phone number. To a Mrs. Brianna Sullivan."

Brianna, raking fingers through her hair, shook her head. "That's me, but I haven't owned a dog in over sixteen years and that dog was three at the time. So, unless you've heard of a dog living, like, nineteen years ... it can't be mine."

"This dog looks pretty young. Sorry to have bothered you."

Brianna's curiosity was mildly peaked. "What breed of dog is it?"

"He's a good-looking dog. Golden mix, would be my guess."

"Weird coincidence. That was the breed of our dog too. Actually, a Golden Cocker mix"

"This dog has some cocker in him, but, like you said, the age is all wrong."

Brianna nodded to herself. She'd loved that big goofy animal. Lost him the same day she'd lost Scotty. "I don't suppose the dog you've got there has two dark, front paws and a darker fur tail?"

"Umm . . . well, yeah. That's exactly what this dog has."

She thought about the improbability of that. "How late are you open tonight?"

"Another hour. I still have to shovel out a few more runs."

Fifty-three minutes later, her hair still a little wet, and not wearing a lick of makeup, Brianna arrived at the shelter slightly out of breath. Not owning a car, she'd jogged the mile-and-a-half distance. Entering the shelter's concrete floors and scuffed long counter office, she found a lone teenager standing behind the counter, talking on the phone. She heard a cacophony of barking noises, coming from behind the far wall. The kid glanced up and, holding up a finger, continued to describe some other dog to the person on the other end.

Five minutes later the teenager hung up the phone and, raising his chin, asked, "You Ms. Sullivan?"

Brianna nodded. "I'm not sure why I'm even here, it's not like the dog here is mine."

He shrugged. "Might as well take a look. Come on, I'll take you back." Gesturing toward another door, he said, "Right through there," and held the door open for her. They entered into what was obviously the kennel part of the shelter. Chain-linked cages flanked both sides of the long building. Renewed loud barking was an assault on her senses. From what Brianna could see, every cage was occupied. And each dog, whether small or large, was wildly vying for their attention.

She walked behind the teenager. His oversized, baggy-assed jeans hung so low on his hips she marveled how they stayed up—didn't drop to his knees as he walked ahead.

"Here we go . . . it's that cage on the left," he announced, both pointing and yawning at the same time.

Brianna positioned herself directly in front of the cage and stared down. In her estimate, he was the only dog in the whole facility not barking. She studied the dog as the dog stared up at her. It really was uncanny how much the animal looked like Larry. Exchanging a quick glance with the teen, she lowered herself down to one knee next to the chain-link fence separating them. Definitely a Golden Cocker mix, it tentatively stepped up closer, sniffing at her fingers pushed through the fencing.

Immediately, the dog began to yelp, wag, and wiggle. He jumped up, pushing his snout through a link opening, his pink tongue frantically licking at her hands.

"Dog's been here for three days . . . first time he's done any-thing like this. Acts like he knows you."

But Brianna wasn't really listening to him. Vision blurring from overflowing tears, she brought her face close enough for the dog to lick. "Can you open the cage for me?"

"I don't know, we're actually closed now."

"This is my dog. I don't know how, but this is Larry. Please, just open the damn gate!"

chapter 14

Commander Jack Landon, securing his own helmet into place, then helping Greg Fischer with his, was just now coming to a second realization. Their spacesuits certainly would provide them the necessary life-support functionality over the next eight, or so, hours, but since all ISS radio communications, including their individual EMU's, utilized the station's main communications hub control unit—one currently no longer getting any juice—unless they were right next to each other, they'd be stuck exchanging basic hand gestures, or writing hand-written notes, to communicate with one another.

Landon activated the integrated light on his helmet and watched as Fischer did the same. The Node 1 airlock brightened all around them. Touching his helmet against Fischer's he pointed toward the open hatch, leading back into the ISS, and yelled, "Need to check on Mirkin . . . see if the ISS is still in one piece."

Fischer gave him a thumbs-up gesture, apparently catching enough of what he'd shouted out.

After the incredibly loud noises—metal scraping hard against metal that he'd heard earlier—he was more than a little surprised to find the station hadn't been breached, and that its internal pressurization was still intact. He studied the narrowed open hatchway through his visor. Their EMU's were ridiculously bulky—ungainly. Sure, it was possible to move about inside the ISS in their spacesuits. They'd trained for it in case of emergencies, but it was a royal pain in the ass.

In the end, it took three times longer than it normally would to reach the Pirs airlock unit. Arriving there, they found Mirkin, perspiration glistening on his brow and upper lip, had yet to attach his helmet. They made eye contact. Floating closer in the weightless environment, Landon barely heard Mirkin yell, "So what the fuck's going on? What's with all these noises?"

Landon, nodding, took Mirkin's helmet from him. The Russian EVU's utilized a slightly different latching mechanism than those found on NASA suits, and he had to fumble with it some. His thick gloves greatly limited his fingers dexterity. On getting the helmet properly seated and latched over Mirkin's head, Mirkin mouthed *thank you*.

Two minutes later, Landon, with Mirkin following close behind, joined Fischer within the somewhat cluttered Russian Zarya module. Pointing to the space around them, Fischer held up his hands and made a face, then gave it a thumbs-up. Landon got his meaning. Everything seemed to be okay, but he wasn't one hundred percent sure. And truthfully, how could he be?

Suddenly, and much too violently, Landon found himself crashing down hard onto the deck. His helmet smashed down face first. His padded EMU absorbed the brunt of the fall, protecting the rest of his body. *What the hell? How is this possible? There shouldn't be gravity . . . not here in space!*

Substantially darker in the module now, Landon figured his helmet light may have broken in the fall. He tried, but failed, to lift himself up, applying what was akin to an upper torso pushup. Even after steadfastly following a set pattern of daily routine exercises, his arms and chest muscles had weakened from months of a zero gravity existence. The three hundred-and-twenty pounds of dead weight added on by his EMU made such an endeavor nearly impossible. Giving up, lying in a prone position on the Zarya module metal deck, he had a clear view of Fischer. He too looked to be struggling, like himself only a moment before. He imagined Mirkin, the most muscular and fit of the three, would be struggling as well.

None of the recent happenings made any damn sense, starting with their total loss of communications with Mission Control. Then the power outage and the subsequent total ISS systems failures. Next had come the series of external noises—as if the ISS was being dragged down a gravel-pitted road. But now the impossible had occurred, the loss of weightlessness, the return of gravity.

While Landon lay there—his finite air supply depleting with each drawn breath—his thoughts raced. *So what can we do? What do I do now?*

Only then did Landon notice a bluish cast to the limited, ambient, lighting within the Zarya space module. He blinked several times in rapid succession, thinking perhaps his visual perception had changed—maybe the air supply was compromised. Although his EMU certainly might be damaged, there wasn't any complex air mixture to get screwed up since their spacesuits simply stored pure oxygen.

Movement!

A darker shade of blue passed within a foot of his helmet. Shadow-like but not a shadow, Landon's eyes tracked whatever the thing was as it moved about the module. It definitely had form—shape. Almost transparent, he could now make out what could be arms and legs, and maybe a head. But it was so very faint; a bluish blur of radiating . . . *energy*.

Two new energy forms joined the first. *This isn't happening. I'm imagining things. I must have struck my head harder than I first figured*, Landon thought.

Suddenly he was being lifted up, rising vertically and standing on his own two feet. Blue energy forms stood on either side, holding him steady. He could feel the pressure of hands gripping his upper arms. The third blue form now stood directly before him. Heart pounding in his chest, and on the verge of hyperventilating, Landon consciously willed his breathing to slow down— his heart rate to normalize. He tried to swallow—tried to think. *What should I do?* And then it hit him; there was absolutely *nothing* he *could* do.

Landon found himself smiling and then, inexplicably, chuckling. This really was happening. Non-Human, alien life forms had somehow infiltrated the ISS. He laughed out loud at the notion. When faced with an equally momentous occasion, Neil Armstrong had declared on taking that fateful first step onto the moon: *One small step for man, one giant leap for mankind.* Christopher Columbus reportedly said something like: *By following the light of the Sun, we left the Old World behind.* Well shit, now's *my* chance . . . and I've nothing to say.

That's odd! Landon hadn't noticed it before but he certainly did now. A substantial portion of the portside bulkhead was no longer there; only an oblong opening, six to seven feet wide by seven to eight feet high, was there instead. Beyond was only blackness. That, at least, explained how these beings, *whatever they were*, had entered the ISS.

No longer seeing any humor in the situation, Landon turned his attention to his fellow crewmembers. But both Fischer and Mirkin were gone.

The energy form in front of him moved closer. So close he could almost make out facial features—eyes, nose, and a mouth— remnants, perhaps, of former, evolutionary aspects. Landon felt the clasp mechanism beneath his helmet being worked on and thought about struggling. Pushing them away. With that breach in the bulkhead, his very survival maybe dependent on his suit's oxygen supply. But he didn't. He quietly stood and let them do whatever they intended to do. He then heard a familiar series of clicks and clacks as his helmet was unsealed, then turned and lifted up over his head. For a moment he held his breath. Closing his eyes, he eventually let his lungs fill up with oxygenated, breathable, air.

Landon asked, "What have you done with my crew?"

chapter 15

Scotty Sullivan chided himself for not being more careful. Yesterday's handcuff stunt was just plain stupid. *Was I just showing off for her?*

He probed the side of his face with the tips of his fingers. No longer tender, he knew if they were to X-Ray his cheek again, they would discover his injuries had all but healed. Yet he'd keep the bandage in place, anyway—no need to draw undue attention to himself at this point.

Scotty felt good. His mind was sharp, his memories once again intact. The re-acclimation process, now fully completed, had taken him days instead of the intended few hours, thanks to that big cop wielding the flashlight. He would need to reestablish contact soon. He thought of Seve and the others and wondered how much time they had left. *Hang on, please! Just hang on a little longer.*

He listened to the latest CNN Breaking News Report, concerning the disappearance of the International Space Station. The drawn privacy curtain blocked visual view of the TV, which was fine. He didn't need to see any of it. He knew all too well what was going on, two-hundred-fifty miles straight up. He knew the oddly pieced together space station hadn't actually erupted in a ball of fire, or disintegrated from an all too quick fall from orbit hitting the planet's upper atmosphere at supersonic velocity. And the crew, he was fairly certain, was fine also. Certainly scared, but okay otherwise.

Scotty thought about the woman again—the FBI agent. He sensed she was conflicted, wondering if he was mentally unstable. A lunatic. A crackpot. He sure could use an ally now, considering all he needed to accomplish moving forward. *Would that be her?* She'd mentioned she would return this morning; even offered to drive him over to where his mother now lived—somewhere off Main Street on the island.

He turned his attention to several seagulls, taking flight off the roof of an adjacent building. Headed toward the nearby Atlantic Ocean, their silhouetted forms were almost black against the brilliant blue sky. Suddenly, a deep sadness fell over him, as he recalled just why he was here—why he had been sent back.

Scotty let his eyes roam over the distant horizon. He could make out cars, moving steadily along the various interconnected streets. Close by, the rooftop of a yellow school bus whizzed past the hospital window. Somewhere near the coast, a motorboat was blaring a forlorn-sounding horn. Life steadily was meandering along within this small picturesque corner of the world; probably not that different from yesterday, or the day before that. But all too soon life—not just here on quaint

Nantucket Island, but on the entire planet—would be coming to an end. The trajectory was indisputable. An inbound interstellar gamma ray burst would blaze through the solar system in a mere instant, leaving nothing behind in its wake. But Scotty wasn't here to save a planet. That would be impossible. He was here to save a species—his own species. To save Humanity—at least to the extent that they wanted to be saved, those who would believe him and accept his presence back as an intergalactic liaison.

Although he didn't personally remember the exact course of events— happening so long ago and being a terrified child at the time—he recalled enough that even today he was surprised he'd survived the ordeal. But survive he had. No longer that same child, nor the same person, he wasn't even completely Human—not really.

Regaining consciousness in an unfamiliar new world—one with a high-level of radiation that would eventually become dangerous to Humans—Scotty would soon transform into something *different*. No, transformed wasn't the right word for it. *Joined* would be more accurate. Indeed, though an aspect of him was still Human, he also was a unique form of *Vallic*. A species that had almost completely discarded embodiment in physical form, exchanging it instead for one primarily composed of energy. Two species now joined, or merged, together—albeit sharing a single consciousness. Most of Scotty's subsequent sixteen years of life on that alien world were lived as a Vallic. Composed of a more hyper-dimensional energy form than one Humanlike, having no crude, obtuse, animal-like, mass.

But his Human self, his complete genetic DNA attributes, still existedand were still accessible. But only when needed, like for teaching purposes—or preparing for this mission.

Thus he'd been able to free himself from the handcuff restraint as easily as a child stepping over a cardboard box.

Suddenly, the hospital room's privacy curtain was pulled to one side as FBI Special Agent Alison McGuire entered Scotty's enclosed space. Looking radiant, and more casual—wearing close-fitting jeans and a red hooded sweatshirt—she smiled and said, "Hey there. Took me a bit longer to get all this stuff." She plopped a large shopping bag along with several smaller bags onto his bed. "I'm assuming you're ready to get the hell out of here?"

"You have no idea how ready," Scotty replied flatly.

"I had to guess your sizes: Waist, shoe-size." She then pro- ceeded to pull out a new pair of jeans from one of the bags, its tags still secured by strings onto a belt loop. She opened a second bag and withdrew white tennis shoes. Another bag held both socks and underwear. The last bag contained a folded blue T-shirt, with a big Nike logo imprinted across the front. "I'll let you get dressed. Let me know when you're done. I'll be out in the hallway. Sound good?"

Scotty nodded, staring down at all the clothes. She'd bought all this stuff on her own—a kindness he never expected. "Um ... thank you!"

"Hey, you can pay me back someday ... if you ever get a job." She smiled, holding onto his gaze for a moment.

A large dark shape moved into the space right behind her. Officer Donald

Platt glared at Alison and Scotty, then down at Scotty's unsecured right arm.

"Who un-cuffed this prisoner?"

chapter 16

P latt moved with all the subtlety of a freight train. Hurrying around the end of the hospital bed, he clipped the bed's far corner with his hip, causing the bed to jerk and shift askew several inches. Maintaining a perpetual sneer, by the time he reached Scotty's right side the mountain of a man had already withdrawn a metal handcuff key from his pocket.

"Don't resist and don't fucking move," he barked, grabbing Scotty's right arm.

Scotty's eyes flashed onto Alison, wondering what she would do. He watched as she reached her hand around to a rear pocket, where she withdrew and then held up her FBI credentials. In that moment, he glimpsed beneath her hoodie, saw a concealed holstered weapon was clipped to her waistband.

"Hold on, officer! Put so much as one hand on that man and I swear you'll regret it. This has become an FBI matter, so stop right there!"

Ignoring her, Platt's vice-like grip grabbed ahold of Scotty's right wrist, twisting and jerking it hard enough around to make him grimace.

Even more determined, Alison took a step closer. Leaning her body across the left side of the bed, she ordered, "Stop!" then held her creds up higher—put them right in his face. "You don't want to push me, unless you want to see your career head right down the toilet from this point on. Screwing with the FBI is never a good idea."

Scotty felt for her. Platt was not only ignoring her authority, he was smirking. Scotty's thoughts flashed back to the earlier beach scenario. Lying on the sand several nights before—naked and defenseless—he was badly beaten; struck repeatedly in the face with Platt's flashlight. He'd watched helplessly as Larry was doused with mace. Now, struggling to keep his growing inner rage in check, he felt a handcuff slap hard around his right wrist; tightening, to the point his flesh was being bunched together and pinched. Platt next grabbed ahold of Scotty's left arm and yanked it closer to him. Alison, looking humiliated and unsure of herself, seemed at a loss for what to do next.

Scotty closed his eyes, relaxed his body, and calmed his mind—detaching all consciousness from the material world: A necessary prerequisite prior to undergoing a physical form-shift. He had undergone the Dyad-Geneses procedure as a child, but being able to *form shift* in the blink of an eye was a feat that took a number of years to fully master. In Scotty's case, considering what he was now tasked to do, he had the unique ability to make dominant either form: Human physicality or

Vallic *energy-based* physicality, pretty much at will. At this point, in his present mindset, he was able to make multiple form shifts—back and forth—all within a perceived instant.

* * *

Alison lowered her creds. She stared in utter amazement. It happened so fast she was having trouble believing what she'd witnessed with her own eyes. One moment Scotty's arms and wrists were forcibly yanked and twisted around to accommodate ratcheting-tight handcuffs. Next, a momentary stuttering of motion, along with a bright flash of blue light, occurred. *Somehow* the handcuffs were no longer secured to either of Scotty's arms. As amazing as that trick seemed, it was nothing compared to the fact that it was the oversized policeman who was now handcuffed to the bed's railing. *Impossible!*

Scotty held up the key to Platt. "Want this?" Instead of handing it over to him, he tossed it over into the room's farthest corner.

Alison took a quick step backward, watching Scotty throw back the covers then swing his legs over the side of the bed. He grabbed up his new pile of clothes and headed out past the privacy curtain. "Come on!" he yelled.

She stood there, looking as calm as she could manage considering what she had just witnessed. Platt's fleshy face was turning a dark shade of red from the exertion of trying to free himself. "Don't cross me again, Platt. Next time, you'll be facing federal charges."

"Bite me, bitch," Platt said back, fuming. He stopped struggling. "Look, I'm doing my job here. What I'm paid to do. And pending arraignment, this boy's due back in jail." His Louisiana bayou drawl was as thick as molasses. "Go now and fetch me that *fucking* key."

Head held high, Alison turned and walked out through the curtain. Past the shocked older man, lying in the adjacent bed, and out into the corridor. Scotty, just then exiting a men's room down the hall, was wearing his new clothes. He'd finger-combed his mop of wetted-down hair. Off-balance, he was struggling to slip on his right shoe when Platt began yelling for a nurse to come help him. The sound of metal handcuffs could be heard clanging against the hospital bed's railing.

Scotty hurried over to Alison, who instructed him, "Elevator's up ahead. Just walk casually, try not to bring too much attention to yourself." *God . . . what am I doing*, she wondered. Only the previous evening she'd had another heated phone conversation with her supervising agent, Donald Price. She could tell he wasn't really listening to her. He definitely didn't give much credence to the incongruities concerning Scotty Sullivan's second DNA profile, ordered by the hospital's physician. As far as he was concerned, the case could now be put to bed. Yet, the missing boy was, in fact, the same person as the man now lagging two steps behind her. *So what?* According to Price, the FBI wasn't social services—most definitely wasn't chartered to help out the homeless. Officially off this case, she was expected back in the office first thing Monday morning. Now Saturday, she figured why not spend the weekend enjoying

Nantucket, this beautiful seaside island? What she did in her own free time—well, that was her business. Price might not see it that way, but he wasn't here and she was.

Down the hall ahead was the second floor's bank of elevators. She heard the soft *ding* of a car arriving. When the door began to slide open, she urged, "We can make it." Once they were inside, she slapped the *Close* door button then the *Lobby* button. Waiting for the car to start its slow descent down, they both leaned against the elevator's back railing.

"How did you do that?" she asked, without looking at him. Her expression was all business. "Jeopardizing my career is not an option, so no bullshit."

Before Scotty could answer, the elevator dinged again and the door slid open. Together, they made their way through the lobby, and exited through the automatic sliding glass doors.

"My car's this way." Alison said, over her shoulder. By chance she glanced up to the second floor of the hospital. A large dark form loomed at one of the windows overlooking the street. *Damn!* Officer Platt was going to be a problem. And this case was getting stranger by the minute.

Alison pointed her key fob at a dark, non-descript sedan parked ahead and heard the doors unlock. "Hop in."

Even before Scotty got the passenger-side door shut all the way, the engine was turning over, the transmission shifting into reverse. Powering backward out of the parking space, she shifted into drive, goosing the engine hard enough that the rear wheels left rubber streaks across the pavement.

"Tell me, damn it. How?" she ordered again, though some part of her really didn't want to know. Unless Scotty Sullivan had spent the last sixteen years traveling with a roving circus—perhaps learning the ropes as a young magician—there really wasn't a good explanation for what had occurred with the hand-cuffs. That's what she was afraid of. Because Scotty Sullivan had already alluded to who he was, what he was, twice, which was too impossible to believe.

chapter 17

Commander Landon had no illusions; he probably was going to die, and probably pretty soon. Hell, that was always a consideration in this line of work anyway. He didn't relish that fact by any means, but he'd already made peace with just such a probability occurring a long time ago. Being strapped to a launching Falcon Heavy rocket, one billowing out five million pounds of thrust, tended to prepare one for the possibility of an early demise. So, at the moment, Landon wasn't scared. Sure, he thought a lot about Jan, his wife of eight years, and his five-year-old daughter, Elsie, and six-year-old daughter, Mia, but mainly he wanted to tell them about what he was experiencing in that very moment—what he was now witnessing. Something amazing.

Within the ISS Zarya space module, Greg Fischer and Peter Mirkin were up on their feet, standing next to Landon. Spacesuits removed earlier, the three stood in their special-ized NASA long johns. Landon suspected they pretty much were experiencing what he was experiencing—a kind of weird, bemused, excitement.

For the moment they could breathe fine. The surrounding ambient temperature was comfortable. There were, by Landon's last count, seven different alien forms scurrying in and out of the Zarya module through the recently made bulkhead opening.

"Any idea which alien is in charge here?" Greg asked.

"Not a clue," Landon replied, watching the nearly transparent, bluish, glowing forms carry various items from the ISS out through the opening.

"I want to know what is out there—out there in the darkness," Mirkin said in low tones, gesturing toward the opening.

Landon shared in the Russian's curiosity, though he had a fairly good idea already. Somehow, the ISS had become situated within the bowels of the alien ship. That explained the earlier loud noises—the ISS seized, then repositioned within this enormous vessel.

"Obviously, we're in some kind of hold area," Fischer said, clearly reaching the same conclusion. "And did you notice? They all have a slightly different hue, some more of an azure blue, some a royal blue, some more . . ."

Mirkin cut Fischer off mid-sentence, sounding annoyed. "Yes, of course we can see that too."

Landon watched a new, different, glowing form enter the capsule, coming to a stop right before them. He was taller than the others.

Landon said, "Hello." *Shit, how profound was that,* he thought. "Um ... can you understand what I am saying?" Landon caught Fischer rolling his eyes in his peripheral vision. The tall alien's facial features were no different from the others, nearly non-existent. Only a faint semblance of eyes, nose, and mouth evident—more like subtle protrusions, having no actual purpose.

"You can call me Halm. Yes, your words are understood, and I trust you can understand mine as well."

The two astronauts and cosmonaut exchanged a quick glance. Landon said, "Yes, loud and clear, Halm." Again, inwardly chastising himself for voicing a second stupid comment. Best now to get right to the point. "What are you doing with our space station—with us?" Landon's gaze concentrated on the alien's face, trying to discern where his voice emanated from.

Halm said, "This must be frightening for each of you. For that, we apologize. In time, you will understand why this encounter was necessary. Necessary for your kind's ultimate survival."

Landon detected no accent, no crazy alien mispronunciations. If he weren't staring at what clearly was an extraterrestrial, the speaker could have been from Los Angeles or Denver.

Fischer asked, "So what are you doing with all our stuff?" He raised his chin in the direction of one of the aliens, carrying off a canvas satchel. Landon knew the satchel contained bathroom supplies: toothpaste, bottled soaps and shampoo, rolls of toilet paper.

Halm turned his attention to Fischer. "Should you need any of these items, we will make them available to you."

"We're not coming back here . . . to the ISS?" Fischer asked.

"It will not be necessary," Halm said.

"Can I ask you something else?" Mirkin asked.

Halm simply adjusted his standing position without answering.

"Your physiology . . . something like energy-based. Yes?"

"That is correct. Our race is called Vallic. We derive from a world called Lorimar, which is approximately six light years from Earth. Your scientists have yet to discover this neighboring area of space. Our physiology is approximately ninety-seven percent dynamic energetics."

"What does the other three percent consist of?" Fischer asked.

"Matter. Our species evolution began much like that of the Human race."

Landon, gesturing toward an alien carrying another satchel, asked, "Can you tell me how forms such as yours, composed primarily of energy, can lift and carry hundred pound satchels full of laboratory supplies?"

"High energy density gravitational waves." Illustrating, Halm extended out a glowing hand and held it there.

Landon, unsure at first what was expected of him, put out his own hand and shook the offered hand. He felt the alien's firm grip. There seemed to be a flesh-like texture to it—in how it felt. "That's . . . amazing."

Halm tilted his head in such a way it conveyed a sense of curiosity. "It was only a handshake, Commander Landon."

After a beat, both Fischer and Mirkin laughed. Evidently, the tall alien had a sense of humor.

Landon asked, "So what now? What are you going to do with us?"

"I assume you would like to make contact with your Mission Control, down on Earth's surface?"

"You'll let us do that? Let that happen?"

Halm raised his chin. "It is understandable you do not trust our intentions."

"I don't know what I believe, to be honest. No offense, but none of us were given much of a choice, how all this went down. Our space station's been damaged. We've been abducted, standing around in our underwear. And I just shook hands with an alien."

"Apologies. Time is an issue, Commander Landon. Recently, the University of Hawaii's Pan-STARRS 1 telescope, on Haleakalā, discovered a 400-meter-long meteor, careening its way through your Solar System. It took Earth's scientists totally by surprise. A lone, interstellar object from outside your planetary system encroaching dangerous close to Earth."

"We're aware of that," Landon said. "It's still being tracked."

"What your scientists have yet to discover is that the gamma ray burst, spanning many thousands of miles, is on a direct, intersecting trajectory with the meteor and this Solar System." Halm gave Landon and the others time to digest those dire implications.

Mirkin asked, "When? How long do we have?"

"Sixteen of your lunar-based months."

"You're telling us that Earth has less than a year-and-a-half to exist? For mankind to survive?"

Halm said, "Those are two completely separate questions, Lieutenant Fischer."

chapter 18

The previous highest-ranking official at the National Aeronautics and Space Administration was the Director of NASA. He'd been fired by the incoming White House administration for reasons still undisclosed. Now filling in, the current *big cheese* was a short, albeit jolly-looking, middle-aged man named Gordon Borkner. Since childhood, he'd suffered from a facial skin condition called rosacea, which colored his rounded cheeks an odd fuchsia shade. He always looked as if he'd just come in from the cold—perhaps building a giant snowman outside—along with his eight, all under the age of twelve, children. All suffered from the same, non-life-threatening, facial skin condition—a whole clan of jolly-cheeked Borkners.

Gordon Borkner worked out of Independence Square, offices within two non-descript buildings in Washington, D.C. His job title was simply Acting NASA Administrator. An appointee from a previous administration, continuing on in this lofty position was anything but guaranteed. This made

Borkner nervous. Made him jittery. The stink of desperation clung to him, like an ill-fitting suit.

For all intents and purposes, Borkner was a politician. He spent most of his time working with other high-ranking, often competing, government officials, jockeying for their own piece of the US budget allocation. In his particular case, to acquire additional NASA funding, not only for the coming year, but for many years into the future. NASA space exploration projects required elaborate financial planning—spanning multiple decades.

So when Acting Administrator Gordon Borkner learned of the presumed demise of the International Space Station, while attending a two-hundred-dollars-a-plate dinner gala— one co-sponsored by one of Washington's major lobbyist groups—he had to immediately excuse himself and head to the men's room. Once there, after ensuring each toilet stall was indeed empty, he yelled out, "Yes! Yes! Yes!" while repeatedly fist-pumping his stubby right arm into the air. Borkner *fucking hated* the ISS program. Hated anything to do with it. Even though five other international space agencies assisted monetarily, *but only barely*, the ISS sucked up far too much of NASA's limited budget. Constant maintenance issues; never-ending resupply missions; the costs added up to more than the GDP of many small nations. Added to that, NASA was everyone's bitch . . . fucking Russia . . . private industry . . .

Attempting to compose himself, Borkner leaned over the nearest sink and peered at himself in the mirror. His rosacea cheeks were damn near glowing and his face certainly didn't portray a look of despair. Before heading back out into the gala affair, he needed to think of something terrible—perhaps an event from his past; something that would sadden him. He racked his brain. But mental images—the ISS blowing up in space from multiple angles, like a professionally choreographed Hollywood blockbuster—kept invading his thoughts. Still giddy, ready to give up, he decided to splash cold water onto his face. After reaching for one of the linen towels, folded up on the counter, he decided to be strategic—study which areas on his face to actually pat dry. Leave just enough moisture beneath his eyes to emphasize the fact that the head of the National Aeronautics and Space Administration was tearful, devastated by the latest news. Inconsolable.

Straightening up to his full stature of five-foot-five and, in an overhand, Kobe-esque, motion—he tossed the wadded towel across the restroom into an available wicker hamper. "Three points," he whispered. Two steps from the exit, he felt his breast pocket vibrate. Withdrawing his iPhone, he checked the Caller ID. *Oh terrific, Mannford.* Paul Mannford was one of the three Flight Directors, stationed at the Johnson Control Center, in Houston, Texas. No one doubted who was actually in charge there. An ex-test pilot, then an ex-Space Shuttle astronaut, Mannford ultimately made all the really big decisions when it came to the ISS—he was also the primary thorn under Borkner's saddle.

"Paul, I just got the awful news. I'm so, so sorry."

"Thank you, sir," Paul said. "Of course, we haven't completely given up hope yet, but ..."

"Oh, I thought it was pretty definite. A terrible, cataclysmic accident had, well, destroyed the space station."

"I don't know who it is you spoke with, but until we have some compelling proof of what actually occurred, we're going to stay vigilant," Paul said. "Every world agency has focused its attention spaceward. Every resource—infrared, radio, X-ray telescopes— of every size and complexity, and, of course, our high-orbit birds are meticulously examining space debris for ... well, anything. Absolutely nothing has been found or detected. Even the worst kind of explosion should have left residual wreckage. It's strange ... some fragments should have been left behind. So, for that reason, I'm cautiously holding back in making a statement. I would recommend your office do the same, if I may be so bold, sir."

"Of course, Paul. I'm here; we're all here to support our incredible NASA team of men and women. Now I want you to keep me in the loop. Updates throughout the day tomorrow, okay? And let me know if there's anything else you need there in Houston, anything at all. We'll make sure the purse-strings remain wide open to get us through this terrible ordeal."

"Thank you, sir. There is one thing ..."

Borkner rolled his eyes, fighting not to tap his foot. "What is it, Paul ... anything."

"I'd like to fly-in the crew's families: Commander Jack Landon's wife, Jan, and his two daughters; Lieutenant Greg Fischer's parents; and Russian cosmonaut Peter Mirkin's fiancée."

"Fiancée?" Borkner repeated, without thinking.

"Yes, sir. She's in Novosibirsk, Russia."

Fuck ... this is going to cost a small fortune. It's not like they'll ever actually see, hear from these loved ones again. Why drag them all the way to Houston only to learn the same inevitable bad news that everyone else is surely cognizant of already?

"Of course, whatever you need, Paul. Get it done."

"Yes, sir and thank you."

"It's an honor to help. And to show my support, I'm clearing my schedule. I'll arrive in Houston this time tomorrow ... the next day, at the latest."

"You're coming here? To the Mission Control Center?"

"Yes. You can give me a tour, since I've never actually visited the Center before. And Paul, best you prepare for a few transitional changes."

"Changes?"

"We'll discuss more about all that when I arrive."

chapter 19

Her lunch shift now ended, her bare arms wrapped tightly around herself, Brianna Sullivan sat within the smoky confines of Captain Jack's cramped, mildew-smelling office. Since Jack was the current owner/manager of Stillworth's Skiff, not to mention her landlord, she had little choice other than to simply nod and listen as he continued to chastise her for the racket above. Even now, she could hear Larry over the piped-in mariachi music, and the nearby kitchen help's banter. The dog's incessant barking was mind-numbingly annoying. She inwardly cringed, hearing Larry switch to howling instead of just barking. *Shit!*

Captain Jack, one of the few people on planet Earth who still smoked a pipe, pulled it out from between his full lips. With dramatic emphasis, he stared up toward the ceiling, and said, "That's what I'm talking about. You know, I've had multiple complaints from our patrons, Brianna. This has got to stop."

"I know... and I appreciate you being so patient with me. I'm trying to work things out with the dog. Maybe hire someone, like a dog-sitter, during the day."

"I don't understand. Why do you need a dog here? With your life, being as it is, I just don't see it. It complicates everything for you. I would hate to see you lose your lease—even your job."

"Now, don't say that, Jack. Come on! I've been here for—well, like forever. I'm loyal. A good portion of these patrons only come here thanks to me. Just give me some time, a day or two." She watched as Captain Jack looked about his cluttered desk for his lighter. His pipe had fizzled out. She glanced around the dreary, wood-paneled office and wondered how he could spend so many hours cloistered in here. Then she thought of something else. "Don't you get lonely, being stuck in here all day?"

The older man looked about his space and shrugged. "No, I like my solitude. People make me crazy."

"Strange attitude for a restaurant owner," Brianna retorted with a crooked smile, watching his thick silver brows knit together. "I have an idea, just for a couple of days." She looked over to the only empty space in the office. "There's room for a small dog bed, right over there. Larry won't bother anyone if he has company. He'll just curl up in the corner and I'll walk him on my breaks. Just for a few days..."

Captain Jack continued to stare hard at the empty corner, as if trying to picture it. "I'm not supposed to have a dog within these lower premises. Health code stipulations and all."

She wanted to tell him he should be far more concerned with the army of cockroaches, which had taken up long-term residence behind the dry-goods pantry and beneath the fry cooker. "Fine, health department shows up tell them he's not your dog. You have no idea how he got in here. But honestly, when was the last time they just showed up unannounced?" Brianna didn't actually know the answer to that, but thought she should throw it out there just the same.

Teeter-tottering his large head back and forth a few times, Jack said, "Fine, we'll try it tomorrow. But no promises. If he annoys me, even a little, you'll have to make other arrangements."

Brianna couldn't believe what she was hearing. She'd made the suggestion out of pure desperation. "You're a peach, Jack. Thank you so much."

"Get out of here before I change my mind. And get that dog to shut the hell up."

She left through Stillworth's Skiff's rear door, crossing over to the steep set of angled stairs. Two people, a young man and a woman, were standing at the top of the stairs, right outside the door to her flat.

* * *

Standing on the narrow outer landing, Scotty Sullivan was able to lean over the iron railing just enough to peer into the apartment's back window. The barking had been going on pretty much non-stop, ever since they'd arrived several moments before. Scotty knew that bark—Larry's bark. He laughed out loud, seeing those familiar brown eyes staring back at him now from inside.

Scotty said, "It's him . . . that's my dog!"

Alison, moving onto the top step of the stairway, nodded unenthusiastically. Scotty ignored her lack of enthusiasm. She'd been miffed, ever since they'd climbed into the car. She wanted answers. *Where exactly had he been for the last sixteen years? What was he doing now in Nantucket? What was his explanation for the bizarre DNA results?* But mostly, *how the hell did he escape from those handcuffs?* But the timing wasn't quite right to get into all that with her. But soon—maybe it would be.

Alison said, "Enough with the damn dog, Scotty! Try knocking again. Maybe she didn't hear you the first time. She could have been in the bathroom, or something."

"Can I help you people?" came a woman's voice from below.

Both Scotty and Alison glanced down to the bottom of the stairs. He saw an attractive middle–aged woman, wearing a Black Sabbath concert tank top, along with faded blue jeans. Her brown hair, cut short, was streaked with strands of gray. Scotty's emotional reaction came on both suddenly and unexpectedly. His throat instantly constricted and he couldn't speak, his eyes welling with tears to the point his mother's image became a mere blur some sixteen steps below him. He heard Alison answer something back. Talking over the dog's barking, she introduced herself.

"Yes, I'm FBI Special Agent Alison McGuire, from the Chelsea, Massachusetts office."

Scotty noticed Alison was holding up her ID. Hesitating, she glanced over at him, not quite sure how to proceed further.

Scotty, blinking away tears, could see that the woman standing at the bottom of the stairs was not listening to Alison; her eyes were locked onto him. Her expression a mix of confusion, hopefulness—and also fear.

"It's me, Mom. It's Scotty."

His mother's legs began to wobble beneath her. Barely clinging to the railing—trying to breathe—she was fighting not to completely fold into herself.

Scotty brushed past Alison, quickly descending the steps two and three at a time. Seeing his rapid approach, Brianna's hands rose up to hold him at bay—her face now angry, full of rage. "You get the fuck away from me!" She took several steps backwards. "Who the hell are you, anyway?"

Scotty stopped on the third step from the ground. "It's really me, honest, Mom. Please don't be scared."

"Oh really! So . . . like after sixteen years, my son casually decides to come knocking on my front door? Bullshit. I don't believe you. Whoever you are? I want you to leave. Now!"

"What if I could prove it . . . that I am your son?"

"I said leave. I'll call the police if you don't . . ."

"Ma'am, I am the FBI." Alison said, from top of the stairs. "He is Scotty Sullivan. Genetic tests, DNA, confirm he is who he says he is."

His mother's lips became a thin red line. Vehemently shaking her head, she shouted, "No. This is a cruel joke. My son is dead. Washed out to sea sixteen years ago."

"Just like your dog up there? Come on, you never believed Scotty was dead. That's why you hired a PI to keep searching for him all these years," Alison said, slowly descending the stairs. "I assure you, Mrs. Sullivan, he is, in fact, your son, Scotty. Now, where exactly he's been living all these years, is something we still need to discuss."

"Show me your feet."

Scotty looked at his mother. "My feet?" She nodded back.

He kicked off one shoe then the other, then peeled off his socks. Standing barefoot, he waited. Brianna took several tentative steps forward, her attention focused solely on his feet.

Scotty peered down at them too, suddenly remembering he had a small birthmark, roughly the shape of a crescent moon, on his left big toe.

A hand came up, covering Brianna's mouth as she drew in a startled breath. She looked up at him—sudden hopefulness shining in her eyes. "Oh God . . . Scotty?"

chapter 20

The three-man ISS crew, unceremoniously escorted out through the opening made in the Zarya module's bulkhead, had Halm leading the way, with two Vallic crewmembers following close behind.

The ghostly blue form of Halm, at least to this point, seemed completely non-threatening, even *polite*, Landon thought. *Or were they lambs slowly being led to the slaughter?* No. He didn't actually believe that. *Why would they bother?* These highly advanced beings could pretty much do with them as they wished at any time—they'd been at their complete mercy. Halm had told them they were here to help the Human race, but Landon was skeptical. Perhaps, though, that was a Human trait, doubting the true intentions of strangers. An instinctual self-protection mechanism with roots dating back to Neanderthal days, when competing tribes were running around naked and throwing spears. And these Vallic aliens were the ultimate strangers. *Again—what was in it for them? Why assist Humanity?*

The hold area was dimly lit, to the point that outlines of what appeared to be towering bulkheads were shrouded in a veil of shadows, cast in near-complete darkness. One benefit now was how much more visible the glowing aliens were to the naked eye.

Landon felt Fischer's presence close to his side. "Have you noticed they don't carry any weapons?"

Landon, keeping his voice low, said, "Well, neither are we . . . so I think they feel fairly secure." He heard Peter Mirkin; several paces behind them, questioning a Vallic being. "Where are you taking us?" Mirkin asked.

"Into the ship proper."

That's a short and sweet answer, Landon thought. Walking for at least a few minutes, he figured it must be some kind of gargantuan hold. "Excuse me, um . . . Halm?"

"Yes, Commander Landon?" Halm replied, slowing his stride.

"Look, it's imperative I make contact with our MCC."

"And that is our intent, as well. But first, it is important that you fully understand the situation. The implications of what is approaching."

"You pretty much told us that. Total annihilation." Just speaking those words made him think about Jan and the kids.

They were approaching some kind of transition point now—not so much a compartment hatchway, more like a circular energy membrane—one that spanned about ten feet in diameter.

"Please wait here a moment while I alter the airlock configuration for your Human physiology," Halm said, as he approached the membrane. An almost imperceptible crackling sound, like static electricity, could be sensed as he passed through it. Landon paused, taking a closer look at the nearby bulkhead. Not what he expected—like riveted metal sheeting or plating—the bulkhead appeared to be molded, an uneven texture to its surface. The coloring, variations of tans and browns, had a natural, organic composition to it. He ran his toes back and forth along the decking beneath his feet, then pushed his heels firmly down into it. *Slightly spongy—organic?*

Startled, Landon felt a hand on his shoulder. Halm stood in front of him. Behind him, the energy membrane had disappeared and he could see further into the ship.

"You're wondering about the composition of this vessel. It is completely organic; necessary for intergalactic space travel. In fact, other than the ISS, and the equipment accompanying it, which are now in this hold, there is nothing else onboard this craft that is not organic. Come, you can pass through now." Halm led the way out of the hold into another part of the alien ship—one with more defined and separate spaces. Here, numerous Vallic crewmembers were moving about, as one would expect on a large ship. But the effect here was magical—sweeps of blue energy visible against a muted dark backdrop of the ship's interior. Landon suddenly became aware of his physicality, his presence among energetics, as Halm had described them. He felt obtuse and lumbering; both out of place and somewhat ridiculous.

Two blue-glowing Vallics, speaking in low tones to each other, were approaching. Only then did Landon notice the Vallic on the left was clearly a female. Her form was slighter—variations, impressions, of having breasts and more rounded hips.

"This is Calma and Bame. They will be assisting you with your education. I must attend to my duties on the ship's bridge." With that Halm strode away.

The female Vallic took a step forward. "I am aware of your greeting customs to shake each other's limbs. She held out her hand and Landon, reciprocating the gesture, took her hand in his. It was small and soft within his grasp. She then proceeded to shake Fischer and Mirkin's hands as well. Bame stayed back, not speaking.

"What's with him? A little shy?" Fischer asked.

Calma gave a quick glance toward her crewmate. "He does not like Humans, or most other alien life forms. Ignore him. He is relatively harmless."

"That's reassuring," Fischer said, making no effort to hide his sarcasm. Landon sent Fischer a quick censoring glare, one that said *try to behave.*

"Please follow us to the Conception Dome."

Doing as told, they fell in behind Calma and Bame and left the area, merging into a wide corridor of sorts. Landon had assumed the Vallics—these *energetic* beings—would move about by walking, maybe even running, much the same as Humans do. But he was wrong about that. Catching but a mere glimpse of their shimmering blue energy wakes—one after another Vallic crewmembers whizzed around at incredible speeds on either side. Landon felt something he hadn't experienced in a long time, not since training to become a navy pilot: Envy. *God, to be able to move about like that; to be so unhindered—so free!*

The Conception Dome was indeed a large, enclosed, domed area. Its size seemed boundless, although Landon was certain that aspect was an illusion. They had entered into a breathtakingly beautiful virtual model. Ultra-realistic, it possessed three-dimensional depth; no floors, ceilings, or walls, they appeared to be standing within the Solar System—almost Godlike. The Sun, orbiting bright-colored planets, viewed from a space perspective.

Mirkin, his Russian accent thicker than usual, held his arms out. Spinning around, he said, "This is truly amazing. Visually stunning!" He walked toward the virtual planets, those positioned farthest from the Sun. "Tell me, what are those other spherical bodies beyond Pluto?"

Bame answered him with measured annoyance, "Six more worlds, ones bordering just outside the Kuiper Belt. Your scientists will not discover any of these worlds until there are further advances with your interplanetary space travel."

Calma said, "You can spend more time in here, within the Conception Dome, later on. But for now, there is a reason we brought you here: For your education. So you can better communicate to your people what is transpiring... that of a cataclysmic course of spatial events." The virtual perspective then changed; as the Solar System suddenly shrank in size, a more distant quadrant of space quickly magnified. "This part of space, you refer to it as . . ."

Landon cut in, "Constellation Ophiuchus,"

"That is correct," she said. The star now coming into view was as large as the Sun had been only moments before. She continued, "Bernard's Star was the third closest star to Earth after your own Sun and Alpha Centauri 3. At six light years distance, this red dwarf was rapidly moving through interstellar space. Eventually, billions of years from now, it would have been as close as 3.8 light years from Earth."

"So this star causes the cataclysmic event you referred to earlier?" Fischer asked.

"No. It is what was behind Bernard's Star. Actually, matching an almost identical, but totally blocked, trajectory. And that was the problem."

In that moment Bernard's Star, with its lone orbiting planet, dramatically exploded.

Landon caught it. *Something* had pierced through the small star system then proceeded on as if nothing had been in its way.

Calma said, "Keep in mind, what you just witnessed has already occurred. Of course, with the speed of light being what it is, it will take six years for a visual confirmation of this event to reach even your most powerful telescopes."

"When did this happen?" Landon asked, his voice barely audible. He was pretty certain he already knew the answer.

"Well over four years ago, at our current frame of reference," she said. "Now, please pay attention. This is what you can expect to occur within sixteen months' time."

Again, the present view of relatively local space shifted. The virtual perspective now showed Sol and the Solar System in the not so far distance. A golden fiery streak, growing larger by the second, could now be seen. Approaching fast, it was headed for the Solar System's encircling Kuiper Belt, consisting of left-over spacial debris—repercussions of the Big Bang—countless rocks and meteors and fragments of ancient, torn-apart worlds. And then it happened; the fiery streak dramatically penetrated one section of the belt. Intense heat radiated outward, until the entire encircling belt began to grow red, then amber, then white. And then, in a singular bright flash, everything within the Kuiper Belt was gone—radiated.

Transfixed, Landon watched the continuing spectacle— the grandeur of the spacial event. But what he saw next made him gasp. He watched in horror as the fiery streak entered the Solar System—and, like what had happened with the Kuiper Belt, radiant heat quickly consumed all matter in its wake. He watched known worlds fragment into glistening particles— **Neptune—Uranus—Saturn—Jupiter—Mars—Earth. He closed his eyes then forced them open.** The destruction took mere moments. In the end, it seemed that only the Sun would endure. But no, sadly he watched as it too began to fragment apart. Glowing solitary embers flittered atop a backdrop of a now dark, lonely-looking section of space.

And as quickly as the fiery streak entered the Solar System, it left—continuing, undoubtedly, onward with unrelenting destructiveness throughout the cosmos. The Kuiper Belt was gone; the Solar System gone. Landon shook his head in disbelief—inevitable doomsday had unfolded right before his eyes.

Experiencing such a deep feeling of loss, Landon's heart physically hurt within his chest. He found it hard to breathe. He couldn't speak—and even if he could, there was absolutely nothing he could say.

chapter 21

Alison watched Scotty and the dog, Larry, roughhousing on Brianna's worn, threadbare carpet. It was a close match—which one had the most energy. It had occurred to Alison earlier that Scotty had a child-like quality about him, and their playing around now only affirmed that assessment.

An hour there already, Brianna's growing frustration was clearly evident in her expression; her numerous questions answered with minimum responses. That was how it all went down in the hospital too. Scotty's evasiveness about where he'd been all these past years had raised more questions than answers.

Now sitting close together on Brianna's couch, they finally could talk in low tones to one another without Scotty overhearing their conversation.

"My take is that there may have been some kind of trauma. And, of course there was. Abducted at such a young age, it's hard to imagine what he went through," Alison said.

"Well, it was hard on all of us. It literally tore our family apart. I lost a husband along the way. Scotty's brother and little sister never fully got over it. None of us are exactly close. And now, all of a sudden, he's here in my living room, playing with a fucking dog that couldn't possibly be still alive," Brianna said staring hard at Alison. "So, what else aren't you telling me?"

Alison pondered the question, mentally replaying Scotty's kooky reference to being abducted by aliens. Going so far as to say he had dual genetic profiles—both Human and alien. But again, he did, in fact, have some genetic anomalies she'd never heard of before. Nor had Dr. Patel, for that matter. And then there was the whole handcuff thing. Alison put a hand on Brianna's knee and spoke quietly: "I know this is a lot to take in. Part of you still doubts your son is even here, that it's really him, right?"

Brianna's eyes, leveled on Scotty, nodded in assent.

"I have to tell you, I've had my doubts as well," Alison said, "To be perfectly honest, I'm not supposed to be involved with Scotty's case anymore. At this point, I am supposed to hand it over to local authorities. The FBI's primary charter is to catch criminals. Build cases strong enough to deliver to federal prosecutors. Since your son's initial disappearance was attributed to him being washed out to sea, there never were any subsequent abduction searches; no big manhunt for a kidnapper. My boss wants nothing more to do with this case. Maybe there are liability issues. Or maybe the FBI dropped the investigation too early. I don't know."

"I never thought Scotty was swept out to sea," Brianna said, scowling. "That was an idiotic premise. I conveyed that to the authorities at the time. Anyone can see Nantucket's coastline is fairly calm— it's not like Malibu, for God's sake. That's why, after getting the runaround, first by the FBI all those years ago then by the local police, I hired Tony. A highly recommended ex-cop, he's a PI out of Boston. And it hasn't been cheap." She gestured around at her flat's shabby surroundings.

Alison hadn't noticed until right then that Scotty was no longer playing with the dog. Both dog and Scotty were sitting quietly, staring back at them. Scotty said, "I'm sorry I've made this difficult for you, Mom. That I couldn't contact you until now."

Brianna didn't say anything. She looked angry—anything but conciliatory.

Scotty turned his attention to Alison. "This is all so much greater than just me. Bigger than the abduction, bigger than anything that has ever happened before on this planet."

Alison let out a breath and glanced over at Brianna, thinking *Oh boy, here it comes again.*

"I am not crazy. I was never abused. I have had a wonderful, full life. But I always missed you, Mom. I missed Dad, Kyle, and Sara . . . missed you all, terribly."

"Just tell me where you've been! Enough is enough, okay?" his mother said flatly.

Scotty gazed back at her apologetically, "You're not going to believe me until I show you exactly *who . . . what . . .* I am."

"Okay . . . then show me."

Scotty closed his eyes. Breathing deeply in and out several times, the corners of his lips rose in the beginnings of a smile. And suddenly—he was gone!

Both Brianna and Alison continued to stare at the chair he'd been sitting in only a moment before. Alison swallowed hard as Brianna's eyes opened as wide as dessert plates.

"I see him!" Alison exclaimed, now leaning forward. "He's there . . . a faint bluish glow. Can you see him?"

Brianna nodded. All color gone from her face, she looked as though she might faint. "This isn't happening. This can't be happening."

"I *am* still here; haven't gone anywhere."

They watched as a near-transparent hand reached out to scratch the top of Larry's head. The dog licked at a face that was nearly impossible to see.

chapter 22

As the Flight Director, at the LBJ Mission Control Center in Houston, Texas, all eyes were on Paul Mannford. All those within the NASA organization were certainly looking to him, but also the general public around the world due to the ever-expanding media coverage mounting by the minute. Mannford wondered if he would forever be defined as the flight director who lost the International Space Station, along with its three-man crew.

Acting NASA Administrator Gordon Borkner had arrived via a private government G6 jet late the previous evening. Mannford noticed the stout little man entering the MCC, with his two-man Secret Service detail, several minutes earlier. *Why,* he wondered, *does he need a protection detail? Do most folks even know who the guy is?* Currently making his way around the control center, Borkner was frequently stopping to shake hands—giving pats on shoulders—letting everyone know that he was their friend, that *he* had their backs. Little did the staff know he was the same government official who'd repeatedly come up short, acquiring the necessary budget dollars for a growing number of them to keep their jobs past the end of the current year.

Mannford did his best to ignore Borkner's disruption. Standing where he usually stood, near the back of the room, where he could best monitor overall operations—the ginor-mous six display screens at the front of the room—and his team of certified flight controllers. Each was tasked with a specific discipline for the *vehicle*—what the ISS typically was referred to by internal NASA personnel. Every console was manned; some there hadn't slept in days.

Mannford scanned his departmentalized teams, including planning, electrical power, thermal control, trajectory, and CapCom. The latter, a leftover term used when there were capsule communications, was the sole communications person responsible for connecting MCC to the vehicle. Wearing head-sets, they sat in front of multiple monitors. Mannford refocused his attention toward the series of giant displays, located at the front of the MCC. Typically, there would be several internal vehicle feeds—say, a particular wide view of a module—also several overall external feeds, viewing the space station from various mounted camera angles. Another feed provided a ground-track map, showing the position of the *vehicle* in orbit. Another could show a space walk, then in progress—or an astronaut, speaking directly with one of the individual MCC department controllers. None of those feeds were active now. Instead, Mannford directed some of the team to provide live feeds from a Space X Rocket, now being prepped at the

LLC—Launch Control Center—NASA's Kennedy Space Center, pictured on Merritt Island, Florida.

Borkner was about halfway through his meet and greets. *Take your time,* Mannford thought, leaning against the back wall and staring blankly forward.

"Hey—just breathe, Paul. We'll take it one day at a time. Okay?" Mannford, turning, found Margaret Haskell, the CapCom's controller, standing on his right. She offered him a still-steaming mug of coffee; his fourth one this morning. He took it from her, reciprocating back her warm smile. They'd been friends for over ten years; had experienced numerous harrowing times—but nothing quite like this one. Margaret was on duty as the CapComs controller—actually talking to Fischer—when their coms failed. When the *vehicle*, ISS, pretty much ceased to exist.

"I know what you're up to," he said.

Margaret feigned an innocent look, both glancing over at her empty chair, which Administrator Borkner was just then passing by. "I'm sorry, but he's such a tool," she said.

Mannford chuckled, but didn't comment.

"You know why he's here—to have you officially make a statement. To finally call it," she said, keeping her emotions in check.

"It's time. Best for the crew's family members, best for NASA personnel . . . and best for the world, I guess," he said.

Margaret nodded. "I had dinner with Jan Landon and her kids last night, over at the Marriot. She's pretty wrecked. Tries to put on a good face for the kids but they know something is up with their daddy ... something terrible." She leaned against the back wall alongside Mannford, her arms crossed over her chest. "It's so damn quiet in here."

Mannford simply nodded. And then each giant screen at the front of the room went black. Everyone present stopped what they were doing, their eyes focused on the blank displays. Mannford, now standing upright, took a step forward.

Character by character, a single line of text scrolled across all six front displays, as well as the individual console monitors.

INCOMING ISS COMMUNICATIONS PACKAGE IMMINENT ...

No one spoke. No one moved ... except Administrator Borkner. Hurrying by the row of consoles, he emerged out at the far end. He then scurried down the side of the room and, within fifteen seconds, stood beside Mannford and Margaret.

"What the hell is *that?*" he asked, clearly angry.

Mannford and Margaret exchanged another quick glance. Mannford could understand hearing surprise, or even cautious hope—*but anger?*

Borkner stared at the screens. Hands on hips, he turned to Mannford, his rosacea cheeks radiating like two red suns. "Someone's messing with our coms in here. Obviously, we've been hacked. Tell me, Mannford, how on Earth can this kind of shit happen within your own MCC?"

Before he could answer, Margaret, her feathers obviously ruffled, said, "No way, Administrator Borkner. What comes in here, that text we see running up on our screens and consoles, came in via a dedicated pathway—telemetry packets, which are highly complex. Basically, we have a locked-down internal loop; one that is funneled into a Level 10 security, a dedicated front-end processor, located in White Sands, New Mexico. And, prior to that, a TDRS receiver/transmitter system, that sends out checksum verified coms packets via an intrusion-locked satellite dish that's pointed directly into space—to the telemetry, right on the ISS. I can assure you, we've not been hacked, sir."

Mannford put up a hand, warding off further explanation from Margaret. "Let's just wait and see what we have going on here. Best you get back to your console, Margaret ... just in case."

"I don't need to be lectured by my own people," the administrator said, obviously still brooding.

"Quiet, sir. Please! Something's happening." Mannford, gesturing ahead, had his eyes locked onto the set of large displays. He heard faint background noises but no sign of visuals. He thought he recognized Commander Landon's voice. Then the screens flickered on and a video appeared, accompanied with sound. The three ISS crewmen were standing close together, apparently dressed only in their temperature-controlled undergarments.

Mission Control exploded with unbridled excitement. Cheers and laughs and even sounds of crying filled the room.

Administrator Borkner, thrusting both arms into the air, shouted, "Quiet down, everyone!" He continued glowering at the startled NASA employees until all center noise became hushed. He stared at the displays. "Can you hear me, Commander?" Borkner yelled."

"Hold on, sir . . . let me get you a headset," Margaret said, back at her station.

"I can hear you sir," Landon said. Both Fischer and Mirkin, who seemed bemused, gave back corresponding thumbs-up gestures.

Mannford looked over to the telemetry console, at Jerry Krupt, working that desk. Krupt shook his head then gave a shrug. The ground-track map was on display; gave no indication of the ISS's presence. *It didn't make sense.*

Speaking into his integrated headset mic, he said, "Margaret, give me an exclusive channel. Too much cross-talk going on." Mannford saw her nod, even though her back was to him.

"Commander Landon, let me be the first to say welcome back. Over"

"Roger that, and thank you, sir. Over," Landon said.

"Ask him where the fuck they are now; where they've been, for God's sake," Borkner fumed through clenched teeth.

The flight crew must have heard him, because both Fischer and Mirkin laughed out loud.

"It's a fair question," Mannford said. "We have zero telemetry on the vehicle. Please bring us up to speed. Over."

On display, Landon glanced at his fellow crewmembers, whose expressions were now serious. "Sir, I suggest you limit our transmission protocols to MCC only."

"Oh, for God's sake," Borkner said.

Mannford heard Margaret's voice in his ear. "We're closed down to the outside world, Paul. Whatever they're about to reveal is for our eyes and ears only."

"Go ahead, Commander. Speak freely. Over."

The silence permeating the room was total enough to hear a pin drop.

"Sir . . . we, the ISS, have been taken aboard another ship. One you do not have the technology yet to detect. We are well above Earth's orbit. The *vehicle* is pretty much in one piece; stored within the confines of this . . . um . . . alien ship."

"Did he just say alien ship?" Borkner asked, staring up at Mannford.

chapter 23

S cotty watched their expressions—amazed and perplexed—appear on both Alison's and his mother's faces.

Alison was the first to speak. "I see him!" Alison exclaimed, now leaning forward. "He's there . . . a faint bluish glow. Can you see him?"

"I *am* still here; haven't gone anywhere," Scotty said, giving Larry another scratch atop his head. He noticed that while Alison now looked immensely fascinated, his mother had become scared. This was all much too much for her, of course. In only an hour she had been reunited with someone claiming to be her long lost son; then told he'd been abducted by aliens sixteen years ago; and now watched him perform an impression of the *invisible man*. She looked like she was going to be sick. "I'm sorry . . . hold on and I'll turn back . . ."

Before Scotty could get the words out, she was up off the couch, holding a hand to her mouth, and running for the bathroom. A moment later, he heard her throwing up into the toilet. Closing his eyes, he calmed his psyche then altered his genome back into a physical Human form.

"So, this really isn't some kind of David Copperfield shit . . . a trick of some kind?"

"I don't know who David Copperfield is, but no, not a trick. Alison, I'm sorry if this is startling . . . freaking you out."

"Don't worry about me. I'm a big girl. So it's true, you really were abducted sixteen years ago?"

"Then why have you aged and the dog hasn't?" his mother asked from the bathroom doorway, using a pink hand towel to wipe the corners of her mouth.

Even now, it seemed, Brianna didn't believe him. Believe her own eyes that something beyond any rational explanation had indeed occurred. Scotty was well aware she still hadn't rushed to the phone to let his father, or Kyle, or Sara know yet of his return. Even recognizing the birthmark on his toe hadn't convinced her, something he personally had long forgotten about. Looking at her now he saw her anger. Sixteen years of pent up pain and frustration—the only person who never gave up hope; believing in her heart he was still alive. She had financially sacrificed. Ultimately lost almost everything in her selfless pursuit to find him. And now, after all the years of struggle were vindicated, she was incapable of letting her insecurities go. At this point in her life, they'd become a part of her—defined whom she had become.

"What I'm going to tell you will sound . . . unbelievable."

"I think we're a tad beyond that, Scotty," Alison said.

"Larry and I were both abducted off the beach by an alien rover ship, down by the water's edge in front of our beach house. That was the last time I saw Larry until I returned a few days ago. Larry has not aged because he was put into a form of long-term storage. I'm not really sure why he was returned along with me. That wasn't part of the plan, as far as I knew."

"You're saying all this was part of some grand alien plan?" his mother asked, taking her seat next to Alison again.

"The alien beings that abducted me are called Vallic. A highly advanced race, their planetary system is light years from Earth. You need to understand that space travel—intergalactic space travel—is commonplace among advanced races within the cosmos. Vast space is ever changing, often violent. Earth has been struck by meteorites a number of times over its relatively young existence, often with devastating repercussions. Twenty-five years ago, the Vallic became aware of what they referred to as a *definitive causation*. An approaching end-of-life scenario for a less advanced species—those who have not yet traveled and propagated to other worlds... I'm referring to Earth Humans."

"So, these Vallic, they're what? Like Greenpeace? They go around helping endangered species?" Alison asked skeptically.

"In the case of Earth, that's pretty much right."

"So what is the... what did you call it, the *definitive causation* that's going to happen to Earth? How does that involve you?" his mother asked. "And why you? Why did they take my nine-year-old little boy?"

"For a while I thought it was purely coincidental, that I was just in the wrong place at the wrong time. Later, I learned that was not the case at all. Specific Humans had been observed and targeted. The Vallic's intention was to find Human individuals they could work with; those that had the right mindset that could be . . . I guess the word is *transformed*. To eventually possess dual genetic dispositions. Something Vallic scientists were still perfecting at the time we were taken. The Vallic, once almost Human-like themselves, had evolved over eons of time, becoming instead an energetic form of matter. Like what you witnessed earlier with me. That form is now my alternate, non-original, genetic state. Possessing dual genetic states, both Human and Vallic, was a recent breakthrough. One that would be necessary to save us; to save us all."

Scotty's mother and Alison appeared totally lost. He further explained,

"There is an extremely large, fast-moving gamma ray burst careening through space, some light years away. The burst is still hidden from Earth, behind a relatively nearby star. Soon, their now common trajectories will deviate away from each other. Then the gamma ray burst will become visible from our most powerful telescopes. But seeing it will make no difference, because not only will Earth be destroyed, so will the entire Solar System."

"When . . . when is this supposed to happen?" his mother asked, her brows tightly knitted together.

"Sixteen months from now."

Alison shook her head. "But it's only speculation, right? They don't know for sure . . . how could they?"

Scotty stared back at her blankly.

"I guess they're pretty smart about such things," she acknowledged. It was a lot to take in. Knowing that within a year-and-a-half, not only could their own lives come to an end, but mankind's as well.

"You're here to tell, um, world governments? Like, help us prepare?" his mother asked, the harshness in her voice softening.

"That's already in process. Undoubtedly, you have been following recent events ongoing with the International Space Station, right?"

They both nodded. "It went missing . . . was somehow destroyed. Some kind of terrible accident," his mother said.

"No, it is fine. The crew is fine. A Vallic space ship is in nearby space. The ISS is fully contained within it. About now, communications with NASA are in progress."

"So . . . you really are Scotty? You really are my son?"

Scotty gazed back at her, seeing raw emotion in her demeanor; tears brimming in her eyes. He nodded, "Yeah, I really, really am."

In a blur, Brianna was off the couch, practically bowling him over. Arms wrapped around him, she hugged him so tightly he had to struggle to breathe. He hugged her back, feeling sixteen years of grief spilling out of her. Larry began to bark, running back and forth within the small confined space. His mother continued to sob, almost to the point of hysteria. Trembling, she struggled to catch her breath. Scotty caught sight of Alison, still sitting across from him on the couch, chewing on her inner lip. She was blinking away tears of her own.

All this was so very *Human*. Life on planet Hope was nothing like life on Earth. Not that it was an emotionally devoid existence living there, just nothing like this. Humans were messy, emotional creatures. A trait he had learned, over time, to personally bury. Now, feeling his mother's love pouring out, and seeing what had to be the most beautiful creature he'd ever laid eyes on sitting across from him on the couch, he felt oddly embarrassed. Overwhelmed suddenly, a part of him craved the quiet stillness—the centeredness of being Vallic, his alternate genetic composition. He'd spent far more years being Vallic in nature than Human.

His mother cleared her throat, finally pulling away. "I'm sorry. I'm . . . I don't know what I'm supposed to do now."

Scotty patted her back several times then awkwardly stood up. "Um, I need to use the bathroom." He glanced to Alison, but she wasn't looking at him anymore. She was staring up, beyond them, toward the front door. An expression of disbelief then anger crossed her face. In the process of swiveling back around, Scotty got a quick glimpse of the big man storming into his mother's flat. He recognized the policeman's face—just as he recognized the large black flashlight arcing its way toward his own head. His last conscious thought, before being struck, was that he really had to perfect the amount of time he needed to change into his more energetic form. The sound of Larry's barking faded out as he dropped hard onto the worn, threadbare carpet.

PART II
WAYS OF THE VALLIC

chapter 24

Sixteen years ago . . .

Nine-year-old Scotty Sullivan tried to make heads or tails out of what was happening to him. To him and Larry. Larry, wet and dankly smelling of the sea, was barking nonstop. Scotty, his arms tightly wrapped around the dog's midsection and his face buried in his tangle of fur, ventured a peek out—at what lay around them. *Not much.* It looked like the inside of a cave—dimly lit, everything mostly a drab, mud-brown color. But Scotty knew he wasn't in a cave, he was in a spaceship. He knew that for sure. His right arm still hurt where *something* had grabbed ahold of him there; some kind of clawed *thing.*

"Okay . . . enough! Stop the barking, already!" Scotty said firmly, yet gently, taking the dog's muzzle in his hand, the way he'd often seen his dad do. Repeatedly shushing him, he stared directly into the dog's brown eyes. Larry, sufficiently chastised, did as instructed, though he continued to mutter low growling noises.

Realizing, at least for the moment, that he wasn't going to die, Scotty slowly rose to his full height—about four-and-a-half feet. Only then did he sense a gentle swaying motion beneath his feet. *They were moving!* Without a doubt, he figured they were no longer hovering above the shoreline, near his family's Nantucket vacation home. As the corners of Scotty's lips reflexively turned downward, he used the back of his hand to wipe away tears and the snot from his runny nose.

"I want to go home now," he said, just loud enough for anyone nearby to probably hear him. But when no one answered, he spoke out even louder: "I want to go home . . . *now!*"

Larry let out a heavy huff before dropping down near Scotty's feet. Apparently no longer sensing any danger, which was somewhat comforting.

"I wish there was a window so I could see out," Scotty said to Larry, taking several tentative steps toward a nearby wall. Placing a hand on its surface, he quickly jerked it away. "Freaky," he muttered aloud. He did it again, only this time letting his palm stay put. The wall's surface, somehow, didn't feel familiar, like he thought it would. It was warm and moist and somehow seemed *alive*. Sort of like how Gomez felt—the skin on his brother's pet box turtle.

Scotty then thought of his mom, experiencing the same feeling of loss. Sadness began to close in around him, like it had moments earlier. He swallowed hard, doing his best to keep fear at bay.

"Hello? Is anybody in here?"

He listened hard, but on hearing nothing back, he continued to explore—taking slow, deliberate steps. The interior of the ship was nothing like what he thought a spaceship should be. Not like those cool-looking spaceships on TV, or the ones he'd seen in the movies. This ship was more like being underground. There were walls, and even what could pass for steps, leading to either raised or lowered sections.

"It's like being inside a big ant hill, Larry," Scotty said, glancing back the way he'd come. But he could no longer see Larry from where he stood. He was about to retrace his steps when the floor began jostling back and forth beneath his feet, forcing him to crouch down. Then, just as suddenly, everything became still, no sense of movement. Slowly, Scotty rose back up. "Larry! Come on, boy, . . ."

Feeling a cool breeze flowing out behind him, Scotty spun around. Instantly confused, he was sure a wall had been there only seconds before. Now he faced a large open space, leading into distant darkness. ,"Crap . . . now this is totally creepy," he said aloud. Again, he called out for his dog. "Larry! Come on, boy!"

Unsure why, Scotty felt compelled to take a step deeper into the open area—then another. He noticed the texture on the walls and floor in here was slightly different. *Smoother*. Less like a mud cave, more like the skin of a melon—a cantaloupe.

Startled, Scotty jumped, feeling something move past him. Close enough he felt something actually brush against his skin. "Hey! Who's there? You're scaring me!" Now he really wanted Larry—wanted him to be by his side. No, what he *really* wanted was to go home. He badly wanted to see his mother.

"Larry!" he screamed at the top of his lungs, not understanding what was happening. *Why wasn't his dog obeying him?* He decided to hurry back and look for him. Quickly glancing both left and right, Scotty sensed *something* near him—something close—even though he couldn't see it. Spinning fully around, he thought, *Wait . . . where'd the opening go? Where's Larry?*

chapter 25

S cotty could now make them out. A bunch of them were scattered all around, like glowing blue ghosts. *But not ghosts—people.*

"Hello, Scotty . . . I know you are scared. Try to relax. You will not be harmed."

Scotty wondered how the alien knew his name. He then noticed the glowing figure kneeling next to him was close enough to reach out and touch. Somehow, he knew she was female. Friendly, her voice sounded feminine. He studied her face—a face that didn't have distinct features. Her eyes, nose, and mouth were sort of there, but not really.

"Can I go home now?"

"Eventually."

"Where's my dog?"

"Safe. You will see him again."

"Why am I here? I want to go home."

"We know that, Scotty. My name is Seve. I promise you, no one is going to hurt you. In fact, you're destined to have a wonderful life."

"I don't know what *destined* means. Where's my dog?"

"Safe, I promise."

"Is this a spaceship?"

"Yes, Scotty, it is,"

"Why does it look like the inside of an animal?"

"Because it is made of organic material. You can think of it as being alive."

"Why is it alive?"

"My people have found that growing technology is far more efficient than manufacturing technology.

Scotty nodded, still not really understanding. "I'm supposed to be home by dark. I could get into trouble."

The glowing figure named Seve glanced away. Scotty sensed he had said something that upset her. He didn't like to hurt people's feelings, but this wasn't his fault. He didn't ask to be here. They just took him. Both him and Larry.

"Listen to me, Scotty. You are not going home for a long time. I'm sorry if that is upsetting to you. Someday you will better understand just why you are here. Why you have been introduced to the Vallic."

"What's a Vallic?"

"I am a Vallic . . . those around us are Vallic. Just as you are Human, we are Vallic. Actually, Vallic-Human . . . but we have time to discuss all that."

"You look weird. You're all weird aliens," Scotty said, lashing out.

"No, you are the alien. There are more of us . . . so the only weirdo is you."

Scotty didn't want to laugh, but he couldn't help it. He liked Seve. Liked it that she didn't treat him like a baby.

"I'd like to show you around. Let you meet some others . . . just like you," Seve said.

"People like me?"

"That's right, the other children that are here. Then it will be time to transform."

Scotty had no idea how to respond to that. What did *transform* even mean? He had toy transformers; cars that turned into robots. Were they going to change him into a robot, or into a car?

Seve stood upright, taking his hand in hers. Her almost invisible hand felt normal enough. Scotty let her lead him off, past a cluster of similarly glowing figures.

"How old are you, Scotty?"

"Nine. How old are you?" he asked back.

"Seven-hundred-and-nine, in your years."

"Wow! You're older than my great-grandma. She uses a walker. Good thing you don't need one of those."

"Yes, that is a very good thing. The Vallic do not age the same way Humans do. In Human years, I am about twenty-nine."

"That's close to my mom's age, I think. At least, that's the age she says she is every year, though I don't know why. Can we go get Larry now?"

"Larry is safe where he is, I promise," she said, as they meandered through a maze, of sorts: Identical-looking spaces, with mud-colored walls separating one area from the next.

"I don't get it."

"What is it you don't *get*, Scotty?"

"Where does everyone sit down? Where's all the furniture; the neat contraptions spaceships are supposed to have?"

Seve stopped and peered down at him. "I can understand why you find these surroundings a bit plain. Boring even, yes?"

Scotty shrugged.

"We will not be in this vessel long. It simply is a temporary means of transportation. And since the Vallic have no definitive mass . . . weight . . . the need to sit, to lie down constantly, isn't there."

Scotty had a lot more questions but decided to hold his tongue . . . for now.

"Come, you will feel far more at home when we reach the Qhuant."

Scotty was about to ask what Qhuant meant when they suddenly passed through a *shimmering* section of wall. Not a wall, really, but something else. Scotty, turning, pointed back at it. "What was that?"

"In your language, I suppose it is similar to an airtight doorway."

"An airlock," Scotty said, glancing up at her.

"Very good. Yes, more like an airlock."

Seve stopped again and held out a hand. This is the Qhuant. A comfortable waiting area. There is a kind of bathroom here and other Human accommodations. And these are the children who will make the journey along with you."

There were four of them. Other little boys and girls he guessed, who were about his same age. Two boys and two girls, they all looked miserable. Red puffy eyes stared back at him. A little boy, a bath towel wrapped around him, was quietly sobbing.

Scotty noticed this area of the ship had actual places to sit down. Part of the wall, protruding outward, created a long bench encircling most of the space.

"Let me introduce you to the others in here." She took his hand again and walked him closer to the group of kids. "Scotty, this little boy on the left, is Ernesto."

Ernesto had dark hair and skin that was darker than his own. Arms crossed over his chest, he was the only one that didn't look scared or sad. He looked angry. "You're fucking kidnappers!" he yelled defiantly. "Where are you taking us?"

Ignoring him, Seve said, "This little girl next to him is Pamela. Say hi to Scotty, Pamela."

Pamela possessed long blonde hair and a homely face. The only one in a dress, there were streaks of red, purple, and green in her hair. Scotty instinctively knew she'd been taken while attending a party. Birthday girl was written all over this kid. Unenthusiastically, she limply lifted her hand to wave.

"This here is Thomas. He is still very upset."

Thomas, the boy wrapped up in a bath towel, kept his head lowered. His exposed arms and legs looked as though they had never been in contact with sunshine. Turning his head away, he wore a pouty expression.

"And next to Thomas is Tori."

Tori seemed the most normal of all four children. Even though she looked as if she'd been crying, she was dealing with the difficult situation there. Offering him a lopsided smile, she said, "Welcome to a whole lot of crazy."

Scotty instantly liked her. She talked like someone older than her years—more like his older brother, Kyle. Scotty offered back a lopsided smile of his own.

"I must leave you now, Scotty, but it won't be for long. I must make preparations for your transformations."

There was that *same* word again. As Seve left, out the same way they'd entered, Scotty stood still.

"You going to just stand there looking stupid?" Ernesto asked.

"Why don't you shut up," Tori said. "Maybe give him a second. It's not like this sort of thing happens to people every day."

Thomas' whimpering began to increase in volume as he wiped his teary eyes with a corner of the towel.

"A couple of the ghost aliens snuck in and grabbed him while his mommy was giving him a bath, then she got a phone call, or something," Ernesto said, mimicking him in a baby-like voice.

"No-o-o! I was giving myself a bath, stupid! My mom wasn't even there," Thomas shouted back.

Ernesto, raising his eyebrows, tilted his head to one side. His deadpan face emphasized his point.

"You can sit down, you know," the girl in the party dress said.

"What are you looking around for?" Tori asked.

Scotty said, "Larry . . . my dog."

"Dead. I'm betting they killed it. I bet they're eating it right this minute. You know they eat dogs in China," Ernesto said.

"You are so mean," Tori said. "And it's Korea. They eat dogs in Korea. But I'm sure your dog is fine. They probably have a different place here for animals."

"Yeah, like a kennel," Pamela offered, sounding optimistic.

Scotty decided to sit next to Tori. As the five young children sat together, lined up on the circular bench, no one spoke for a while. Then Ernesto said, "At least I wasn't kidnapped wearing only a pink towel."

Scotty saw Tori roll her eyes, trying not to smile as she glanced toward the rather pathetic-looking Thomas.

Scotty wondered if he was the only one on the verge of totally freaking out here. Suddenly, as a bleak sadness built up within him, he was afraid the other kids would see the tears now welling-up in his eyes. He knew they would make fun of him, call him a big baby. But right then, all he wanted was to feel his mother's arms wrap tightly around him. For her to make all this somehow go away. Perhaps tell him all this was nothing more than a bad dream. But he knew it wasn't a dream. And he knew things were going to get worse—a whole lot worse.

chapter 26

S cotty realized he was probably the youngest of the group. The other four kids looked as though they were maybe a year or two older than him. Pamela might be as old as twelve or thirteen. She definitely was older than his big brother Kyle, who was eleven.

Seve reentered the room as silently as a ghost. On seeing her glowing presence, the boy in the towel leaned forward and demanded, "I have to go home! I have to go home now!"

"Come on, we all want to go home, Thomas," Pamela said, resting a reassuring hand on his bare shoulder, sounding and acting motherly.

"Speak for yourself," Ernesto said. "Me? I'm not going back there. They can take me wherever they want."

Thomas, shrugging Pamela's hand away, continued on as if he hadn't been interrupted, "And can I get something to wear other than this towel? I'm cold," He then looked over at Ernesto, his teeth chattering, and said, "You don't want to go home because nobody wants you. You live in an orphanage."

Pamela made a face. "They're not called that anymore. They're called group homes . . . or foster homes."

Scotty didn't know what either one was about. Never before had he even considered that some kids didn't have a regular home to live in with their families—parents, and a brother or sister. Maybe both. He looked at Ernesto, the boy with the darker skin. He knew he was African-American. He also knew there were some people who called them other names. Bad names—like the N word. His brother Kyle once used the N word and got his mouth washed out with soap and then sent to bed without dinner.

"How do you even know where he lives?" Scotty asked Thomas.

"Mind your own business," Ernesto shot back.

"We live in the same neighborhood. In Ohio," Thomas said.

"May I have your attention, please?" Seve said.

"Hey . . . how is it you speak like an American?" Ernesto asked, narrowing his eyes. "Why don't you sound like an alien?" The rest of the kids also turned to Seve—their interest peeked. It was a good question.

"A number of Vallic individuals, including myself, have spent time amongst Human beings on Earth. I lived in the United States. Other Vallic have lived there too, also in other Earth countries."

"Bullshit! You wouldn't exactly fit in. Looking all glowing like you do and hovering around like a spooky spirit. No way, alien lady," Ernesto said.

Scotty and the other kids laughed. Ernesto was funny, even if he didn't intend to be.

"I am one of the very few Vallic from my home world who underwent a special genetic modification . . . a medical treatment. One that has taken years to perfect and is dangerous to undergo. I chose to do this for you, too."

"I don't even know you, alien lady," Ernesto shot back, a freaked-out expression on his face. Again, a few more giggles could be heard.

"Not you, specifically, Ernesto, but all Humans."

Scotty watched Seve as she gestured to another crewmember to come over. They spoke between themselves. The other crewmember, clearly a female, stepped closer and stood silently for several moments. Then, miraculously, she materialized into a Human—a woman. Wearing clothes, she was dressed in a formfitting uniform, of sorts. And like Ernesto, she appeared to be African-American. She turned to Ernesto and smiled.

"Holy crap! Jennet?" Ernesto asked, his words barely loud enough to hear.

Scotty, now totally confused, stared first at Ernesto, then at the Human-looking woman, then over at Seve.

"Wait . . . you know her, Ernesto?" Tori asked.

Ernesto's smart-ass demeanor all but disappeared. "Yeah . . . she works at the foster home. She's one of the volunteers there."

"How did you do that?" Scotty asked her.

"That's a very good question, Scotty," Jennet said. Taking a step closer, she knelt down onto one knee to be at eye-level with the children. "What if I told you that each one of you, in time, will be able to do the same . . . do what I just did?"

"I'd say you're on mind-altering drugs," Ernesto said, although his belligerent tone had clearly changed.

"We're going to be ghosts? Just like you were a minute ago? Ah, no thank you." Tori said, shaking her head.

Scotty studied Jennet . . . or whoever she was. She seemed nice enough, but he wondered if she was tricking them. Maybe it was some kind of elaborate trap . . . like in Hansel and Gretel? The old lady in the cottage who was fattening the children up so she could eat them later.

Jennet stood, nodded to Seve then walked away.

Seve focused her gaze on Scotty. As if reading his mind, she said, "In time you will learn to trust us and come to understand just why you were chosen. I am sorry we had to take such drastic measures."

"Yeah, like kidnapping us," Tori said.

"So you will take us back home again soon?" Pamela asked.

"In time, but not soon. It is best you come to terms with that fact right now. Go ahead and cry. Mourn for the life you knew, for it is gone. We understand how difficult this is for you; how it will continue to be difficult for some time to come."

As if on cue, Thomas began to weep. Once again, he used the corner of his towel to wipe away tears. Scotty was starting to dislike the sniveling brat. Although to be truthful, the boy's constant crying and complaining presented an example of someone he didn't want to be anything like. Perhaps Thomas' behavior was the reason he wasn't bawling his own eyes out.

"You mentioned before something about a transition coming?" Tori asked.

"Yes. We will leave Earth's upper orbit soon. Prior to that, you and me—all of us, even this vessel—will temporarily be converted from obtuse matter into pure raw energy." She pinched the skin on her arm. "This step is necessary for us to travel at the speed of light, and even, effectively speaking, beyond that."

Thomas stopped whimpering long enough to interject, "Einstein's theory of relativity. It's impossible to travel faster than the speed of light."

"You are a smart boy, Thomas. It's *something* like that, although old Albert didn't live long enough to theorize on the possibilities of a factored progression of light energy."

"You're going to change us into light?" Tori asked, giving a skeptical sideways glance

"We all will be converted to an energetic form of ourselves. Typically, this process is much easier for the Vallic since we are only three percent matter to begin with. Now that I have Human DNA, along with my Vallic DNA . . . that complicates things somewhat for me. Just the same, all of you, and me, will be converted into a form of energy and then stored in what is referred to as an atomized macro-structure. Then we will be ready for our intergalactic space journey."

"Please don't take us! Just let us go home. Please!" Tori pleaded.

It was the first time Scotty witnessed seeing Tori acting her age—like a child. He momentarily wondered how long it would be before he too started pleading. Begging to go home to his family; to his mother's warm embrace.

So this spaceship we're in won't fly off to the stars? Like in Star Wars or Star Trek?" Scotty asked, changing the subject.

"No. Sorry, Scotty. What you have seen in the movies and on TV does not actually work. Physics do not support that reality. It would take us hundreds, even thousands of years to get from one point in space to another. We also may journey through various wormholes to cut our travel time way down. Only pure energy . . . such as light energy . . . could survive such a trek. I can explain more about this later. For now, please come with me. It is time."

chapter 27

They moved together as a group—Seve in the lead, with Pamela and Thomas close behind her, followed by Tori, Scotty, and Ernesto, still-griping, bringing up the rear. They passed through a number of compartments, such as they were, of varying sizes. Once they'd progressed deeper into the spaceship, Scotty noticed something that would pass for a kind of technology. Elevated, organic-looking protrusions, rising up from the floor, or extending out from the walls. Somewhat rectangular in shape, Scotty thought they could be consoles or control panels. On closer inspection, beneath a thin, top surface membrane, things blinked and shimmered with hundreds of tiny illuminations.

As they continued deeper into the ship, he saw other faintly glowing crewmembers bustling about. They turned and watched expressionless as the small cluster of young Humans moved passed them. Scotty's fear of what was coming next had become an all-consuming dread; his heart was hammering faster and harder in his chest and his rapid breathing was making him feel woozy. Startled out of his worrying thoughts, Scotty heard Thomas plead again. Louder now, his annoying, whiny voice filled the space around them.

Two Vallic crewmembers suddenly joined their procession, each taking ahold of one of Thomas' thin white arms. The boy began screaming louder, wildly thrashing about. Seve momentarily glanced back at him then continued on.

At some point Tori fell behind and now walked by Scotty's side. He asked her, "Are they going to kill us?"

"Why are you asking me?" she asked back, then added, "It wouldn't make sense . . . going to all the trouble of kidnapping us, only to then turn around and kill us here on the ship. Why do that?"

Scotty nodded. Her explanation made sense. He felt somewhat comforted.

Coming to a stop, they evidently had reached their intended destination. This compartment, by far, had the most technology. The walls and ceiling were ablaze with blinking, glowing, illumination. So much so, that Scotty could easily make out what appeared to be submerged branch-like veins, or arteries running deep within the depths of various surrounding surfaces. *This vessel truly is alive,* he thought.

Another glowing Vallic figure entered the same compartment. Moving with unhurried purpose, he headed directly toward them. He was larger, more imposing, than any of the aliens they'd encountered up till now. Scotty and Tori instinctively moved closer to one another. The typically talkative

Ernesto, now silent, huddled closer in too. *There's something really dark and foreboding about this big alien,* Scotty thought.

They watched as he quietly conversed with Seve. Not speaking English, their voices steadily began to rise in volume. Seve was now shouting, standing up to the far more imposing figure. Their dispute continued until finally the larger Vallic spun around and reached out for Thomas. The boy flew up, the alien's glowing fist securely clenched around the youngster's neck. Eyes wide and filled with terror, Thomas stared back at his captor in disbelief. His little hands desperately ripped, clawed at the alien's fingers tightly gripping his constricted throat. A tiny whimper escaped through his gasping mouth when his pink bath towel dropped to the floor below. Now naked, his skinny legs frantically flailed and thrashed about. Then came a definitive, singular, sound: *Crack!*

Thomas no longer struggled. A limp ragdoll, his body was then held up for the other children to witness.

The large alien slowly lowered his arm, one hand still clutched around the dead boy's neck. Moving away without looking at Seve, Thomas's limp body—only a lifeless carcass— was dragged along at the alien's side.

Both horrified and paralyzed with fear, Scotty continued to watch, trying not to breathe, to stand perfectly still. He wanted to scream. Wanted to run and hide, hoping his mother or father would somehow hear him, would come and find him up here in space. His mind raced, as if a highly charged electrical current was coursing around and around through his brain. Mental images of everyday good and normal events entered and left at such lighting speed he wasn't able to hold onto any one of them. He only knew what was occurring was far more than any nine-year-old should have to endure. Mere hours before his life was normal. Kyle tuning out the rest of the world while playing video games on his PlayStation; Sara sitting at the kitchen table singing a silly song she'd learned in pre-school and drawing in the new coloring book she'd just convinced Mom to buy her at the Stop and Shop. *No . . . this stuff doesn't happen to someone who's only nine!* Scotty swallowed hard then hoped it wasn't that loud, not wanting to attract the attention of the big alien.

He briefly wondered where Thomas was being taken. Perhaps he'd be tossed out into the lonely blackness outside these walls—out into space where he'd drift forever and ever.

Scotty, upon feeling Tori's fingers tightening within his own, wondered when she'd taken his hand in hers. Staring into her terror-filled blue eyes, he saw his own scared reflection stare back. He noticed she was trembling then wondered if he was, too. Ernesto's voice, only inches away, was barely more than a whisper, "This is so much worse than I even thought."

Seve was saying something. Scotty wondered how long she'd been speaking. Tori, pulling her hand away from his, took a step closer to the female alien.

"I am sorry. I know that was a terrible thing to see. It should not have happened . . . not like that. Best you learn early on that not all Vallic appreciate other life forms . . . ones different from their own. Especially Humans."

The remaining four children listened intently, not daring to speak.

"All I can say is there is a reason you are here. It is important, beyond anything you can fully understand at your young age."

"We understand enough to know you just murdered a little kid right in front of us," Ernesto said.

"I suppose that should be a warning to you . . . to all of you. You are here to learn. You are here to eventually help others on your planet. Help your species to survive. If it is determined you cannot do that, that you are incapable of doing that, then you may face a fate similar to that of poor Thomas. What Horran has done.

"Is that who that was . . . his name is Horran?" Scotty asked.

She nodded. "The leader of this team. And I am sorry, but I will not be able to save you in the event he intervenes. So be good children and do as you are asked. Learn and complete each task presented to you and do so with a positive attitude. Do this and you will live a long life. Eventually, you will be returned to Earth. But I assure you, when that day comes, you will find it just as hard to return there as it was to leave. Over subsequent years you will learn to do things no other Human has accomplished before. You will become far more than what Earthlings are presently. Someday, you all will be sole examples of how the Human race can survive."

Seve turned away as another Vallic crewmember approached. They spoke together in friendly low tones before she turned back to face them. "It is time."

"Time for what?" Ernesto asked.

"For each of us to make the transition. Do not be afraid. You are safe . . . the procedure will not hurt."

"Why would you even say that . . . that it won't hurt? I didn't think it would until you said that," Ernesto said.

Scotty asked, "Where's Larry? Can I get my dog back first, before the, um, transition?"

"Seriously? Again with the dog?" Pamela shot back.

"Larry has already gone through a similar process, Scotty," Seve said. "Now it's your turn."

Scotty was taken aback—learning something had already happened to Larry without having prior knowledge. He felt a deep uneasiness within, creeping in from all sides.

"Scotty, why don't you go first?" Seve asked, in an upbeat voice. Almost as if suggesting he be the first to head into a classroom, or jump into a swimming pool.

Scotty glanced over at now stone-faced Tori, then at Ernesto, who merely shrugged, looking more than a little relieved that it wasn't him going first.

"What do I do?"

Seve held out a hand, "Come with me, child."

Scotty hesitated as long as he thought he could get away with it, then reluctantly moved around Pamela's protruding party dress and took the alien's outstretched hand. Seve gave it a gentle squeeze then led him in the opposite direction from where Thomas's body had been dragged off by the towering alien. *That's at least something*, he figured. They entered through a separating, thin, translucent layer, consisting of a kind of energized particles, and his skin tingled as they passed through it. On the other side the walls came together—what amounted to either a hallway or a passageway. Twenty paces later, they moved into another compartment. In some ways it seemed pretty much the same—but different too—the illumination in here far brighter. Combinations of tiny lights were blinking on and off, patterns being made, but he didn't understand what they meant. Only that, on a more active level, more of the same weird alien technology was going on here.

At the center of the room was a humongous-huge white worm—maybe maggot described it better. It emitted a sweet, sickening smell that made Scotty want to gag. Faceless, its bloated-looking body was a series of large, puffy, inner tube-like connected segments. Scotty continued to watch the thing, realizing it was actually moving. *No, it was only breathing. And it was beyond disgusting.*

Scotty glanced up and found Seve looking down at him, watching his every expression. "It looks worse than it is. We call it a Porthwamp."

To Scotty, the *thing* couldn't possibly look any worse. Towering high overhead, it easily was as wide as three side-by-side SUVs. Clearly, it was both an animal and a *thing*—maybe even a machine, of some sort. The Porthwamp had little lights glowing on and off within its flesh. It also possessed a wide-open, gaping mouth.

Seve smiled. "That is the entrance."

"No! There's no way anyone ever willingly goes in there. I'm not going in there . . . not ever."

Looking bemused, Seve said nothing, as she pointed to a large, integrated, 3D display taking place within the enormous maggot's surface membrane. Scotty was seeing views that he assumed were other areas on the ship. His attention was drawn to one display, in particular, showing multiple rows of seed-like objects. *Pods?* Lined-up, one-after-another, each had a small clear section, an irregular window, set into its top portion. Inside each, Scotty could just barely make out their faces: sleeping Vallic crewmembers. To Scotty, they looked identical to one another, and wondered, *why even bother with windows since they all look the same?* Then it occurred to him, *maybe not so much for others to look in, but to enable the crewmembers to look out.*

"What's going to happen to me, Seve?" Scotty asked nervously.

"You're going to walk through this entrance gate and step onto the yellow circle. There, your body will be scanned. Scanned down to its smallest components—to the very atoms that make Scotty, Scotty. Even your thoughts, memories, emotions, will be scanned then stored into a virtual representation of you . . . an atomized organic macro-structure. Those pods, or structures, you noticed back there on the display are actually *symbolic* versions of something that does not have actual mass. We think of them as virtual *place holders.*"

Scotty appreciated that Seve wasn't speaking to him like he was only nine. And, for the most part, he understood what she was saying. He didn't *like* any of it, but he understood. "Okay . . . then what?"

She paused, staring at him for several moments. "Well . . . then we totally obliterate your physical body."

Scotty felt as if he'd been slapped in the face. He struggled to breath. "You said you weren't going to kill me . . . to kill us." Fear, which had slowly begun to subside, now rushed back in him like a quickly approaching tidal wave.

Seve shook her head. "No, no, you won't be dead. Not really, since everything that makes you *you* will already be stored. There cannot be two Scottys, not two of anyone. This is just part of the process. Once '*all of you*' is properly stored into your associated atomized macro-structure, then the rest of the crew, including me, will be similarly transformed. This spaceship, with the help of the Porthwamp, will follow pre-programmed instructions, transform into what amounts to pure energy constructs. At that point in time, everything in here will become nothing more than meticulously organized, arranged, energy. This Porthwamp transmits that energy when it's left behind. Alone here in space, it will fire-up our energy—light beams deep into the cosmos, to a distant point light-years away. Then, closer to another planet within another planetary system, the whole process is reversed."

Scotty asked, "Can I do all that . . . but do it with Larry?"

chapter 28

"Are you ready?" Seve asked.

"Wait. You mean, like right now? We're doing this right now?" Scotty asked.

"Yes. It is time."

Scotty looked about the compartment, at the *alive* walls, with their strange creases and ridges, then at the narrow passageway they'd traversed through to get here. He wanted to say goodbye to Tori, even to Ernesto. Then he thought of his family—*were they worried about him?* Did they even know he was gone, maybe never to return? *Would they think he was dead?* Would he soon, in fact, be dead? He thought of Thomas, of his recent horrific demise, then thought of the pink towel, lying in a heap on the floor.

"I'm ready, I guess. But do I really have to go inside there? Inside the Porthwamp's mouth? I mean . . . it totally reeks. I feel like gagging just standing out here."

Seve stared down at Scotty for several long beats—her glowing, featureless, face somehow conveyed understanding.

"I have high hopes for you, young Human. You may be one of the ones chosen ... one of the ones, someday, who will guide your species toward new and exciting distant frontiers."

"So, we can stay together?"

"Stay together?" she repeated, slightly tilting her head to one side.

"Pamela, Tori, Ernesto, and me ...," Scotty said.

Seve, raising her head up, slowly nodded in understanding. She stepped over to the second display—one which seemed to show nothing other than a bazillion, gray, oblong seedpods. Scotty had seen geometric computer screensavers before not much different from this one. Seve did something with the controls and, as the image began to zoom in, Scotty's eyes widened and his mouth dropped open. It wasn't a screensaver after all. The oblong shapes, now coming into view, were simply more seed pods like the ones he'd seen on the other display. There were thousands of the things. "Where ... who's ..."

Seve finished his question for him: "Who's in these other pods? It's approximately three hundred Human children, all from Earth, who were taken over the last few months. As to where the pods are physically located ... well, they are right here, on this ship. But they could just as easily reside somewhere else. What you are viewing has already been converted into the purest form of energy. These pods would easily fit onto the head of a pin.

"You're going to put me into one of those pods?"

Seve said, "Larry is in one of those pods."

"Oh ... well can you put my pod next to his?"

"I can certainly try," Seve answered.

"Say goodbye to Tori for me, okay?"

"You'll see her soon enough. Now stay where you are. You do not need to do anything more than to remain perfectly still." Seve placed a soft hand on Scotty's cheek and held it there a moment. "Can I give you a little advice, Scotty?"

"Sure . . . okay."

"I've had the opportunity to study your kind, your people, over the last year or so. I learned much about the evolution of Human beings. About what makes certain individuals, throughout your sordid history, stand apart from others. Which men and women made their mark . . . made a difference."

"Like Michael Jordan?"

"Sure . . . but others, too. Great leaders like George Washington, Winston Churchill, Nefertiti, and Julius Caesar. When you transform, back into a material form, you will be on another planet. Let me give you some good advice. You are not there to make friends. You are not there to form a community. You Humans have a saying that I like: 'Hit the ground running.' Let there be no mistake about what you have been chosen to do, and that is to win. Prevail over all others. And, most important, survive. If you truly wish to see your family again, also help others on your home world, you need to play by a new set of rules; even to the point of being ruthless, if necessary, in achieving your goal. Do not forget this, Scotty. You will be tested every step of the way . . . stay cognizant of that and you may prevail."

"I don't understand a lot of what you just said. I don't know what cog ... ni ... zzzant means," Scotty said.

"Do not worry about that now. You will understand in time, young Human." Seve, exhaling a deep breath, turned and walked away, leaving Scotty alone on the yellow circle.

He waited, about to holler out another question, when he felt something *strange*—an electrical current course throughout his body. Suddenly, in a flash, he was somewhere else, lying within a small enclosure. Above him was a small window—one he could see out through—though all he could see were the other nearby pods.

Before everything went black, he wondered if Larry was there, nearby ...

* * *

Scotty blinked his eyes open, feeling both confused and disoriented. *Something must have gone wrong.* Whatever was supposed to happen inside the pod—hadn't happened. *Or had it?*

He then realized he wasn't in a pod at all, although it sure was dark wherever he was. It obviously was night time and he was outside. Barely visible, he sensed more than saw tall trees rustling overhead—swaying back and forth from unseen winds. Strange, but he didn't feel wind gusts brush against his skin—his face. He heard sounds of chirping birds; night time wildlife somewhere up above. *I must be back on Earth! They took me back! I'm back home!* Exhilarated, Scotty tried to sit up—but nothing worked. He couldn't force his arms down to his sides, which would enable him to push off. In that one moment

Scotty Sullivan truly felt panic. Did he no longer possess arms, legs, or even a body? *Oh God, I'm dead.*

Seve you lied to me.

The trees rustled overhead with an intense, angry thrashing that both frightened and delighted Scotty. *I think I felt that!* It was very subtle, but he felt a slight breeze lightly touch his face, also something pointy, sticking him in his lower back. *A twig? Sharp rock?* Once again, he tried to move an arm and this time he had at least minimal success. I have arms.

As the seconds and minutes ticked by, more and more bodily senses and functions returned. It took a full hour's struggle before he was able to fully rise into a sitting position. Glancing around, he took in the surrounding landscape. His first thought was straight out of his mom's favorite movie: *Toto, I've a feeling we're not in Kansas anymore.* Second, were Seve's parting words: *You will be tested every step of the way.* Just knowing he was being tested changed everything. He labored to his feet, resolute to indeed survive what would come next.

chapter 29

S cotty wondered why he was deposited here. Left alone this late at night in some kind of creepy wilderness. At least he was back on Earth, and that was encouraging. He was sure someone would be along soon to help him.

Unsteadily, he rose to his feet then realized he was dressed in different clothes. Not his own rolled-up jeans, faded tank top, and tennis shoes. He made a face. *Who did that—changed my clothes?* His balance still unsteady, he stood and listened for sounds from the others. Perhaps Tori, or Ernesto, or Pamela were nearby? Scotty thought of his dog and, on the off-chance that he too was nearby, called out, "Larry! Here boy! Come on, boy . . . Larry!"

Again, Scotty tried hard to listen for a familiar sound above the rustling wind. He slowly turned around, giving his immediate surroundings a closer inspection. In the moonless darkness, he approached what appeared to be the wide trunk of a silhouetted tree. Stepping up to it, he stuck his palm out and felt its rough bark against his skin; a strong pine scent invaded his nostrils. Blindly, stretching his arm even higher up, he touched a low-hanging branch. A cluster of long pine needles brushed against his wrist. Even further up, his fingers touched a hanging pinecone. At least, it *felt* like a pinecone.

Scotty refocused his attention on his clothes, what he was wearing. His best guess, standing alone in the darkness, was that he was attired in some kind of dorky overalls. He couldn't make out what color they were. And he was wearing boots, instead of his old Keds. Sliding his hands into the overalls' two side pockets, he found them empty. He checked out a top chest pocket as well, and, patting it, could feel something inside. He fiddled with the opening—not exactly a zipper, but something similar. Reaching several fingers inside, he pulled free what felt like a little matchbox car. He had close to a hundred of them back home packed away in a shoebox, since he was now too old to play with them.

Using his fingers on both hands to examine the contours of the small object, he realized it was something entirely different. Roughly shaped, like a flattened-out bird, he wondered at first if it was—*somehow*—still alive. He felt warmth, emanating from its winged, almost aerodynamic shape, but it was some kind of device, he was sure of that. Flipping it over again, along its bottom surface, his fingers felt a slight indentation. *And a button.* He pressed it and immediately felt the object gain weight—its dimensions increasing. Letting the object drop freely from his hand, he took a step back from where it landed on the ground.

Scotty leaned forward, noting that the ever-enlarging device was also kind of glowing. Mesmerized, he watched it continue to expand in size. The wind had subsided substantially—night sounds coming alive to the point of distraction. When all further growth finally ceased, it had become roughly four-feet-wide by six-feet-long in size. Nearly transparent, it still resembled a flattened-out bird. One with its stubby wings more defined, and an elongated tail. As a soft '*ping*' sounded, a separate circular section began to rise up several inches from the device's mid-section, illuminating a circle in a brighter shade of yellow. The familiar looking, stepping stone-sized circle was identical to the one he'd stood upon within the alien ship. *Terrific.*

Scotty debated whether to step up onto it, or not. Sure, he realized he was supposed to do just that, but he wondered if he should wait. Perhaps Larry was around somewhere, or the other kids with him on the alien ship. He contemplated what to do since, truthfully, he had no idea what would happen if he stood upon the circle. He might be whisked back inside another pod, or even onto a spaceship somewhere. Frustrated, he blew through puffed-out cheeks and studied the surroundings; everything was unchanged, still black as pitch. Shaking his head, he stepped onto the yellow circle.

Immediately things started to happen, the contours of the device were changing. Tempted to jump off, Scotty watched as it assumed completely new contours. It wasn't long before he realized the bird-shaped-thing was in the process of encircling him. Materializing all around him—into some sort of enclosed, tear-drop-shaped vehicle. *Or was it more like an animal?* Staring out through its clear, membrane-like surface—first left, then right—he noticed the stubby wings had taken on a more defined shape. Yes, the bird vehicle definitely was some kind of aircraft or space vessel, but it also was *alive—or sort of alive*. In front of him, a bright futuristic dashboard appeared just below a thin, translucent membrane. Scotty smiled. This was far *cooler* than any video game or space tech he'd ever seen.

The enclosure, or belly area, was fairly roomy. Scotty figured it was about the size of a short stubby bus. Everything inside and out was soft to the touch—and also see-through. As he looked about the confined space, he questioned why whoever had made the thing hadn't designed built-in seats. And then wondered, *what am I supposed to do now?* As cool as the craft was, it would quickly become—he tried to remember the big word for it—oh yeah, *claustrophobic.*

Enough light was generated within the enclosure, and spilling out beyond, that Scotty could make out the nearby landscape and surrounding big trees. His heart began to race, even before he fully comprehended what his eyes were now steadfastly locked onto. Not five feet from where he'd previously stood and touched the pinecone, was some kind of creature, perched high upon a tree branch. Its eyes, glowing green, reflected back the vessel's illumination. Its face, matte black, looked as if it had been smashed flat in a horrific car accident. Its nose—nearly nonexistent—consisted of two small nostril holes. Below it, were thick lips, surrounding a gaping mouth. Scotty, staring, was certain the creature was incapable of closing its jaws, possessing so many protruding teeth and six or seven-inch-long fangs.

The creature, becoming restless, stirred and suddenly stood upright on the supporting branch. Rising up to its full height, Scotty figured it wasn't quite as tall as himself. The creature scratched between its legs where, comparative to its overall size, existed enormous private parts. Genitalia that swayed and hung down like a colossal pendulum. Its long, curved claws were busy scratching there when the creature began to scrutinize the night.

Scotty caught something moving about in his peripheral vision. Staring out the front of the craft, he watched a different kind of animal hop into view. But it wasn't a rabbit, as he'd first suspected, but something closer to a large insect, one with hair and oversized transparent wings. As it slogged along, its two forward pinchers constantly scissored open and closed. Scotty in that one moment knew—beyond any doubt—he was not on Earth. *He had no idea where he was.*

chapter 30

"I'm impressed. Having survived even this long on your own, is commendable, Scotty," a female voice said, filling the confined space.

Scotty spun around, finding Seve standing behind him. More accurately, a full-size projected image of Seve. Every few seconds, her glowing form pulsed erratically with static.

"As you've undoubtedly guessed, I am not actually there with you. Not until the Romper was activated did we confirm you were safe."

"Romper?" Scotty repeated.

"That's what we call the transport vehicle you're standing within."

"Seve, there's a . . . scary animal. Up in the trees. I was right next to it. It looks like it could eat me."

"That's a Kammie. Intelligent, and yes, it is a very dangerous life form indigenous to this world. Kammies are meat-eaters. They don't like loud noises . . . something to keep in mind."

"So, I'm not on Earth? What world is this? Where am I?"

"You are about eight light years distance from Earth. Larger than your home planet, by about one-third, it is remarkably similar. There are large oceans, continent landmasses, magnetic north and south poles, a relatively mild climate, and a highly diverse, thriving ecosystem."

"What's it called?"

"We call it Hope,"

"Okay. Am I the only one here? Am I alone on Hope?"

"No. There are approximately three thousand other Human beings here along with you."

Scotty nodded back, then turned and looked out through the side of the nearly transparent Romper. "You're referring to the abducted kids who were in the pods on the ship. The pods that you said could all fit on the head of a pin."

"That is correct, plus several thousand adults who have been here some time already. Everyone here has been transitioned back into material forms . . . as you have been."

"So why are we here? When can we go home?"

"Scotty, it is time you come to realize that this—that Hope—*is* your new home. Someday, it may become home to millions of Humans."

"Wait! You said that I'd be able to return to my old home, um, Earth," Scotty said.

"That will depend on you, Scotty. And even then, it will only be for a short while. We already spoke about this, remember? The people that travel back to Earth will have a very important mission. As I mentioned before, Earth, unfortunately, does not have much time left. It will not survive an impending cosmic disaster. Something we can talk more about in the days and weeks to come."

"So wait . . . just tell me this. The people from Earth will come to planet Hope to live? This will be their new home?"

"Some people, but not all. We will do our best to communicate the seriousness of the situation; demonstrate what exactly is going to occur. Scotty, my people, the Vallic, are committed to helping other beings on worlds similar to Earth. But only if they want to be helped."

Scotty mentally flashed back to the imposing alien on the ship. His arm outstretched—then snapping the neck of poor Thomas.

"This fast-moving gamma ray burst that will strike Earth, has already destroyed numerous other planetary systems along its path . . . and it will continue to do so, for millions of years to come. So far, getting Vallic teams ahead of this gamma ray has been problematic. With your Solar System, Earth, and systems farther on we believe we will find more success."

"Oh . . ." Scotty mumbled, weighing the dire seriousness of it all.

"We have found it is a matter of trust—or, more accurately, mistrust. The people of Earth will not trust the word of an alien race that their world will soon be coming to an end. We have witnessed far better outcomes when someone of the same species delivers the message. Someone who is a natural leader who can manage such an important undertaking—that of saving an entire species from extinction."

"No one would believe me. I'm just a little kid."

"Yes, right now you are. But by the time you are an adult, you, or someone even better qualified, will need to be ready."

"I don't understand. Why can't you start moving people off Earth now if it's going to get so dangerous there? What are you waiting for, Seve?"

"There are certain things you still do not understand. Not yet. Your Human race will require a specific environment to survive in. A planet nearly identical to Earth would be best."

"Yeah ... like Hope. You already told me how perfect it would be here."

Seve shook her head. "Well, as similar as this planet is to your own, there are some monumental differences here as well."

"Like what?"

"Like, during the day, when dual Sun-like stars rise on this side of the world, the radiation produced from them is much too strong to survive in for long. Along with that, some of the indigenous life forms here would devour Humankind in short order."

"Like the Kammie?"

"The Kammie would be the least of their problems, I'm afraid," she said.

"This planet doesn't sound like a good place for Humans," Scotty added.

"Maybe not perfect, but it will have to do. Our scientists are in the process of perfecting what we refer to as Dyad-Geneses."

"What's that?"

"Later, Scotty, after the other children have been retrieved and we meet at the congregation site."

Scotty didn't know what congregation meant, but suddenly, as the Romper craft began to rise off the ground, he no longer cared. "Where are we going?

"To retrieve the other children, scattered here in the area," Seve said.

A spotlight then came on at the front of the vessel, illuminating the forward landscape. Silently, the craft began to move—more like glide—several feet off the ground. Again, the terrain looked somewhat Earth-like. But there again, maybe not. Squinting his eyes to better see out into the darkness, he saw what at first appeared to be regular evergreen-type trees—but no. These were actually crazy weird in shape. They didn't grow straight up like normal trees should, like on Earth, but these grew just as tall, and then bent back downward again—in effect, making tall oblong circles. He saw a number of the trees grew out into multiple connected circles—having a kind of curly-cue pig's tail effect.

A hillside, not far away, had large outcroppings of dull gray rock. At least rocks were the same here. He thought of home. He thought of Massachusetts.

"Seve?"

"Yes, Scotty?"

"How did I get into these retarded-looking clothes?"

"Onboard the ship. When it first arrived here, in Hope's upper orbit, you were extracted from your pod. You awoke, although you do not remember it. You were then dressed in those clothes and immunized for this particular environment." Seve, noting a confused expression on his face, added, "You were given medicine so you wouldn't get sick while here on Hope."

"And then you just sent me down to the surface by myself . . . even with all the dangerous animals lurking around?"

"That's basically correct. Time is short and we are forced to hurry. In fact, the ship has already moved on. Left for another endangered planetary system. Understand, there are just too few of us Vallic to stay around here. As I mentioned before, it will be survival of the fittest from here on in. Now hold your questions until later."

The Romper had picked up a bit of speed, forcing Scotty to reach his hand out to steady himself. Several times he thought he saw something *strange*— caught in the spotlight—little more than a fast-moving blur. A creature he had nothing in his memory bank to compare with, other than it was alive, dark, and moving fast. Bigger than a bear, even a gorilla, but smaller in size than an elephant. He glanced back at Seve's projected image but found it gone—Seve was gone.

The Romper, beginning to slow, descended, setting down onto the ground. The craft wobbled at first then steadied. Glancing around, the landscape looked similar to what he'd first seen when he awoke not so long back. When the Romper's side door slid open, Scotty didn't move. In fact, he searched for a way to shut the door since there were big man-eaters running about outside.

Encircling the top of the Romper, additional lights pulsed on illuminating a circle thirty to forty feet into the trees and into the low-lying scrub brush. The tree's long black shadows cast away from the Romper like reaching limbs. Scotty peered out, trying to see something, anything, out of the ordinary—something that might resemble another kid. Then he saw it: Two legs extending out from a cropping of trees. Scotty closed his eyes, took in a long breath, then slowly let it back out. It didn't help any that he was still scared; too scared to go out there. Moving over to the open doorway, he stood at the threshold and shouted, "Hello? Can you hear me?" and waited.

A full minute passed before he tried again, "Hey . . . you need to wake up and get yourself over here, come inside where it's safe."

The extended-out legs didn't move. Whoever it was didn't stir. Scotty recalled something Seve had told him: *Let there be no mistake about what you have been chosen to do, and that is to win. Prevail over all others. And, most important, survive.*

Crap!

Scotty stepped down from the Romper's open doorway. Glancing left then right, he took one slow step after another. Hearing something behind him, he spun around in time to see the Romper's door slide shut.

chapter 31

S cotty hoped that none of the forest animals, the man-eaters, would come near. That the Romper's high-powered lights would keep them at bay, at least as long as it would take him to get back inside the craft. First, though, he needed to awaken the kid, still sleeping soundly in the trees up ahead. *It'll be nice to have company*, he thought.

At ten feet away, Scotty held up and yelled out, "Hey kid . . . you need to wake up. We have to leave here pronto."

But still no movement came from the legs' unseen owner, as they extended out into the light. The rest of the body, hidden from view, was behind two closely joined together tree trunks. Scotty tentatively approached—stealing quick glances left, right, and back over his shoulder—sensing some predator's eyes were watching his every move.

Reaching the extended-out pair of legs, Scotty found that they indeed were a small kid's legs. He or she was wearing the same retarded-looking overalls as himself. He remembered now that their color was called khaki. Grandparents wore khaki.

He stepped closer, spotting a darkening stain at the waistband. Something rust-colored had seeped through and into the fabric. Then it hit him. His nostrils flared at the rising acrid smell—like pennies—like copper. Unconsciously, Scotty grimaced, and took another half step to the left. Now able to peer around the closest tree trunk, he inwardly prayed that what he was seeing wasn't Tori. He *liked* Tori. He continued to stare down at what he now knew was a dead kid. A corpse. But there was no way to determine just who it was since the body's torso wasn't even there. *Something had eaten it!* Appearing black in the tree's dark shadow, glistening entrails lay on the ground—like oversized pasta noodles snaking off into the darkness.

As both hands flew up to his mouth, Scotty wanted to scream. Wanted to cry out for help, but Seve's words came back to him: *Prevail over all others. And, most important, survive!*

Scotty forced himself to keep quiet, taking one shaky step backwards then another. His too rapid in-and-out breaths—almost like panting—made him feel light-headed. Like he'd just run a mile. He continued to stare down at what was left of the unknown kid.

Hesitating, Scotty shot a quick glance off to his right—*Did a shadow just move over there in the trees?* Or was it only his imagination, working overtime? Taking a few steps back—not daring to take his eyes off the dead kid's appendages—Scotty swallowed hard with some difficulty. His constricted throat was dry. He mentally had to use every bit of willpower to slow his breathing rate down. He told himself he was going to be fine;

that he was going to get back into the Romper and leave this place.

In the process of taking the next step backward, he bumped up against *something—something unmistakably alive*. Startled, he screamed to high-heaven, spinning around to face whatever kind of man-eating monster had snuck up behind him. Scotty's nine-year-old clenched, white-knuckled fists came up, ready to defend himself.

"For God's sakes, Scotty! What are you doing? You scared the crap out of me," Tori exclaimed, looking both frightened and annoyed at the same time.

Scotty, relieved, was forced to bend over, his hands on his knees, to catch his breath. Without looking in that direction, he lifted an arm and pointed to the unmoving legs. "I don't know who it is . . . dead. Seriously, you don't want to look."

He heard her walk over to the tree line. A moment later he heard her retching and throwing up. Only then did he sneak a glance in her direction. She too was bent over, her hands on her knees. They exchanged a long look.

"It's Pamela," she said.

"How can you tell?"

Tori pointed in the direction of the second tree. "Big clump of hair back there. The strands are died purple."

"Okay, we need to get out of here . . . we're in danger," he said, straightening up while scanning their surroundings.

Tori looked deeper into the woods. Scotty watched as a fearful wariness settled into her eyes. Giving him two quick nods, she said, "Yeah, you're right." And hurried back his way.

He saw tears on her cheeks. Her stare leveled onto the craft. "What is that thing?"

"It's called a Romper."

Approaching the craft, she gave him back a quick scowl. One that asked—*and how would you know that?*

"It's how I got here. And Seve was inside, though she wasn't . . . um . . . really there."

After another scowl, Tori approached the side of the nearly transparent Romper craft. As the door, almost dutifully, slid open, Tori looked back at Scotty.

"It's safe . . . hop in, we need to go." As Scotty followed her inside, the overhead lights immediately switched off. The outer landscape suddenly fell into darkness, with only the forward spotlight staying on. Scotty looked at Tori in the dim light—watched her as she glanced about the compartment and then back at him. She's probably eleven or twelve, he figured. She was small—small body, a small nose and mouth. But her eyes were large, super-expressive. She *spoke* with those eyes without even uttering a word.

"What now?" she asked, taking in the complicated illuminated dashboard.

"We'll probably be sent where another kid was dropped off by the aliens."

"Seve told you that?"

Scotty nodded. "She said that we're going to be pretty much on our own down here. The spaceship, the one we arrived on, has already gone to help others."

"Really?"

"Yeah. She said there are thousands of Humans here."

"Where is here?"

"We're on a world called Hope, a long distance away from Earth. Everything will be explained more when we next meet up. I can't remember what she called the place. She did say that half the people here would not survive."

"Half?" Tori asked, and Scotty nodded back.

"Why is she telling you all this stuff and not me?"

Scotty shrugged. "Probably just likes *me* more than *you*."

Tori gave him a *ha ha* expression, then, crossing her arms over her chest, said, "I can't believe Pamela is really dead. I've never seen a dead person before ... like for reals, not like on TV."

"I didn't know her. But she seemed nice enough," he said.

Now it was Tori's turn to shrug. "I only knew her for a few hours. To be honest, she was kind of weird. Like she had, um, issues. That's what my mom would say. She had issues."

They looked at each other with sadness. Tori's mention of her mother brought his current, desperate situation back into the forefront of his thoughts.

"Sometimes I wonder if I'm dreaming. If all this is really happening to me," Tori said.

Changing the subject, he said, "Seve said some of us will go back to Earth; some of us children ... someday."

"Oh, and I suppose that will be you?" Tori asked, her eyes challenging.

"I didn't say that. Only that whoever this person might be . . . he or she needs to survive; not give up. That type of thing."

"Well, I'm not planning on giving up. Maybe I'll be one of the ones returning to Earth."

The Romper now was decelerating. The surroundings outside were no longer thickly wooded forests. On the distant horizon, silhouetted against the glow of an approaching dawn, were gently rolling hills. *They look far less foreboding*, Scotty thought. The Romper, touching down, wobbled like it previously had.

"So now what?" Tori asked.

When the side door slid open, Scotty said, "I think this Romper's like a bus. "We should look for another kid." Tori's eyes widened.

Scotty stepped outside just as the overhead lights turned on, illuminating the surrounding landscape. And there, standing several paces in front of him, was Ernesto, who stared back at Scotty with surprise.

"Some pervert dressed me in this *onesie*," he said.

Tori, standing in the open doorway, said, "Pamela is dead."

Ernesto's expression instantly changed. In that one moment his tough, street-kid demeanor evaporated and he once again was a vulnerable youngster. Scared and unsure about what was happening, like Tori and Scotty.

"We have to go," Scotty said. "There are man-eaters out there." He gestured with his chin, toward whatever existed out there beyond the Romper.

chapter 32

The auto-piloted Romper made three more stops along the way. Three more kids, ranging in age, were coaxed to hurry onto the transport craft. From what Scotty gleaned, from each of the two girls—Courtney and Tiffany—and from the boy, Trent, was that they all met the female alien, Seve, on the spaceship. Also, that they were abducted exclusively within the United States.

Curious about something, Scotty moved through the huddle of kids to get closer to Tori, now talking to the newest boy, Trent, whom he'd overheard was also nine. Chatting together, sitting cross-legged on the floor, she looked up as Scotty approached. Kneeling down right in front of her, she raised her brows at him questioningly. Scotty held up two fingers and gently poked the upper right side of her chest.

"Hey . . . knock it off, perv!" she said.

Scotty readjusted his aim, about to poke her again, when she slapped his fingers away. Holding up a balled fist, she looked angry; more than ready to throw a punch.

"Was there anything in that pocket, Tori?" he asked, ignoring the fist now threatening his face.

"What are you talking about?" Tori asked with a sneer.

"The Romper craft we're in now, I had it in my pocket. When I woke up it was right here." Scotty patted his pocket.

Tori's eyes shifted toward his chest pocket then back to his face. "This craft . . . in your pocket? Bullshit!"

Scotty turned his attention to Trent, also poking his chest pocket. *Nothing was in there either.*

"Hey! You need to stop poking people like that!" Trent exclaimed, but with far less fury than Tori exhibited.

"Honest! I'm telling you both that when I woke up there was this little bulge in my chest pocket. About the size of a matchbox car, I took it out, discovered a little button on the bottom and I pushed it."

Standing above them, Ernesto said, "You're smoking the ganja, kid."

"No . . . really! The little device began growing, expanding right in my hand. It got too heavy to hold on to so I dropped it on the ground. It stopped growing when it was about the size of a bath mat. Then a yellow circle rose up." Scotty looked up at Ernesto then over to Tori. "Do you remember another yellow circle?"

Tori nodded but looked uncommitted, while Ernesto just shrugged. Trent said, "Yeah, I remember the yellow circle, back on the ship." Ernesto rolled his eyes.

"Well, I stepped up onto it, the circle, I mean. And, like right away, things began to happen. This Romper craft began to take shape all around me."

"Why did *you* get a Romper, and not us?" came a voice above him. It was Tiffany, her dark-red hair pulled back into a ponytail. Her freckled face made her appear younger, Scotty suspected, than she actually was.

"Are you saying you're special . . . more important than the rest of us?" Tiffany asked.

"No, I'm not saying that at all. I have no idea why I was given the Romper device and you weren't."

"Seems like you are saying that," Courtney said, standing next to Tiffany. Both girls glared down at him.

"Hey, if my boy says he had a Romper in his pocket, he had a Romper in his pocket," Ernesto said, coming to his defense.

"The point I'm trying to make is this: It seems the aliens . . . those Vallic . . . are taking some pretty big risks." He looked at Tori. "You and I know what happened to Pamela. What if it had been her, holding the Romper device in her chest pocket?"

"Who's Pamela?" Courtney asked.

"A chick who no longer has a chest pocket," Ernesto said flatly.

"So, what's your point, Scotty?" Tori asked.

"I don't know if I have a point. It just seems like . . . it's all so unorganized. The kidnapping. Our abductions. What they want from us . . ." Scotty said.

"They want something from us?" Courtney asked.

"You didn't know? We're here to save the world, Missy," Ernesto said.

"My name is Courtney, not Missy, and that's ridiculous. As far as I can tell, *none of us* are that special. I know I can't do anything *special*," she said, with a self-conscious laugh. "I can't even ride a bike."

That drew a moment of silence from the group.

Scotty, studying the faces around him, couldn't argue with her on her point. Why were they chosen, when there probably were far more intelligent, talented, capable kids to choose from back on Earth?

"I guess we'll find out. I think we've arrived," Ernesto said.

Standing up, they gazed out together toward an approaching green valley. A mile or so wide by several miles long, it lay nestled between two long, towering, rocky cliffs. Beyond the valley, two bright stars, one red and one bluish, were just beginning to peek over the horizon. Scotty noticed the temperature within the Romper was becoming uncomfortably warm.

"Bunch of buildings down there," Tori said, pointing a finger toward the center of a lush-looking valley with its high wind tussled grasses. "The first sign of civilization since we arrived here. Maybe this won't be so bad."

Ignoring the buildings, his attention was focused instead on the towering, inward-facing cliffs. Studying the surface on the right, he noticed black holes, too many to count, and he was pretty sure they were entrances to caves. Then he was sure—the early morning sunlight exposed clusters of erect figures, standing within several of the dark openings. *Perhaps alien residents observing their arrival?*

"Rompers!" Tiffany shouted way too loud for the confined space.

Scotty had just noticed them too . . . dozens of them. More of the same quasi-transparent crafts were now descending into the valley below.

"Look at them all . . . more abducted kids," Courtney said.

Multiple handfuls of dark standing figures were silhouetted within each Romper. "Sure hope there's a few black brothers aboard a few of those," Ernesto said.

Scotty marveled at the sight—so many fast-moving, teardrop-shaped craft were descending from various directions. Sunlight sparkled off their reflective surfaces.

"Oh wow . . . that's really pretty," Tiffany said.

They watched as six preceding rover crafts descended down—disappeared on the other side of the tallest of five building structures. Suddenly, their own Rover craft banked left abruptly, coming around to what looked to be a four-story, pre-fab-type, building. Below lay a football-field-size cement pad. Mid-center were two ginormous, angled up, open metal doors. The Romper descended straight down.

It was a huge subterranean cavern. So large, in fact, he wasn't able to see where it ended in any direction. Scotty watched as the Rompers preceding theirs now began flying in single file. They moved in the direction of what looked to be some kind of large parking lot that was quickly filling up with more identical-looking craft. One by one, the forward positioned Rompers took their turn; first slowing—hovering in place a moment—then descending straight down into what appeared to be pre-determined landing slots. Scotty estimated there were about a hundred of them, lined-up in perfect symmetry. Glancing back, he saw a line of Rovers following along behind their own—plus others just now descending through the open doors.

Their Romper landed with a muffled *thump* sound. Immediately, when the side door slid open, throngs of children could be seen, moving toward a tall bank of distant windows built into the side of the cavern.

"I don't like this, something's not right," Ernesto said.

"You know, you don't always have to be so negative," Courtney replied.

"Really, Missy? Well, I've got news for you. That's not a Wal-Mart over there. Just sayin' . . . we should be prepared for the worst."

Scotty was with Ernesto on that. He felt it too. Once they entered that structure he wondered if their lives would ever be the same.

"You guys can stand there with your thumbs up your butts. I'll go first," Tori said, stepping outside and quickly moving away from the Romper.

By the time he caught up with her, the others too were running, catching up behind them. Side-by-side, Scotty and Tori exchanged a quick glance as they followed behind a bunch of kids—kids that didn't look all that different from them. They moved like cattle, or sheep, in through a tall, wide, metal archway. Scotty was struck by the fact that once again no one was giving them directions. No adult telling them to either do this or do that—go this way or that way. Like he'd done when stepping onto the yellow circle back in the forest, these kids were making decisions on their own; handling circumstances remarkably well . . . considering. *That's when it struck him.* Maybe he and the others had been pre-selected. Not because they were the brightest, or the most athletic, or anything like that. But because they were, on the whole, more level-headed than most other kids. Perhaps emotionally better equipped to deal with such craziness, like being abducted. He thought about Thomas. The Vallic sure judged that one wrong and the poor kid paid, losing his life. Scotty quietly said, "Note to self—no emotional outbursts going forward . . ."

"Huh?" Tori asked, staring at him.

"Nothing . . . tell you later."

"Oh crap! Look! Didn't I tell you this was a bad idea?" Ernesto said.

chapter 33

S cotty, along with throngs of other kids, entered into what would best be described as an immense arena: an arena with no seating, no large overhead TV screen, and no sports-playing field in the middle. Just a massively large, basically circular in shape, open room that had been dug and chiseled into what seemed to be solid subterranean rock. A raised platform, positioned in the center of the space, had vague figures standing upon it. Ernesto had noticed them when they entered. The ambient light within the chamber was relatively low, which allowed the ones on stage to be barely noticed: Seven faintly glowing Vallic aliens. One was instantly recognizable, not by his facial features, which were pretty much indecipherable from the others, but by his towering, brooding, stature—his overall unnerving presence truly radiated darkness.

Oh God, not him . . . not that Horran guy, Scotty thought.

Then, as if the alien leader had tuned specifically into Scotty's mental wavelength, out of what could easily be hundreds of other kids there, the ghostly form raised his head and looked directly at them—at *him*. Scotty wondered if Horran could actually see, or maybe sense, the fear his presence was provoking within him. *Nah, how could that be?*

"This way," Tori yelled, above the noise. Waving a hand over her head for them to follow her as she plowed deeper into the crowded mayhem. *How does she know where to go?* Scotty glanced back, making sure the others were still in tow. He heard different languages being spoken within other groups congregating nearby. *Did that mean these kids were from all over?* That the mass abductions truly were an international operation?

"Hey! Hold up . . . maybe we're supposed to be right here," Tori's unique, high-pitched voice exclaimed.

It took Scotty a second to find Tori amongst the other kids. Locking onto her, she gave him an exasperated expression back. "I think we're supposed to stand right here. I don't know for sure, but that's what I think. Look around you . . . it just makes sense."

Scotty looked at the spot she was standing on, then at the children around her. *How in the world did she figure out that this was the exact place where they were supposed to stand?* But join her they did. Scotty, Ernesto, Tiffany, Courtney, and Trent squirmed around the increasingly bossy girl, clueless as to why.

"What are you doing?" Scotty asked Ernesto, who was repeatedly rising up on his tiptoes, first looking left, then right, and then behind them.

"Need to seriously punch a dook."

Scotty frowned and shook his head.

"Squeeze a steamer . . . bust a grumpie . . . drop the *kids* off at the pool!"

Scotty still didn't get it.

"He has to take a crap, stupid," Trent said, bewildered by Scotty's ignorance of crude slang expressions used for going to the bathroom.

"I suggest you hold it in a while," Tori said, keeping her eyes forward, on the Vallic aliens standing on the platform.

For the first time, Scotty took in the myriad of faces around him. Listened to them talking amongst themselves. Everyone standing near him seemed to be American. Not far to the left was another large cluster of kids. Hearing their accents, he guessed they were from either England, maybe Australia—he really couldn't tell the difference. *So*, he thought, *maybe everyone in here has automatically gravitated to a particular area, one occupied by kids from their own country*; small, separate, nation clusters, distributed evenly around the arena? There's still enough room for ten times as many kids in here, Scotty figured.

Like a constant buzz emanating from a giant beehive, low murmurs—from too many kids talking at once—suddenly grew into distinct, louder voices. Heads spun around, as if given a silent command to do so, to get a glimpse of who was entering through the arched entranceway.

"It's the adults," Tiffany said.

Now that's interesting, Scotty thought. Unlike the kids, who were roughly within a narrow age range of nine to twelve, the adults were all ages. Some youngish—maybe in their twenties—and some older, with grey hair or bald. *Strange.* A part of him wasn't thrilled to see them here. Almost as if they'd encroached into *something* intended only for kids. But Scotty knew that was silly. It wasn't as if anyone of them was given a choice.

There were tons more adults than children. Enough to completely fill up the arena. As they filed in, Scotty was surprised at how little attention they gave the kids. And something else too; he had the distinct impression all these grownups had been around here longer. Studying their overalls, it was evident they weren't as new here as the kids. Most had worn areas and some stains, even small tears in the fabric.

"Geez . . . they won't even look at us," Tiffany said, sounding more insulted than hurt.

Scotty knew what she was saying; none of the adults made eye contact with the children, or even offered a sympathetic glance in their direction.

Horran was on the move. A hand raised over his head to get everyone's attention, he walked the outer circumference of the raised platform. When he spoke, his voice was deep, thundering out over the watchful crowd and just as loud as if he were speaking into a microphone.

"I am Horran. I am the shepherd of this operation . . . and only that. I am not your commander, your boss, your chief, or anything else. Those that need to be told what to do will not last long here. You will learn the language of the Vallic. You will exclusively speak the language of the Vallic—or not speak at all. Your religious views will remain private, never to be discussed here. Not ever. There will be no time for any cultural, religious, racial, or even regional mindsets. The punishment for separatism will be swift."

Horran let that sink in.

"Too much is at stake for those residing on Earth. For the Humans there."

Moving to the center of the platform, he continued, "Some rules you must follow: Do not take it upon yourselves to either direct or command someone else. Be mindful of another's unique place here. Not every individual here thinks or acts or responds in the exact same way. Those in this room are accountable only to themselves and those back on Earth. Not to others here. Half of you will not survive the week." Again, Horran let that sink in. Scotty noticed it was only the children in the room who abruptly stood taller. Quizzically, they looked around—as if they couldn't possibly have heard right. The adults, seemingly unaffected, evidently had heard the same talk before. But Scotty had heard right. The large alien just said it, plain as day, that half of them were going to die.

Horran continued, "We are not looking for gratitude." Scotty and Ernesto glanced at each other. *Gratitude?* Ernesto mouthed, wide-eyed.

"Getting in front of the gamma ray this far has been a challenge. With Earth, we believe, things will be different. Understand, in an attempt to save your species, Humans still on Earth, hundreds of Vallic have already perished. Sacrificed their lives . . . for you. Hundreds more will perish when they reach other star systems, repeating a similar pattern of what we are planning here—saving endangered, intelligent, life forms. Those other worlds are also standing in the path of certain destruction. It is now our destiny to help these alien civilizations as much as we can. And to do so indefinitely, if necessary. You should know that it is us, the Vallic people, who are fully responsible. We are to blame for that fast-moving gamma ray burst now traversing the cosmos, causing cataclysmic destruction in its wake. Leave it to say, it was an interstellar experiment gone very wrong. Our technological arrogance, and subsequent insensitivity, will remain a Vallic disgrace; a burden we must shoulder for eternity. I apologize for all the Vallic, and I apologize that you were singled out to save Humankind on your planet. Not a second thought will be given about terminating any of your lives if you do not willingly serve the greater good of this operation."

Horran stood quiet, then took a step backward, rejoining the six other glowing, nearly transparent, Vallic forms.

A female Vallic took a step forward, assuming the spot Horran had just vacated. "I am Seve, some of you already know me." Taking an additional step forward, she lifted her hands up in front of her torso, facing the mesmerized crowd. Following a momentary bright-blue flash, Seve was no longer just a faintly glowing alien. She was now in Human form—and she was a Human that Scotty knew quite well.

chapter 34

How? How was it possible that Seve was actually Ms. Keeler? She'd been an elementary school substitute teacher for his class no less than seven times over the past year. Both pretty and smart, he'd always preferred her to his regular, full-time teacher, Mr. Ashwhile—more commonly referred to (behind his back) as Mr. Ass Wipe.

"Hello everybody. First of all, to our newest arrivals here, the children, welcome to the planet Hope. There are a number of logistical items we will be discussing after we take a short break. You'll notice there are twelve temporary toilet cubicles set up along the back wall. Those that need to go can do so now, then hurry back."

With only a few exceptions, most of the kids within the arena made a fast dash toward the rear of the room, including Scotty and the rest of his Romper craft contingent. Lines formed and grew. From his spot, now just four kids back from the cubicles, he was able to assess the portable toilet units. Although not too different looking from any port-a-potty back on Earth, he was fairly certain he'd find a difference once inside. Doing one's business publicly certainly must have progressed some within this futuristic society—one where spaceships and Romper craft were commonplace.

When it was his turn, he studied the exiting Asian girl's face—looked for clues on what he could expect to find inside. But she didn't make eye contact. She simply trotted down the three little steps, brushed quickly past him, and scampered off into the masses of those behind him. Once inside, Scotty closed and latched the door and looked around. His nose was immediately accosted by the familiar smell of acrid chemicals laced with shit and urine. He involuntarily grimaced, noticing the all too familiar toilet seat. But instead of a hanging roll of white TP off to the side, it was a roll of something the color of moss. Scotty realized he wouldn't be finding any super-futuristic kind of technology while in here.

Twenty minutes had passed before everyone had returned to their former position within the arena. Scotty spent that time studying the seven beings standing up on the raised platform. They'd spent the same time pacing back and forth, periodically altering between both their physical and non-physical forms. It was an amazing sight. One moment a mere whisper of rustling blue energy and the next, in Human form, walking tall about the stage with a purpose. They too were dressed in overalls, similar to those worn by the abductees—only theirs were a darker-green shade of color. Horran was just as imposing in his Human form as he was non-Human. Tall and broad shouldered physically, his muscular chest and arms tautly stretched out his overalls.

"Look, they walk right through each other . . . did you see that?" Tori asked.

Scotty hadn't noticed that she'd been standing next to him ever since her return from the port-a-potties. Nodding back, he said, "Yeah . . . I didn't understand what they were doing at first." Continuing to watch the spectacle, he found it occurred when they were in their Vallic state, crossing within each other's paths. Their energies, joined momentarily, became amplified; their co-mingled forms becoming brighter. *The sight was dazzling.* Some of the kids oohed and aahed, even clapped their hands when that happened.

Seve was back, standing where she'd stood before the break. With her palms up, again facing all the onlookers, she said, "I am no longer Vallic."

The loud murmuring crowd settled down quickly and quieted down.

"Relinquishing one's congenital species—one's very form of beingness—was beyond difficult. For me, growing up on Lorimar, on that beautiful world, being a Vallic, was all I ever knew; a world where billions of advanced, ethereal beings cohabitated together in tranquil harmony. It is amazing what can be accomplished when there are no wars, no strife, and no hatred. Creativity blossoms to unimaginable heights. Incredible advances in technology can result when existing in such a state. The Vallic routinely traveled to planetary systems light-years away. We began to alter the natural progression of things.

Terraforming alien worlds we liked, or atomizing uninhabited worlds we did not like with bombardments of dark-matter projectiles. The Vallic pushed their advanced technology out to distant space . . . but there was a fine line that should never have been crossed."

Seve stopped speaking long enough for the six others on the platform to join her, three standing on either side. In unison, they all switched back to their Vallic energetic states.

"Children, the grownups you see in this arena have been here for quite some time now. Like you, they were abducted from all across the Earth. Each was observed going about their individual lives and assessed for their viability as a candidate. But no one here was accepted if their unexplained departure would cause undo attention within the media. No one was acceptable if they were too famous, or overly temperamental, or had a mental illness, or suffered a physical impairment. They needed to be highly intelligent, and each needed to be an expert in their respective field. Please look upon the adults that are here now."

Scotty and the others did as asked. For the first time, he saw acknowledgment in the adults' eyes. The adults turned their larger, taller bodies around to glance either this way or that way to see them all. But there were no smiles on their faces; no friendly nodding of heads that he expected to see. If anything, mild irritation was their most common noted expression.

"For the first time we have gotten far enough ahead of the gamma ray. So, each adult here has an important job to do; one that determines if the Human race can survive the changes coming. Look at them. They are nervous their individual efforts will not be enough . . . that there won't be sufficient time. Time to complete their job responsibilities prior to the eventual migration of Earth beings to Hope, all within a timespan of eighteen years. That is when the gamma ray burst will impact your solar system—Earth. This planet needs to be made far more hospitable. Transporting large and dangerous life forms from all around this world to a separate, secluded, continent must be completed, one we call Tyline. Other adults here are working to lower the surface radiation levels being emitted from Spar and Lore, our nearby stars, through manipulation of meteorological climate variables. Others here are devising new and advanced technologies that will allow for large masses of people to rapidly undergo the genetic alterations that will be necessary for survival on Hope. This Vallic/Human meta-morphosis is called Dyad-Geneses. I have gone through this metamorphosis and so have my colleagues here."

As if on cue, those on the platform simultaneously changed again into their Human forms. Horran stepped forward and began to speak. "We, those you see up here upon this dais, were required to go through a form of Dyad-Geneses. We all did so, so we could better interact with the beings back on Earth through the whole selection process. We looked Human to those there because we were both Human and Vallic. There is no technology available that will allow one species' genome to completely convert to another. Technology available today will only append another genome onto one's own. Do you understand?"

Heads nodded. Some children said, "Yes," or "Yeah," or "Uh huh."

"Now ... here on Hope, because the daytime radiation levels are still so high, our Vallic forms are necessary. This way, we are less affected. But it truly is a hostile, dangerous, world for Humans. Thousands of Humans have died here. Subsequently, the surviving Human adults on Hope have all undergone Dyad-Geneses."

As if on cue, within that same single instant, each adult standing within the arena became transformed. Scotty took in the thousands of faintly glowing, bluish energy forms around them. The kids in unison roared and cheered and clapped.

Seve raised her palms higher into the air. Within several moments the room had again quieted. "Children, starting today you will be called to relinquish your earthly Humanity. And you will accept becoming something new, something completely different. Something we call, Vallic-Human. I too am Vallic-Human. Horran and the others up here are Vallic-Human. And all the adults out there, originally Human, are now Human-Vallic. Understand, it is a medical transformative process, one that is relatively quick. It also is incredibly painful and debilitating for several days ... maybe even weeks. You must be prepared for that. I propose that you have never experienced anything like it before. I am sorry for that. And I am sorry that not all of you will survive. The Dyad-Geneses process, this technology, is very new and being used far earlier than it should be. But we have no choice ... you have no choice.

Unfortunately, less than one-half of you will survive." She let her words take hold on the quiet, subdued children.

Scotty had heard these same dire words spoken before. Somehow, until then, he'd dealt okay with the increased levels of stress and tension building up within him by doing something akin to compartmentalizing, terminology he would learn much more about later in life. He was unconsciously adept at relegating some portion of his mind over to the alien craziness while still remaining sane. For now, though, he just closed it off, like shutting an annoying, yipping puppy behind a closed door. Sure, you could still hear him, but it was somewhat more bearable. Perhaps being with the other kids now made it all easier to handle. They were in this together; he wasn't alone. There was a common strength in their sheer numbers. But growing anxiety—just how and when this Dyad-Geneses thing would take place—was making it hard for him to breathe. It was all too unbelievable—asking much too much of young children. First, they'd been forcibly kidnapped, and now they had to undergo some kind of excruciatingly painful procedure. One that necessitated them never really being a hundred percent Human again!

Scotty's spiraling, out of control thoughts squirmed through the tiny cracks and spaces around and beneath the closed door of his mind. He knew he was on the brink of totally losing it. Maybe he should permit the tears to freely well up in his eyes—to overflow and make wet tracks down his cheeks—and let the dripping snot run rivers out of his nose. Yes . . . he could then fall to the ground, a whimpering mess. Curl into a tight ball, screaming and shrieking for his mother to come ... *save me, Mommy!*

"That is going to be so cool! Look at them ... they're like ... like fucking superheros up there!"

Scotty paused in his internal, emotional landslide just long enough to shoot an angry glance toward Ernesto. The brash black kid's excitement was definitely real—he wasn't faking it. How the kid could solely lock onto the more positive aspects of Seve's speech, ignoring all the horrific other prospects— probable death, following ensured agony—he had no idea. But clearly, he had managed to do so. Now taking in Ernesto's raptured, smiling grin, made Scotty almost want to laugh out loud. The total absurdity of it all. But then, suddenly pulled back from the brink, Scotty discovered his moment of terror and anguish had gone. Scanning other children's faces, those near and far, it was clearly evident that some kids were already toppling into a bleak emotional abyss. This too was just another test, he was certain of that. Immediately thinking of young Thomas on the ship, he wanted to yell out to them. *Don't fall apart ... don't crumble ... be strong!*

chapter 35

At least with a school assembly, the school principal would tell you when it's over. Tell you to stay with your class and go back to your classroom. This gathering, or whatever *this* was, ended with no further instruction. No steps to follow; no directives on where everyone was to go next. The raised platform was now empty and all the adults in the room were quickly filing toward the exit. What remained behind were small islands of children. A number of them had begun to cry. Other children were folding into themselves—lowering their bodies down onto the rock surface beneath their feet.

"Don't they know that's a real bad idea," Ernesto muttered, under his breath.

Only then did Scotty see Horran, and several of the others who'd been up on the platform, lurking amongst them, partially cloaked within their Vallic energy forms.

Scotty was startled by Tori's sudden outburst: "Get up everybody and stop your whimpering!" Heads turned in their direction—uncomprehending faces cemented in various expressions of misery.

Scotty found himself chiming in before he even realized he was doing so: "They'll kill you! They have no use for the weak here. We've seen it happen. It's a test . . . everything is a test. Get up!"

"Try to be brave . . . or at least act like you are," Tori added.

Scotty was encouraged. Their words seemed to have an effect. Kids now were indeed rising to their feet. Most of the whimpering had subsided, except for two children still crouched down on the ground at the far side of the arena. Scotty and Tori, after exchanging a concerned glance, started walking in their direction. Horran's unmistakable Vallic form was also on the move.

Running now, moving through and around various clusters of kids, Scotty yelled out, "Hey . . . get up! Just stop crying, we're going to help you!"

The two kids, a boy and a girl—both probably about his age—had fallen deeper into total despair. Their earlier whimpering and crying had escalated into a loud sobbing and wailing. The boy, certainly used to the same attention-getting act working on typical adults, was now screeching—flailing his arms and legs about. It was a full-on tantrum. Not to be outdone, the girl began to mimic his loud screeches, only hers were far worse—a shrill, eardrum-shattering sound that went far beyond irritating.

Scotty was the first one to reach her. When he and Tori knelt beside her, Tori's arms quickly encircled the screeching girl. Immediately, she began quieting down, sobbing into Tori's embrace.

By now, Horran, and one of the other Vallic, had reached the yelling boy. They each grabbed an arm then raised the bellowing child off the floor with such ferocity he squealed out before quieting in shock. But his silence came much too late. Greedily, the towering Horran forcibly jerked the boy closer to himself.

Scotty whispered, "Oh no ... please ... you can't ..." but his words were cut short. He watched as the boy's body began to swing around in circles, held onto by a single frail arm. Around and around—faster and faster—and as the centrifugal forces were just reaching an apex of speed ...

"Horran!" Seve, visible in her Human form, suddenly appeared relatively close to Horran and the doomed boy. Horran hadn't yet released the stricken boy's arm. Hadn't killed the child as he most assuredly intended to do.

Seve looked away—disgusted. Her gaze fell upon Scotty. She said, almost imperceptivity, "I apologize. It will take time for us to fully assimilate Human DNA into our ... *beingness*."

Scotty wasn't aware that a number of other children had come closer until he heard someone choking-back sobs. He looked back to see who it was. *Tiffany*. Something in Scotty's warning glare caused her to quiet down. Ernesto, moving closer to her, whispered something in her ear. She sniffed once, then silently nodded. By the time Scotty turned back around, Horran was already dragging the boy away by one arm. Wide-eyed, the boy stared back at them in terror, a winding river of urine trailing behind. Scotty was keenly aware that Horran's action was nothing less than another show of force, almost identical to what befell poor Thomas. Another example of what would happen should any of them act badly. He didn't know if the boy would survive. Maybe Seve somehow would be able to save him.

When Scotty turned back, Seve was gone. Now he took in the hundreds of faces surrounding them, all children, no one older than eleven or twelve. They'd gotten the message—loud and clear.

Ernesto asked, "What now? We supposed to hang around here or what? Should we leave like the adults?"

"I think we need to find a place to live," Tori said.

Scotty said, "The caves . . . that's where everyone lives here."

"And just how would you know that?" Courtney asked, tightly clutching the arm of a very uncomfortable-looking Trent.

"He's right," Tori said. Where else would people live around here? The building we passed when we arrived here is like way too small to house all the adults and kids." Tori lowered her voice so only those closest around her could hear: "We need to find a vacant cave. Now, before everyone else gets the same idea."

Ernesto asked, "Hey you . . . crybaby girl, what's your name?"

The small girl physically shrank away from the renewed attention. Scotty recognized her as the same Asian kid who'd exited the port-a-potty just prior to him going in. She looked like a perfect China doll. Her hair, so black and shiny, had perfectly trimmed bangs hanging just above her eyes. Wondering if she was wearing a wig, he quickly dismissed the idea as stupid. When she spoke, English words weren't leaving her mouth. Scotty had no idea what language it was. She was still jabbering when Ernesto, looking annoyed, held up a silencing hand. "You need to find your group—your own people. Someone who can understand what the hell you're saying."

She stared back at him. First looking hurt, then something akin to a rising sense of defiance showed in her expression. In broken English, she said, "I understand you an asshole. And my name is Jill."

Scotty said, "Let's just go. Um . . . start heading for the archway. But make it seem casual-like." Nods all around, the group began walking, like they weren't in any particular hurry. Someone, from another cluster of kids, yelled out, "Where you guys going?"

"Just taking a look at something over here for a minute," Tori replied back, as the five children kept moving ahead. Then Jill was hurrying after them, making it six.

Ernesto spoke without moving his lips, "Boy . . . that didn't sound at all lame . . ."

Once they'd reached the arena's arched entrance, Scotty turned, giving an aloof glance over his shoulder, and found a fast-moving stampede of kids sprinting after them. He yelled, "Run! The secrets out!"

"Where are we going? Tori yelled back, sounding out of breath, the first to enter into the garage.

Scotty hadn't noticed another way in or out of the garage other than the way they had arrived. He said, "We need a Romper." He watched as Tori, still in the lead, veered left down an aisle of the tightly parked teardrop shaped crafts. "Where you going?" he yelled, hearing hordes of kids coming though the archway behind them.

Tori spun around—just long enough to shoot back an angry-looking face. "To our Romper! You just said..." then she got it. It didn't matter which Romper they took. They were all the same.

Ernesto hurried through the open sliding door of the closest Romper, the others pushing and shoving in behind him. The door remained open. They looked at one another with bewildered expressions.

"Terrific!" Tiffany said, gesturing out to the other Rompers, also filling up with kids.

Scotty and Tori moved forward to the front of the craft then stared down at the darkened dashboard. She poked it in different places, but nothing happened. Scotty noticed a raised yellow circle, smack dab in the middle of the dashboard; placing his open palm onto its surface, he was quickly rewarded when it illuminated enough to silhouette his hand. Little lights and indicators on the dashboard had awakened—the Romper was coming *alive*.

chapter 36

A pleasant feminine voice emanated all around the confined space—a voice speaking rapidly in an unfamiliar
foreign language. Tori leaned in over the dashboard and asked,
far louder than necessary, "Romper, can you speak English?"

"Yes, that is within my linguistic capabilities. How may I
assist you?"

Scotty leaned in, and asked, "Can you take off? Like right
now? Get us in the air . . . take us out of here?"

Tori, first throwing a furrowed-brow-scowl his way, added,
"Can you take us to the caves?" Scotty then instantly felt a
subtle vibration, emanating from somewhere beneath them.

"Hey, we're going up!" Tiffany exclaimed, stating the
obvious.

Steadily lifting, above all the other, still-parked, crafts,
Scotty watched as heads spun around to follow their progress.
All showed exasperated faces; several children were silently
yelling, pointing their fingers up—emphasizing *they're getting
away!*

The Romper scurried along through the subterranean space—pretty much at a consistent speed. Obviously a self-driving vehicle, since there was no gas pedal, steering wheel, or anything like that evident, Scotty wished there was something he could do to make it go faster.

"I feel guilty . . . that we didn't help any of the other kids," Courtney said, her voice coming from somewhere in the back.

Scotty shrugged. He'd experienced a fleeting pang of guilt too but pushed it aside. Once again, he recalled Seve's parting words: *You are not here to make friends. You are not there to form a community. You Humans have a saying that I like: 'Hit the ground running.' Let there be no mistake about what you have been chosen to do, and that is to win.*

"Looks like someone else figured it out," Ernesto said, glancing back through the Romper's clear glasslike membrane. Scotty, following his gaze, found not just one, but three Rompers, close behind them.

Their own Romper slowed, then hovered and began to rise. A golden swath of daylight poured in from above. Scotty, looking upward, could see the wide-open, big metal doors now come into view. Within seconds, they ascended outside through the opening, traversing around the same buildings he'd noticed earlier. With both stars higher in the sky, the brightened valley was alive in a carpet of brilliant emerald green. What Scotty had surmised earlier to be a field of tall grasses, clearly, now, were treetops instead—trees so densely packed together that one was almost indiscernible from another. He wondered how tall the forest trees were; how far below them was the ground?

"There must be, like, a few hundred caves. Some clearly occupied," Tori said, "You can see people milling about over there in that one, and look . . . over there, too."

Scotty, following her outstretched finger, noticed a few dark figures moving about in the darkness. He scanned the towering cliff side, then asked, "Romper . . . take us to an unoccupied cave, okay?"

The same pleasant voice replied, "There are currently twenty-two unoccupied settlement dwellings. Direct access to any of the dwellings is not permitted."

"Well, then, how do we get to them?" Scotty asked.

"If you wish, I can transport you to the bedrock platform. From there you can make your way to individual dwelling sites. Those that are unoccupied will be so indicated."

"Whatever *that* means," Tiffany commented.

By now a long procession of Romper craft were following closely, though several moved away in an adjacent direction.

"Go! Take us to the, um, the bedrock platform," Tori ordered.

Their Romper changed course, heading now in the same direction as six or so other Rompers. Approaching the cliff, they swooped lower, dropping beneath the emerald-colored treetops. Scotty was surprised, noting the trees' height—*really* tall. The ground was another few hundred feet below them. The dense forest appeared dark and ominous. From his new vantage point he could see what must be the bedrock platform—a flat stone outcropping that already had twenty or thirty Rompers parked atop it. Those who'd arrived were already filing out of two of the craft.

No sooner had their Romper touched down, the door sliding open, when Scotty and the others made a fast-dash for the cliff. An entrance, cut into the rock and flanked by a stone pillar on either side—looked to have been recently shored up. Scotty heard laughing, echoing off the stonewalls. Tori, the first to reach the short flight of steps leading within, ran in without looking back. Scotty, fast on her heels, entered a chiseled-out tunnel that was surprisingly cool inside and smelt dank and something else—maybe minerals, he guessed.

Kid's laughter far up ahead must have been contagious because he heard Tori giggle a few times—which made him laugh, also. The chain reaction continued on behind him with Tiffany laughing the hardest.

The tunnel led into a large circular vault, of sorts. In turn, it offered them a choice of ten tunnel offshoots. Each one had stairs, rising up into darkness.

"How does anyone find their way around this place?" Ernesto asked. "I'm already lost."

Tori, comfortable being in the lead, charged straight ahead into an opposite opening and scrambled up the steps. There was enough light to see where they were going, but just barely. Soon the stone steps were even steeper, a winding spiral staircase. In no time at all Scotty found himself huffing and puffing. He didn't want to be first, needing to stop and catch his breath. No one ahead was laughing, now. Another ten minutes had passed, Scotty guessed, before they emerged from the confined stairway into a wider passageway. Bands of light filtered down from high above—perhaps from above the cliff. Both Tori and Scotty were now bent over, hands on his knees, panting.

The other kids in their group finally trudged their way into the passageway. Scotty had forgotten about the little Asian kid, Jill, who, had apparently adopted their group as her own.

Scotty said, "I can see wooden doors all along here . . ."

"The Romper said unoccupied caves were clearly marked," Trent said, already moving off to the left. Ten paces away he said, "Oh . . . I get it."

"Get what?" Tiffany asked, following after him like a puppy.

"There's a plaque, hanging down on a string. Says occupied." Trent kept going down the passage without waiting for her to catch up.

Scotty said, "Maybe we should check it out, too, by going a different way." Tori nodded then sped past him, running in the opposite direction of Trent. Four doors down they reached the first door that had an off-kilter plaque, reading 'unoccupied.' Tori, hesitating, looked to Scotty.

"I'll go in first," Scotty said. Since there wasn't a doorknob, or a handle of any kind, he shoved the door inward. The door was heavy, so he had to put all his weight behind it. Fresh air and daylight greeted him as he stepped into an area that was both wide and deep. Directly across was the mouth of the cave, one of hundreds he'd spotted from the Romper. Around the oblong space were beds— no, more like cots. A folded stack of two or three khaki overalls lay at the foot of each cot. There were also individual night tables, holding small lamps.

He stepped aside making room for the others to enter when he noticed a little kitchen area off to his right and one of the port-a-potty units off to the left.

Tori said, "Home sweet home," then ran toward a cot in the middle of the cave and flopped down onto her back. Squirming around a little, she smiled. "Not too bad." She raised her head, "Well, what are you waiting for?" She pointed to the cot next to hers.

God she's bossy, Scotty thought.

He watched as the rest of the kids ran in to claim their own cot. Tori had been right; the cot wasn't all that bad. Scotty, glancing over, noticed she was up on her elbows intently staring at *something*. Judging by the seriousness of her expression, Scotty sat upright—scrutinized their surroundings. He almost missed seeing her—Seve's energetic *Vallic* form, standing at the foot of Tori's cot.

"You two will go first," she said looking at Tori and then Scotty. "Best you both say your goodbyes now ... just in case. And we need to hurry."

chapter 37

Hovering right outside the mouth of the cave was a different kind of vehicle, one that was small and dark. Of course, in keeping with other Vallic technology, it looked oddly organic in nature. It also looked a whole lot sleeker than their bulbous Romper. Scotty briefly wondered if it was capable of traveling into space.

But he was simply avoiding what was coming next, he knew. Scotty had to force himself to deal with the situation now at hand. The children were up on their feet, hugs being exchanged all around. He didn't want to start crying while saying goodbye. The truth was, he barely knew these kids—hadn't known any of them long. *So why, then, was saying goodbye so difficult?* He knew why. Because Horran had made it perfectly clear: *Half of you will not survive the procedure.*

Scotty turned to look at Tori. He hadn't realized just how small she really was. He saw that her overall pant legs were rolled up into cuffs above her boots. Standing on tiptoes, she was giving Ernesto a hug as wet tear tracks reflected off her cheeks. Ernesto simply looked terrified. *Was he thinking the same thing?* Scotty wondered. *Will it be Scotty who returns . . . or will it be Tori?*

Seve quietly stood off to the side, patiently waiting.

Sniffling and looking defiant, Tiffany approached her. "How can you do this? Have a bunch of little kids go through something like this? You know what? You're all barbarians . . . you're cruel, and I hope all of you burn in hell!"

It was impossible to get a true read on Seve's expression, since she was in her mostly featureless Vallic form. She continued to hold Tiffany's staring contempt a moment longer before turning toward Scotty and Tori. "You ready to go?"

Tori said, "No!"

Scotty shrugged, "I guess."

They followed Seve toward the sleek, awaiting craft. Tori took Scotty's hand in hers—intertwining their fingers—still openly weeping. Perhaps her tears made it easier for him not to cry.

The craft was suspended in mid-air, about a yard out from the side of the cliff. Seve leapt across into an open hatchway. She stood aside and signaled the two children to do the same. Tori turned and gave one last wave to the other kids—tossing out another choke-filled goodbye—then jumped across. Scotty jumped right behind her, not looking back.

The craft was equipped with three rows of seats in the rear, plus two seats in the forward cockpit area—one now occupied by a male Vallic form. Seve moved to the far side of the vessel and took a seat. Tori sat next to her while Scotty sat across from them, in the row of seats that faced toward the back. As the vessel sped away from the side of the cliff, Scotty avoided looking back at the mouth of the cave—at the kids standing there, who were, most assuredly, waving goodbye.

Through the membrane windows, Scotty could see they were heading toward the buildings at the other end of the valley. The craft rose above the treetops, banked into a tight left turn, then, moments later, descended sharply down. Scotty watched as the pilot maneuvered the craft beneath the tallest building, which he could see was standing on stilts. A parking garage was below, with a handful of similar-looking vehicles inside.

Was this really happening? Scotty glanced across at Tori, now looking straight back at him. If one of them had to die, he hoped it would be him. He'd never met anyone like her before. Someone so confident . . . *so alive.*

* * *

Now seated in some kind of medical facility, Scotty fidgeted in his chair. Seve was speaking to him. Re-focusing his attention on her, he asked, "Can you repeat that please?"

"I said there are numerous outposts similar to this one. Several on each continent actually, although most support staff have already moved on. You know, to help out on other worlds . . . worlds further away than Hope. The staff, those who remained behind such as myself, will be staying here indefinitely. So, you're stuck with us," Seve said, giving him an easy smile.

Scotty nodded up at her. She was standing—actually leaning—within the open threshold of a nearby doorway. Seve was again in her Human form—Ms. Keeler—his always-chipper substitute teacher at Whiteoak Elementary School. Five minutes earlier, Tori had been escorted away by someone who definitely was an Earth Human; a baldheaded man wearing glasses. Staring now at the closed door of the adjacent room, he wondered what they were doing in there to Tori.

"When you wake up, I want you to remember something," Seve said.

"What's that?" Scotty asked.

"That it will get better. That you are stronger than you think."

"*You mean if I wake up,*" he wanted to say, but didn't. "So, this is some kind of hospital?"

"Of sorts. It is where I went through a similar Dyad-Geneses procedure."

"How long were you here . . . after you woke up?"

"Several weeks. Look, there's nothing easy about this, Scotty. Over and beyond how much it hurts, you will be learning how to operate in a whole new type of existence. Having another, separate body. It is beyond weird . . . not something I can explain. But you'll see."

She then gave Scotty an offhand facial expression, remarkably similar to one his mother would have given. Seve, or Ms. Keeler, who was about his mother's age, looked nothing like her. He had to force himself not to think about home; about the family he probably would never see again. He badly wanted to tell Seve he wanted to go home—*needed* to go home. "I wish Larry was here with me," he said instead.

Seve, sympathetic, offered up a melancholy smile.

"How come grownups here never tell us what to do?"

"We've learned from past experience that doing that does not facilitate the best outcome. Better to encourage independent thought and action—even bravery. Those that can handle what happens here, and all the turmoil to come, will be far better suited for what comes later, years from now. So, don't expect to be coddled or mommied. The good news, Scotty, is there are no bosses here, no one barking off orders."

"And Horran, he'll deal with the kids that don't handle things all that well?" Scotty asked.

"Maybe, but not just Horran. What's out there, too," Seve, staring out the closest window, added, "You have no idea how dangerous it is here."

"What's out there?" Scotty asked, not even trying to hide the dread in his voice.

She thought about that. "Remember back in school, when we talked about Earth's Cretaceous Period?"

"The last part of the dinosaur age, right?"

Seve nodded. "But this is Hope, not Earth. There are none of the same plants or animals here. The genomes are completely different. But DNA has a tendency to evolve similarly, even on different worlds. At least on the ones sharing similar climates and world gravitational properties. But nothing is exactly the same here. You will see. Yes, it is an amazing, wondrous, planet, but one that must be tamed before the people of Earth will be able to survive here."

The door adjacent to theirs opened. The same baldheaded man, now wearing a long, white lab coat, hurried out and quickly shut the door behind him. Scotty tried to glimpse inside Tori's room, but he wasn't able to do so.

The baldheaded man said, "Let's go, buddy! Your turn!" then disappeared into the room next to Tori's.

"Is she okay . . . did she . . . ?"

"We won't know for a while. Don't think about Tori right now. Think about being strong . . . about seeing Larry and your family again. That can happen, you know. Honest," Seve said.

Scotty rose to his feet, desperately wanting to believe her.

chapter 38

Two weeks had passed. Much of the first week was a nightmarish blur. At times the searing pain had been so intense Scotty wanted to croak—had prayed to just be allowed to die. The new Vallic energetic aspects of his physiology continuously burned, like having acid poured onto various points of his skin all over his body. At times, he thought he could actually smell the odor of charred flesh hanging in the air. A full week passed before he was able to sit up in bed without throwing up or blacking out.

There was much Seve had not told him about what was to come. For instance, she hadn't mentioned the simple fact that within hours after the procedure, his physical form would start metamorphosing. With the successful indoctrination of Vallic DNA into his physiology, he would start to change; not change from one type of species into another, but would have both species present within him at the very same time. He remembered the doctor, whom he now knew was named Dr. Miller, had mentioned at one point that the radically different genetic makeups of the two forms weren't playing well physically with each other. And, for some reason according to the doctor, that was a good thing.

Seve entered the room and Scotty wondered if this was the first time she'd visited him since he'd arrived here. She was in her Vallic state. *Something about her was different.* He stared up at her face and noticed she was smiling—a smile that reached her eyes. *But how was that possible?* The Vallic did not have prominent features—at least, not like Humans. He wanted to comment on this bewildering observation, but couldn't; he was not able to speak vocally since undergoing that god-awful procedure.

"Good morning, Scotty. You look much better today."

So she did visit me, he thought.

Seve reached out and took his hand, then looked at his arm. Still the same to the touch, splotches of nearly transparent, blue-glowing areas speckled his skin. Half Vallic and half Human, he also knew from his own observation that he was spotted similarly pretty much all over his body.

"Still burns?" she asked.

Scotty nodded rapidly to emphasize the point. *Yeah—burns beyond anything I've ever felt before.*

"Has the physical therapist been in everyday?"

Scotty nodded again then furrowed his brow.

"I know it's painful, not at all fun; but the only way you will be able to maintain two separate genome forms is through mastering your mental state— mind over matter." She pointed to one of the larger Vallic formations, showing on his upper arm. "This is a good one here. Let me see how you transform that particular area from Vallic to Human ... can you do that?"

Scotty shook his head no.

"Come on ... do it for me."

Scotty went through the mental steps that Nemon, his female Vallic therapist, had been teaching him how to do. For hours and hours, in fact—over the past few days. He focused his concentration solely on that one glowing, see-through, bluish splotch. The first step was to inwardly acknowledge how that one Vallic area felt compared to the areas of Human flesh surrounding it. Only by being keenly aware of both physical states individually, would he be able to take the next step. Second, he had to erase all doubt from his psyche. He had to believe he could make the change. Even the slightest doubt, or uncertainty, would foil such attempts. And finally—the most difficult part—he had to mentally call-up a myriad of chemically produced metabolic enzymes, which would act as a catalyst for converting one DNA genome structure for the other. He had no idea what any of that meant, but his therapist had repeated it so many times by now it was forever etched into his memory. But, in time, he'd been taught to detect mentally induced micro-changes within his physiology. It took several minutes before the Vallic splotch began changing genetically— molecule by molecule anatomically—making the necessary internal alterations to become the dominant, Human, physiology. He watched as the splotch became more and more solid. Eventually he was studying what appeared to be normal Human skin. Even tiny arm hairs had reemerged.

"Excellent!" Seve exclaimed.

Exhausted, Scotty exhaled a long breath. He closed his eyes, deflated it took so much effort to transform such a small part of himself. *How would he ever transform his entire body*, like Seve could do in an instant? He shot a sideways glance toward the opposite wall—the wall of the room adjoining his—where he knew Tori had undergone an equivalent procedure. He hadn't asked about her and no one had volunteered any information. Some part of him suspected the answer anyway. He'd survived—she had not, otherwise, they would have told him, right?

As if reading his thoughts, Seve said, "You know, over the last two weeks each of the others in your group has also gone through this same Dyad-Geneses procedure. Mortality percentages were better than average."

Scotty shook his head, not understanding what she was saying.

"Fewer, on average, died. But yes, several did not make it, I'm sorry to say, Scotty."

He thought of them now. A weird group of kids he barely knew, not having spent that much time with them. Still, for some reason, each and every one of them had become immensely important to him. In some ways, perhaps, even more so than his own family. These kids had shared the same unimaginable obstacles he had; abducted away from their families; whisked off from everything familiar. Facing the same high odds of dying from some kind of monstrous medical procedure. He thought of them now: Tiffany, with her ponytailed dark-red hair and freckled face. One of the brave ones, he liked her. Then there was Ernesto, the skinny black kid, who was always hyper and moving around. He was also funny; pretty much said anything that popped into his mind. Courtney and Trent, somewhat similar to each other in looks—blond hair and rather plain looking—were more on the shy side. He didn't know Jill, the Asian kid, well enough to form much of an opinion about her yet. And then there was Tori . . .

He read the sadness in Seve's expression. He closed his eyes. Felt a familiar tightening within his chest—deep sorrow taking ahold of his heart. *No.* He didn't want to know which kid—*who* it was—he would never see again. It was better not knowing.

"Well . . . you two are by far the farthest along."

Scotty opened his eyes—held her gaze. He waited until she said the words aloud.

"Tori is fine . . . and she wants to visit with you. She's already walking. Well, trying to walk. Says you're a," Seve tapped her chin with one finger in a very Human-like manner, ". . . I'm trying to remember the actual word she used . . . oh yeah, *wuss.* She said you were a wuss."

Scotty blinked away sudden tears of happiness. He opened his mouth and tried to speak. An undecipherable croaking sound escaped. But at least it was something audible. He tried again, "Can . . . I . . . see her . . . now?"

Seve, smiling, stood up and nodded. But instead of walking toward the door in her Vallic form, she walked straight through the opposite wall and disappeared from view. *Show off,* he thought.

It was a good five minutes before he heard a commotion out in the hall. A moment later, Tori, holding on to Seve's arm, hobbled around the corner—a broad smile on her face. A face that was strangely segmented—left side Human, right side Vallic. Seve was right—Tori was progressing, physical therapy-wise, at a far quicker pace than he was. But by the time she plopped down into a chair at the side of his bed, she looked totally spent.

"You look terrible!" she said.

"You look weird," Scotty croaked back.

"I'm farther along than you are . . . than any of us."

"I'll catch up. I'll be farther along than you in a day or two."

"Uh huh . . . yeah, right," she said, exaggeratedly widening her eyes. "Jill is dead . . . so is Courtney, and so is Trent."

Scotty's eyes shot up to Seve. Glaring at her, he was suddenly angry— infuriated—and he didn't know why. Seve had just told him that their mortality rate was better than average. She'd led him to believe that fewer had died, and he'd figured maybe one, two at the most. And now he'd just found out he'd never see three kids, perhaps friends, again.

"Sorry . . . Seve told me you didn't know. Thought it best to just tell you. Rip the Band-Aid off . . . real quick-like."

Scotty brought his attention back to Tori. Weird being able to see through half of her bluish, glowing, face.

Tori changed the subject. "Watch this . . ." She closed her eyes and within moments both distinctive halves of her face began to switch. The left side, which was Human flesh, was becoming fainter and beginning to glow, while the right side was becoming more solid—signs of flesh already visible there.

Narrowing his eyes, Scotty scrutinized the transformation, akin to how any one of the doctors there would have made the observation. It was incredible. The speed in which she'd made those physical changes. When completed, her thin brows shot up. "I learned how to do that yesterday. Go ahead, you can say it: I'm amazing. Seve says I'm a superstar." Tori leaned in, "Okay . . . your turn. What can you show me?"

"That's enough for today, kids," Seve said. "Scotty showed progress to me earlier. And, for your information, Tori, he, too, is a superstar."

Tori nodded, not trying to hide her disbelieving smirk. Rising to her feet, she held out a fist.

Scotty went ahead and fist-bumped it. "Tomorrow, I'll come see you."

"Yeah, sure you will," she said. Turning and hobbling away, she declined to take Seve's extended-out arm for support.

Five minutes later, Seve reentered the room, along with the baldheaded Dr. Miller, both now in their Human forms. He was holding what resembled a beehive in one hand, only this beehive was far smaller, shaped like the curled horn on an animal—like that on a ram.

The two moved closer. The doctor placed the ram's horn beehive-thing on the bedcovers in front of Scotty.

"What is that thing? Scotty asked.

Neither answered the question. Instead, the doctor said, "You're getting fairly healthy. Clearly, you will be one of the survivors here."

"Yeah, I already know that," Scotty said, a little bewildered.

"That means you will need your own Orand-Pall," Seve said, placing a hand atop the hive-like thing. "It is how we communicate with one another when we are apart."

"Like a cellphone?"

"Well, not really. An Orand-Pall will allow you to speak, indirectly, to anyone anywhere . . . even to those on other planets. Or to those on spaceships." Seve raised her sleeve and gestured toward something circular lying beneath her skin. The doctor then did the same, exposing his own round circular pro-trusion, like a big, puffy coin, just beneath the skin. Scotty probably wouldn't have noticed either, if they hadn't brought them to his attention.

"What do you mean by indirectly?"

"That it's more like you tell the Orand-Pall something and then it, in turn, tells the other person's Orand-Pall. It goes back and forth like that," Seve said.

"Sounds confusing. Why not just talk to the person directly?"

"It's complicated," Seve said. "An Orand-Pall can do certain things that we cannot. One of the things it *can* do is read your thoughts."

Scotty made a face. "I don't want anything reading my thoughts."

"Well, it only happens when you're communicating. Scotty, your Orand-Pall will become a part of you. Will be more loyal to you than anyone, anything, could ever possibly be," Seve said.

Scotty shrugged. "Okay. So ... can I see it?"

Seve and the doctor exchanged a glance.

"You first need to understand the Orand-Pall is alive. It's not a *thing*—not a device."

"Really? So, it'll be more like a pet?"

The doctor, showing an annoyed frustrated expression, said to Seve, "I have a lot of work to do, others to attend to."

"Hold out your arm, Scotty. No, your other arm and try not to move, okay?"

Scotty began doing as asked then pulled his arm back. "Is this going to hurt?"

"No, you won't feel much of anything," the doctor said, unlatching a cap from the wider end of the curled ram's horn-like *thing*. He impatiently waited for Scotty to reposition his arm, his forearm facing up. "Now, don't move!"

Scotty began to wince even before actually seeing what the *thing* looked like. The doctor tipped the ram's horn-thing up and jiggled it. Out the *thing* came: Perhaps a bug, of some sort, or maybe some kind of crab? Scotty furrowed his brow as it began to move—to scurry around. It had hundreds of tiny legs, like a centipede's legs, all around its circumference. It was using long, hair-thin antennae to feel its way around. Dark red, maybe purple, it was just about the most disgusting creature Scotty had ever seen. But he really didn't mind bugs all that much. And *this one was fascinating.* Unlike anything he'd ever seen before.

"You say it's smart?" Scotty asked, as it came a little closer to his legs, lying beneath the bedcovers.

"Very smart. Bred for only one purpose," Seve said.

Scotty smiled as the tiny creature tentatively moved even closer—its antennae seemed to be reaching out for him like teeny outstretched arms. He laughed, "I think it likes me—" barely were the words out when the Orand-Pall hopped onto his still outstretched forearm. Scotty screamed; tried to pull his arm back and shake the thing off. But both the doctor and Seve were firmly holding his arm in place. He couldn't move it. Eyes wide, Scotty watched as the small creature began to burrow beneath his skin—using its countless legs like miniature saw blades. As blood began to seep through the two-inch slit in his skin, Scotty screamed louder—tugged harder—trying, vainly, to retract his arm.

"Stop fighting it, Scotty!" It won't hurt you," Seve ordered.

"It *is* hurting me!" He watched in horror as it wiggled, shimmied sideways beneath his skin, like a burrowing sand crab. "Get it out of me!" he screamed, watching the last semblance of the Orand-Pall disappear beneath his skin. Then, five or six errant antennae, like wet spaghetti noodles, slurped out of sight into the bloody gash on his forearm.

Dr. Miller used his index finger to apply yellow goop along the length of the still open wound. Almost immediately, the wound began to close—to heal. Scotty could still feel movement within his arm. "It's moving around in there," he cried out in alarm, staring up at Seve then the doctor.

The doctor, replacing the cap on whatever the ointment crap was, said, "Good, it's just getting comfortable. Getting a lay of the land, so to speak."

chapter 39

They were now back in their cave dwelling, still feeling the lingering effects from their respective procedures. Conversation was kept to a minimum as each quietly contemplated what they had endured and what was yet to come. All of them now were exhibiting partially Human and partially Vallic physiologies; arbitrary areas—transparent splotches like glowing energetic voids—on what was, other than that, their normal flesh. Tiffany appeared to be missing an eye, and part of her nose. Scotty's right hand was gone from sight.

Scotty glanced toward the three empty, though properly made-up beds. Beds, belonging to those who didn't survive the procedures: recently departed Jill, Courtney, and Trent. Their empty beds only underscored the seriousness, the life and death nature of present life on Planet Hope.

He watched as a slow-moving Romper passed the mouth of the cave outside. Four or five individual adults could be seen standing within it—being transported somewhere. Receiving the impression they were not Human, originally, he pondered on that. There were the Vallic-Humans and there were the Human-Vallics. The latter were the Earth Humans such as himself, Tori, Tiffany, and Ernesto, plus all the other kids and adults who'd recently gone through the Dyad-Geneses procedure. The former, the Vallic-Humans, from Lorimar, were the original aliens: Seve, Jennet, Horran, and others—those who had gone through their own version of Dyad-Geneses. Thinking some about it, Scotty could not recall a time when the two differentiated groups, not even individually, *hung out* together. Although often friendly, they were not friends. The Vallic-Humans were on Hope for a specific reason; an obligation that required them to dedicate what still remained of their lives to a singular cause. In their words, it was to assist Earth Humans survive the impending, catastrophic, spacial calamity coming. Scotty felt, and often could see, the sullen resentment on their faces—especially in their eyes. Perhaps not so much in Seve's but definitely in the others. But that was okay. He didn't really blame them.

The remaining Human-Vallic children, those who survived the most recent Dyad-Geneses procedure, had been delivered here to their respective dormitory cave dwellings to regain their strength—and to physically prepare for what was coming next. Something Seve referred to as a DNA Inculcation Infusion—*big* words that Scotty didn't grasp. She said it was more commonly referred to as *smart dunking,* which certainly made it sound less scary. Hopefully, it would be a lot less painful than Dyad-Geneses.

The previous morning, when Seve dropped by to check on them, she arrived holding a large box, one filled with gifts. Although thinking about it now, none of the items were wrapped, like all true gifts back home on Earth. There were several packs of playing cards, a stack of coloring books, cartons of crayons, spiral-bound drawing pads, pencils, a stack of paperback books—geared to either boys or girls tastes—and an assortment of odd toys, like Slinkies and Lego kits, and even a Mr. Potato Head. Scotty pictured Seve and Jennet, ghost-like, pushing a store cart around the various aisles of a toy store.

Ernesto, after rifling through the assortment of toys, looked up at Seve and shook his head. "What is this crap? You think we're fucking five-year-olds? Lady, for your information, I play Assassin Creed and maybe Gears of War on Xbox 1 ... I wouldn't even know what to do with a damn Slinkie." Scotty nodded his head in agreement, though he wasn't totally against the Lego kits, or even the Mr. Potato Head.

Glancing now around their cave dormitory—noting the toys and coloring books strewn about on the beds and on the ground—all Scotty really wanted was to be back home. To be with Larry, sitting now on his own bed, knowing his mother and father, his big brother and little sister, would never be far away again.

Scotty heard Tiffany speaking in low tones to Tori, but couldn't make out what they were saying. Ernesto was asleep on his bed. The Mr. Potato Head box had been torn open, its plastic parts assembled and laying atop the bedcovers near his pillow.

A shadow fell across the mouth of the cave. One of the more aerodynamic transport crafts was maneuvering closer in. Then, to Scotty's surprise and unease, Horran stepped across the open hatchway and into the cave.

Horran stood tall in his energetic form as he looked about the dorm quarters. His gaze fell upon the still-sleeping Ernesto. He waited a moment before using a nearly transparent foot to jostle the sleeping boy's bed. Ernesto groggily muttered something then quickly sat up, noting Horran's towering form near him.

"Sorry . . . um . . . what's going on?" Ernesto asked, looking up at Horran, then toward the other kids.

"It is time. Bring nothing with you," Horran ordered.

"Where are we going?" Tori asked.

"You will see soon enough. Up, all of you. Get into the Arrow Wing."

Scotty stared at the now waiting, hovering, craft. It actually kind of looked like an arrow wing.

"Where's Seve?" Scotty asked, as he pulled on his boots and rose to his feet. "I thought she was going to take us to . . . to be smart dunked." He still didn't know what the phrase meant, but he knew he'd feel lots more comfortable if Seve was around.

"Seve is not feeling well today."

It took Ernesto the longest to lazily drag himself into a seated position and pull his boots on. Looking around, he asked, "Are we ever coming back here?"

Horran didn't bother to answer, although he may have shrugged—hard to tell. One by one, the four kids jumped across and into the awaiting craft. Horran, following behind, on his way forward into the cockpit, moved right *through* both the kids and the seats. "Take your seats," he said, as he got his own bulk situated at the controls, powering the sleek craft away from the rocky cliffside. Soon, they were rising high up within the valley.

Scotty, seated between Tiffany and Ernesto, looked straight forward and through the cockpit window. He watched as they moved across, then past the buildings where they underwent their recent treatments.

"Where we going?" Tiffany asked, as she fiddled with a mostly invisible ponytail, securing it in place with a bright neon-pink elastic band.

Scotty, noticing they were moving beyond the valley now, raised himself higher in his seat so he could get a better perspective of the ground below. It was pretty much all orangey-colored rocks and sand. He'd heard the term barren used before, and he was pretty sure that's what this area was too. It looked hot—like a place you wouldn't want to be caught dead without a big jug of water . . . maybe a weapon of some kind, too. Undoubtedly, there were all sorts of alien killer animals, hiding among the towering rocks and dark nooks and crannies.

The Arrow Wing's sudden descent caused Tori and Ernesto to simultaneously groan. Scotty, too, felt it in the pit of his stomach. He closed his eyes as a pang of nausea lingered, then slowly passed. The craft banked tightly left, revealing the ground below coming up fast and the perfectly spaced dome structures, maybe ten in all, that looked like tiny tan-colored igloos. Only then could he see people in their Human form, milling around down there.

Horran, after putting the craft down gently, was quickly up and out of his seat in a blur. Even before Scotty could move out of his way, Horran was walking right *through* him. A sensation Scotty decided he definitely didn't like, it somehow felt like he'd been rudely intruded upon.

Once outside, standing in the intense midday heat, the four kids were clustered together in a small group. Each held a hand up, shielding their eyes from the glare rising off the white sand.

The Human adults gathered in close and stood before them. Scotty noticed that Horran was already heading back to the Arrow Wing.

One of the men stepped forward. He looked like a character out of a movie. His long hair, turning gray, was messily pulled together into some kind of bun at the back of his head. A *boy-bun*, he'd heard them referred to. He also had the palest blue eyes Scotty had ever seen. But perhaps his most noticeable physical attribute was his broad, welcoming smile, which put Scotty instantly at ease.

He said, "Hello. I am Professor Hank Stiles. But just Hank is fine. Bill, here, is on my left, and that's Gail and Caroline, on my right. Today is an important day for you." He stopped speaking long enough to let Horran's Arrow Wing take off then fly away.

"Each of you will be taken into one of these hard-huts behind me. The four of us are chiefly here to assist you with your individual procedures. There is nothing to be afraid of. This won't hurt a bit, I assure you."

"So why are you in your Human form?" Ernesto asked.

"Simply to show you that we too are Human ... Human-Vallics, just like you. To show you that you can trust us, which will be key as you embark on your individual DNA Inculcation Infusion processes."

"Smart Dunking?" Scotty asked aloud.

"That's right. Let's just call it that, for now."

"So, what's this all about, Hank?" Tori asked impatiently. "It's like a thousand degrees out here. I can feel sweat dripping down under my armpits."

Hank nodded. He turned left then right and simultaneously the four adults turned into their Vallic energetic forms. He said, "Each of you has been assigned a learning guide. You will go with them now to a hard-hut where they will assist you in disrobing and getting situated within the brine vats."

Before anyone could object to what sounded pretty awful to Scotty, the adults were on the move. Gail made a beeline toward Tori, and Caroline toward Tiffany. Bill, who Scotty remembered as dark-skinned, approached Ernesto, while Hank stayed put, his eyes focused on Scotty. The kids exchanged nervous glances with each other before moving off with their *learning guides.*

"Come with me, son ... our hard-hut is the closest one here."

A lot of the things Hank mentioned were currently racing around in Scotty's mind. But the words *disrobe* and *brine vats* were among the most significant.

chapter 40

S cotty followed Hank, once again back in his Human form, around to the side of the hard-hut where the big metal hatch was located. Off in the distance, he caught sight of Tori, walking behind Gail's Vallic form. As if feeling his gaze upon her, she looked back over her shoulder and gave him a quick wave before disappearing around another hard-hut structure.

"This way, Scotty," Hank said, swinging open the hatch door. Noisy, complaining hinges gave Scotty pause before entering the darkened space before him.

"It's all right, son . . . don't be afraid."

Stepping inside, Scotty's nose was instantly accosted by a myriad of strange odors. That, and the near-total darkness surrounding him were freaky. He waited for Hank to swing the hatch door shut before saying, "Smells like an old shoe in here."

"Oh, come on, Scotty. Both you and I know it smells a whole lot worse than that."

As Scotty's eyes slowly adjusted to the dim light within, he took in the domed space overhead. What looked to be a square pool of sorts took up most of the floor space—about five times the size of a hot tub. He heard liquid sloshing sounds and could just barely make out a bit of movement. Everything had the same drab greenish color—the vat, the dome, even Hank.

"What's that stuff on the walls . . . the ceiling?" Scotty asked.

"I guess the closest thing you could relate to is that it's a kind of moss. And it's alive," Hank said, stepping closer to the side of the dome and placing his open palm upon it. "Try it . . . put your hand on it."

Scotty did as told, and, sure enough, it was mossy. A spongy texture that tickled his skin. "It's kind of gross feeling."

"If you think that's gross, just wait 'till you get in there."

Scotty followed the line of Hank's outstretched finger. "Do I really have to get in there, into that disgusting slop?"

"Yeah, the brine vat. Enticing, huh? Let me tell you something that will make this a bit easier for you." Hank walked around the vat's narrow edge—a walkway of sorts that surrounded the brine vat—until he stood directly across from Scotty. "Five minutes after you're in there, you'll be immensely contented. You'll feel whole; you'll feel relaxed; and you'll feel happy, like this was the one place in the world you always wanted to be, but you didn't know it until right then."

"Well, why *am* I going in there in the first place? What's it for?"

"To learn . . . it's as simple as that. Assist you in fulfilling your destiny, going forward. To help those back on Earth, you'll need to be a whole lot smarter than you are now. You're going to have to know how to do many things that nobody on Earth has even a clue about."

"And all that *gunk* in there is going to teach me that?"

"Actually, it is. That gelatinous goop is a concoction, which was made specifically for you. Basically, it is your DNA, countless nucleotide strings infused with what we call memory proteins. We call them mempops, for some reason. Anyway, the mempops will find their way into your body, into your physiology through your epidermal layers, and through various open orifices," Hank pointed to his own eyes, nose, and mouth, "and soon you and that gunk will be like one entity."

"I'll absorb memories? That's weird."

"More like factoids. DNA has the capacity to store an incredible amount of data. You'll simply know things you never had to learn on your own."

"What kind of things?"

"Things like there are over two hundred galaxies in the known, observable, universe. That neutron stars are incredibly dense; in fact, one spoonful would weigh a billion tons. That the average person takes about 680-million breaths during their lifetime. Your heart will beat over three billion times by the time you're eighty. And that there are seven extra-terrestrial worlds, all located within six light years of Earth. Three of those worlds visit our home planet on a regular basis. But just knowing such albeit interesting facts will not be enough. You not only need to learn *the what* of things, but also *the how*. How to do certain things with your body . . . primarily, your new Vallic body. And for that, you will need full sensory, and musculature interaction with the goop medium."

"Okay . . . I don't really understand, but that sounds cool."

"Time to get started. I'm going to step out for a minute. Get yourself undressed then slide into the vat. Again, it will feel strange. Yeah, even a little disgusting, but it is necessary."

Scotty watched Hank exit the hard-hut, closing the hatch door behind him. Staring at the awaiting, thick greenish liquid, he made a face. Behind him, he noticed a wooden bench and a few cubbyholes he guessed were to store his clothes. He started to get undressed, removing his boots, socks, overalls, and underwear. Once he had his things stored in the cubbyholes, he hurried over to the edge of the vat naked. Sitting on its edge, Scotty let one foot slide into the dark muck. Grimacing, he said, "Ugh," then reluctantly slid the other leg in too. Then, as the rest of his body followed, he found it was fairly deep. He figured that not even standing on his tippy toes would he be able to reach the bottom. At this point, his head still remained above the goop. The stench was pretty overpowering. Allowing his body to lean back farther into the goopy stuff, he then let his head go all the way back. He felt his ears filling up, all sounds becoming muted. His legs floated up as the rest of his body became more horizontal. Suspended, his extended-out arms floated on either side.

Maybe this isn't so bad, he thought to himself, letting his eyes slowly close. The subtle bobbing motion was making him sleepy.

"Scotty . . . can you hear me?

Scotty opened his eyes to find Hank sitting on the edge of the vat, his legs crossed Indian style.

"I want you to look straight up, to the very top of the dome. Can you do that for me?"

Scotty blinked a few times then let his eyes focus up there. "How is it that I can see outside now?"

"You're not actually seeing outside. The moss surface is stimulated. You're seeing a flashing of colorful bioluminescent bacterial growth, which, in turn, creates the three-dimensional images you are seeing now. Highly realistic, looking as if you were right there."

"Yes, I am right there."

"I'm glad, Scotty. I want you to relax even more now. I want you to allow yourself to fully interact with your surroundings."

"Wow ... I see an elephant. Wait ... It's not an elephant, is it?"

"No, it is not. It is a Towheff. Bigger and far more danger-ous than any elephant you'd find on Earth. It is an animal that has existed on planet Hope for thirty million years. But you already know that, don't you, Scotty?"

"I do know that. How do I know that, Hank?"

"The slime, remember?"

Scotty observed the ginormous animal. It appeared to have a thick gray hide, like those found on an elephant, but its head was oddly shaped. Flaps of drooping hide, like loose pages of a book, hung down on either side of its broad face. He also noticed it had a mouthful of sharp, pointy teeth. *A carnivore.* "Hank, I think the Towheff has noticed me."

"Yes, it most certainly has. Do you know what Towheffs like to eat?"

"I do. I know everything about Towheffs. They eat various indigenous plants, but also eat a number of animals. Basically, whatever it can catch it will eat. Towheffs have an insatiable appetite. How do I know that word? Insatiable?"

"Pay attention now, Scotty!"

"The Towheff is charging! It's coming right for me!"

"Run, Scotty! Search your memories for the absolute best way to evade it. How to outsmart it."

Scotty was *there*, standing fifty yards away from the charging beast. Already he could feel the thunderous beat of its heavy stride, vibrating up through the ground. He looked around—searching for somewhere to hide. Seeing no trees and no rocks to hide behind, he ran—pumping his arms and legs as fast as they would go—unaware he was actually running within the confines of the vat. It was all a part of the DNA Inculcation Infusion process. Scotty, noticing his arms and legs, found he was an energetic form, striding fast across a hard, sun-cracked, desert field. "But how does the beast even see me, Hank?"

"How do you think?" the distant voice asked back.

"A form of heat sensory . . . not so different from infrared detection."

"Run faster, Scotty. The beast is gaining on you."

"It can smell me, too. A Towheff has stereo olfactory glands on its snout . . . amazing directional smell detection!" he said breathing hard.

"You have mere moments to survive, Scotty. What will you do now?"

"I see a pond up ahead. I am so tired . . . can't catch my breath. I don't want to die."

"Search your memories, Scotty. How have others evaded capture in similar circumstances?"

"I'm too tired to remember. I can't run any farther."

"Then you will be eaten alive, Scotty. Is that what you want?"

"The Towheff is afraid of deep standing water!"

"Yes . . . that is correct, Scotty."

Scotty could feel the beast's hot breath upon him as it too quickly approached, could smell its foul odor. He didn't dare look back. The pond was close now, and larger than he'd initially thought. Fifteen paces away—he ran even faster. Gave it everything he had.

"Scotty? Why, would you suppose, is the Towheff afraid of the pond?"

"Oh no . . ."

chapter 41

About five years later ...

T he mobile power pallet, *MPP*, zoomed along ten feet
off the ground at close to two hundred miles per hour.
Another banking turn was coming up and Scotty tightened
his grip on the nearest leather-like tether strap, so he wouldn't
be thrown overboard again. He shot Tori, standing at the controls, a weary glance. They'd be trading places within the next
hour. She was talking on the hand-held—giving an update to
base camp, located some two thousand miles away across the
Macosian Ocean.

Basically, MPP's were little more than large flat slabs of
metal, forged from trathion-tunston—a rigid metal compound,
highly abundant on planet Hope. The rectangular-shaped,
thirty-foot by sixty-foot MPP craft was powered by a Vallic
organic power plant, equivalent to a two thousand horsepower
engine back on Earth.

Scotty's arms were getting sore from having to hold on tight for so long. This particular trek was one of hundreds he'd been assigned to over the past few years; part of the redistribution of Hope's less-than-friendly indigenous life forms. Preparation for the day when Humans would start to arrive on planet Hope in droves. But that was still years away.

Scotty stared out across the rushing-by, non-descript, arid plains. The terrain could have been the high desert in California or Arizona—but this was Tyline, one of the larger continents on planet Hope. A continent perfectly suitable for the Liapalese organism, now strapped down and taking-up most of the MPP's usable surface.

Scotty wasn't a fan of any of the dinosaur-sized Liapalese species. The creatures didn't even look real. With eight stubby legs, overstuffed, toy-like bodies, they looked harmless enough. Their small heads were taken up by a singular, large, round feeding orifice, encircled by countless shark-like, but usually hidden, teeth. He'd recently learned these creatures were nearly identical to something called a Tardigrade species, found back on Earth. Only the Earth organism was tiny, almost microscopic in size. Similarities, other than their relative appearance, were found in the simple fact they both were almost indestructible; the stinky, disgusting creature that he and Tori were in the process of transporting would outlive most other life forms. It was a species that would be around for billions of years—one resilient to extreme temperature changes, and unaffected by high-doses of radiation. The problem was a Liapalese would be just as content eating Humans as eating tall trees or shrubbery.

Like so many other predatory creatures on this planet, it would now find its new home exclusively on the continent of Tyline.

Scotty, glancing over at Tori, yelled over the wind, "Set it down . . . let's take a break. And we need to feed the Liapalese."

Tori at first didn't acknowledge she'd even heard him. He continued to stare at her glowing form, standing within the phone-booth-like cab area, when she finally acquiesced with a single nod of her head.

Typically, each of the surviving Earth abductees preferred to live life every day as an energetic Vallic. In fact, there rarely was a reason to transform back into Human physicality, other than to keep in practice. Being Human was not only physically limiting, it was also cumbersome and awkward in comparison.

Scotty could hear Tori *singing* again. The girl loved to sing—never embarrassed that she couldn't hold a note, went off-key, and destroyed just about any song she attempted to vocalize. He smiled to himself. She'd awakened him in their dorm-cave two mornings back, bellowing out *Happy Birthday* at the top of her lungs. Tiffany and Ernesto squawked, throwing their pillows at her. Scotty had just turned fifteen. Tori, seventeen, had never shown any romantic interest in him. Still, they were the best of friends. Scotty often wondered what she'd do, or say, if she knew just how head over heels in love with her he really was. But it wasn't worth the risk finding out.

The MPP decelerated to the point Tori was able to set the craft down with well-practiced proficiency.

Tori came out of the cab, skirted the tail end of the bound creature, then together she and Scotty jumped down to the ground. Like a number of other Human-Vallic girls here, she'd snipped the pant legs off her overalls. Now short-shorts, they accentuated her thin legs.

"Can we get away from it for a few minutes?" he asked, already heading away from the MPP and the struggling, constrained, Liapalese. Without the constant headwinds, associated with going two hundred miles an hour, the odor had quickly become overwhelming.

"This is going to be tricky. Tell me . . . when has a two-man team ever successfully released something of this size?" Tori asked. "Hell, it took eight of us to get the beast up onto the MPP!" then continued to look at him, apparently the question wasn't simply rhetorical.

"We'll be fine. We'll stay out of sight, out of its way until it moves off," Scotty said, sounding more sure of himself than he actually was. The problem was these catch-and-release assignments weren't meant for a team of less than ten. But over the last five years, the population of original Vallic had decreased from over one several hundred worldwide to less than a hundred worldwide. And it wasn't only the hunting and capturing of beasts, like the Liapalese, that caused the rapid decline in attrition levels. It was bad science. While the Dyad-Geneses process seemed to work relatively fine for Humans—having their DNA merge with Vallic DNA—things didn't seem to work as well the other way around for the Vallic. The typically calm, good-natured Vallic were constantly having inner fights with their far more barbaric alternate Human selves. Their newly acquired DNA had both physical and emotional repercussions, which had only worsened over time. Surprisingly, what was killing so many of the original Vallic-Humans, was their inability to deal with their new, less evolved, Human emotions—anger, anxiety, and an oft crippling sadness. Sadness, to the point many hundreds of Vallic-Humans decided to commit suicide rather than deal with their newfound, overwhelming emotions. Scotty remembered the first time he'd witnessed an unstable Vallic back onboard the ship, when Horran ruthlessly killed the young boy named Thomas.

"Did you hear me?" Tori asked.

"Sorry . . . what?"

"There's only so much that can happen while we're in our Vallic state . . . so . . . we'll be fine," she said.

They both knew that was bullshit. Sure, it was safer than being a clumsy Human, but by no means perfectly safe. He'd witnessed a Russian kid just last week inhaled suddenly into a Liapalese's feeding orifice. Almost like he'd been sucked into a jet engine, it was horrific.

Even after five years, none of the kids were fully accustomed to their Vallic forms yet—certainly not enough to make a necessary physical adjustment all that quickly. Existing as an energetic form required one to constantly adjust the output of gravitational forces around them. Whereas, being in the Human state when walking, one would simply utilize the weight of physical matter, along with maintaining the proper balance, and other natural properties. But being Vallic, one had no mass to speak of. Instead, they must learn how to direct a myriad of opposing, outward, forces—directing gravitational waves. Still,

Scotty wondered if he would have been able to survive that unimaginable Liapalese ordeal. He was better accustomed to being in the energetic Vallic state than any of the other abductees—even Tori, although she probably wouldn't admit it.

"Let's finish this and get back," he said. "Seve says something's up tonight . . . we all need to be there."

Together, they headed back to the MPP and Scotty couldn't help but laugh, noting Tori's disgusted face as the beast's horrific smell enveloped them once again.

"We really should take it inland a few hundred more miles. Finding a mate for that big beast here . . . in this remote an area could be difficult," she said.

"Tell me about it," Scotty said, without thinking. Immediately, he regretted saying it—felt his Vallic cheeks turn hot.

Tori, glancing back at him, asked, "What did you say?"

"I said we shouldn't worry about it. Do we really care if there is one less impregnated Liapalese?" Scotty could feel her gaze linger on him as they got closer to the MPP.

Tori then asked, "How do you want to do this?" Thankfully, she'd changed the subject.

Scotty took in the Liapalese—all the crisscrossing straps securing the creature atop the craft. "I say we remotely release all the straps at once then hide under the pallet until the thing wanders off."

"We should feed it first," she said. "I remember being a kid and my mother wrestling with the vacuum cleaner hose, sucking up potato chips, crayons, and dimes from beneath the couch. I don't want to be a potato chip today."

Scotty laughed. "I'll do it . . . feed the thing first. It'll only take me a few minutes." With a running start, he jumped up onto the pallet and moved around the creature's mountain of restrained flesh to the other side, then opened one of the long metal bins. Inside were the few remaining feeding rations for the Liapalese, contained within edible, celluloid, sacks. With the sudden presence of direct daylight upon them, the five sacks began to stir. *Gammy-tow larva.* The maggot-like critters were a welcomed delicacy for the Liapalese.

"Hey . . . I'm going to feed it two of these sacks, then place the other three sacks off in the distance—you know, lead it away so we can . . ."

Scotty was interrupted mid-sentence, as Tori's lips pressed against his own. His heart racing, he mentally comprehended what was now happening. He already knew that a Vallic kiss was something special and a constant subject of interest and discussion among the other boys back at base camp. Ernesto was a virtual kissing bandit, if he could be believed; a fan of kissing the Honduran sixteen-year-old girl, who lived three caves over.

Scotty returned Tori's gentle kiss, breathing in her faint floral scent. He felt the tip of her tongue explore, find, then tease his own. She'd obviously done this before—little doubt about that—but he didn't care. She pulled him in even closer and he felt her chest against his. A moan rose from deep within her, but as quickly as the embrace started, it ended.

Tori pushed him away with surprising force. Looking out of breath, giving him a lopsided smile, she said, "Now you can go and feed the damn beast." Showing off, the way she often did, she walked right *through* the Liapalese, then he heard her jump down to the ground, some thirty feet away.

Scotty smiled and shook his head. It was one thing for an original Vallic to do such a thing—walk right through doors, or walls, or even each other—but it was no easy task for a Human-Vallic. Make a mistake and you're dead—molecularly merged within a foreign mass. *I could have done it*, he thought, studying the rising bulk of the gray animal—*probably.*

Leaning into the bin to grab the top sack, he heard Tori scream, "Scotty!"

chapter 42

Without giving it a second thought, Scotty's energetic form raced through the Liapalese; exiting out of it on the other side, he jumped down to the ground. Fists clenched, ready for whatever dangers awaited him, he spun around looking for Tori.

He heard another scream, this time farther away to the north, and yelled out, "Tori!"

Far in the distance he saw a plume of dust and took off at a full run, briefly thinking of the hand-held communications device still back within the MPP's cab. *But who would he call, anyway?* No one else was close enough to help.

Scotty ran faster, trying not to think about what was happening to Tori. Who or what had taken her, and why he no longer was hearing her calling out for help. As a Human-Vallic now, he was able to move much faster than he could before the Dyad-Geneses procedure. Not so long ago, Ernesto and he had timed each other's quick sprints. Both had reached running speeds the equivalent of sixty-five-miles per hour. Right now, he knew he was running even faster than that. He was running to save Tori's very life.

Chest burning, he was beginning to tire—he'd run at least three miles. The windswept plume of dust ahead was now near enough for him to see what was causing it—a fast-moving band of hairy Kammies; at least five of them. *Damn!* Scotty thought he saw Tori's faint blue glow—her body draped over the shoulder of a lagging-behind beast. *Why,* he wondered, *hadn't she simply escaped—moved through him like she did the Liapalese?* Nearing exhaustion, Scotty powered on forward. Apparently, the Kammies were tiring as well since he was closing in on them. Then his breath caught in his chest, realizing why Tori hadn't escaped. Why she was still confined, held in the clutches of the trailing Kammie. She appeared to be unconscious and in a partially physical Human form. *How was that even possible?*

Over the years he'd seen the awful carnage even one Kammie could produce. He remembered back—back to when they'd first arrived on the planet. There'd been several late-night raids into their dorm caves. Kammies were suspected of climbing the sheer cliff walls and entering the caves late at night, then absconding with young Humans—boys and girls. Later, what was found of their remains, sometimes many miles away, was beyond grisly. Little more than shredded flesh and pulverized bone. But once the dorm caves became inhabited by Human-Vallics, the Kammie raids stopped. They had no interest in the energetic Vallic forms. *So what happened to Tori then? Why was she stuck like that—half Vallic, half Human?*

As the Kammies slowed to a stop ahead, Scotty, re-energized, sprinted right into their fray. He'd never actually accomplished what he was planning to do now. But it was something he'd seen Horran do on more than one occasion—bring down big alien game without a weapon. Should his own timing be off now, by even a millisecond, it would be all over for him. He'd be dead; unable to save Tori.

Scotty zeroed in on the largest of the five Kammies. Not slowing down, he plowed right into its thick dense body; instantly, he felt himself passing inside its physical form. He already knew there was much he still didn't know about his Vallic capabilities. But what happened next was unexpected, beyond comprehension. Relative time was altered—*somehow*—and he was watching himself. Watching everything move in slow motion around him. *This is truly amazing*, he thought, briefly wondering if he could actually stop time completely. He forced himself to snap back to the present. It was only then—timed to the precise moment when he was about to emerge from the doomed Kammie's opposite side—that Scotty transformed one lone part of his anatomy—a fist that was now fully Human. With all the pent-up fear and fury, building within him since he'd first heard Tori's screams for help, he now punched out with his clenched fist, unleashing a singular, volcanic eruption of shattered bone and brain matter that spewed forth from the Kammie's destroyed cranium. Scotty's driven momentum carried him all the way through the now dead beast's body unscathed. His timing—perfect.

The four remaining Kammie beasts stood paralyzed at what they'd just witnessed. Eyes darted back and forth, from the dead, nearly decapitated, Kammie body on the ground, to Scotty.

"Put her down, you hairy motherfucker," Scotty spat, pointing a finger at the beast carrying Tori's body over its shoulder. Debating with himself about just killing them all anyway, he had to fight against the strong impulse. Standing alone in the middle of the pack, Scotty heard their low growls. Grotesque lips stretched, then curled back, revealing yellowed teeth—fangs dripping with syrupy strands of mucous. When sinewy muscles suddenly tautened along their animal limbs, readying to attack, Scotty didn't hesitate. The closest Kammie, a female, followed the same fate that befell her larger companion, when Scotty passed in and through her. Her head exploded, as if hit by a cannon ball. A swath of blood red gore rained down upon the remaining three creatures.

Scotty watched as Tori's inert body was gently placed onto the ground. The three beasts quickly scurried away, going off in opposite directions. He took a tentative step forward, then another, then knelt down beside her. He hadn't seen her face in its Human form for over a year. Tori had become even more beautiful. Gently, moving several strands of hair away from her eyes and face, he let his fingers linger there—touching her cold, lifeless, cheek.

PART III
RETURN TO EARTH

chapter 43

Present Day: Nantucket Island, Stillworth's Skiff

S cotty revived as he was being manhandled over to an exterior stairway. His head hurt—throbbing—where Officer Platt had smacked him again with his damn flashlight. Still incoherent, he only now could feel his legs—*thump thump thump*—painfully dragging along behind him. *I don't have time for this. Earth doesn't have time for this . . .*

Scotty, transforming from Human physicality into his Vallic form, felt himself falling free—right into and through Officer Platt. As he emerged out of Platt's front bulk, he continued on, rolling head-over-heels down four more stair rungs to the sidewalk below—little more than a spinning blur of blue energy. Rising to his feet, he immediately transformed himself back into his Human state then spun back around, waiting. It took a moment for Platt's mind to catch up with what had just happened. Wide-eyed, the policeman fumbled for the gun at his hip.

"Don't do it, Platt!"

The command came from the landing above. FBI Special Agent Alison McGuire, her own weapon drawn, was pointing it at Officer Platt's substantial center mass. At the railing, Scotty's mother tentatively stepped into view beside her. Her eyes, focused intently on Scotty, conveyed a lifetime of worry, unanswered questions, and something else . . . a mother's love.

Larry's loud barks broke the momentary standoff. The golden retriever turned the corner above them, lumbered down the top few steps, then got held up behind Platt's substantial backside. What happened next was completely unexpected. In one fluid motion, Larry too transformed into an energetic state. In the midst of jumping right into and through Officer Platt, Scotty quickly stepped to one side. After the big dog awkwardly landed onto the concrete beside him, he felt the full impact of the animal's weight lean into his legs. Larry was back in his physical canine form. Staring at him, Scotty realized his dog had his own unique story and wondered if he'd ever know it.

Scotty stared up to see three gaping mouths. He settled his attention onto Platt. "You're either going to help me, help us, or you're going to die. There is far too much at stake here. Decide right now. And if you ever touch that flashlight again, I'll take your head off. I've done that kind of thing before. Trust me."

He avoided looking at Alison and his mother. This was a side of him they would not have expected.

* * *

All four were back now in the mother's cramped apartment. Scotty sat cross-legged on the floor, with Larry's head lying on his lap, while Alison sat next to his mother on the couch. Officer Platt had to shoehorn his large hulk into the lone adjacent chair. For close to an hour, for the most part, Scotty was the only one speaking. He started from the beginning—what he remembered of that fateful day when he was a nine-year-old boy, playing on the beach with Larry. He spoke of the rover craft—of his abduction into a massive, living, spaceship—then spoke of alien beings that were little more than wisps of blue energy. He described the arduous medical procedures he and others endured to become a Vallic-Human. He told them of the alien called Seve, and then of the intolerant one, called Horran. He chronicled the years spent on a distant world, called Hope, and of the other abducted children he'd met there: his friends Ernesto, Tiffany, and Tori. He spoke of the reason for their abduction. The ramifications of an arrogant alien race—the Vallic—whose experiments had gone terribly wrong, resulting in a tremendous gamma ray burst, currently shooting out through space straight toward countless planetary systems—inhabited worlds unaware of what was soon to come.

Scotty took a moment before continuing, "Um, may I have a glass of water?" suddenly thirsty.

"Of course . . . anyone else?" his mother asked.

"Yes, thank you, Mrs. Sullivan."

"Just call me Brianna."

Alison nodded. "Fine . . . Brianna, then."

Brianna, sidestepping between the couch and the coffee table, headed off to the kitchen. Scotty felt Platt's eyes boring into him. Then his wooden chair creaked as he wiggled about, trying to make himself comfortable. Up to this point, the policeman had made no effort to hide his growing skepticism, expelling overly dramatic, yet barely audible, huffs and uh huhs . . .

"Are you going to tell us the rest of it?" Alison asked. "Like what now . . . what you're doing here?"

Brianna, after handing both Scotty and Alison a glass of water, retook her seat on the couch. Breathing in a deep breath then slowly exhaling, a bemused smile crossed her lips.

Scotty saw that his mother, for the moment, was just happy to have her son back.

"I'm here to assist those who want to survive—assist them in making the transition that will enable them to live out the balance of their lives on another world."

Platt shifted his weight again. The chair under him swayed and creaked louder. Red-faced, the man's agitation was growing by the second.

Alison said, getting to her feet "Okay . . . that's it! You and I are going to swap. Up with you, Platt. You can take my seat on the couch. Come on, UP! She came around to the chair and waited for Platt to extricate himself. Once Platt was settled in on the couch next to Scotty's mother, Platt continued, "This is all a load of horse shit. Aliens? Come on ... you must really think I just fell off the *dumb-fuck* truck."

Alison, brows knitted, said, "So ... you didn't see what I saw? What *we* saw?" Her tone incredulous, she continued. "The guy can turn into a ghost. He literally dove right through you back there on the steps."

"Clever magic—some *Siegfried and Roy* kind of shit. Hell, they could do a lot more than what he did and they did it with man-eating Bengal tigers." He shifted his eyes onto Scotty. "No, I don't buy any of this crazy BS, mister! And the sooner Ms. FBI here understands that, the sooner I can do my job and take you in."

Scotty had no problem with Platt's skepticism. There would be many others following. Perhaps most Humans on planet Earth would find his story pure fantasy. "What would it take for you to believe what I've told you is true?" Scotty asked, turning first to Platt, and then Alison and his mother. Although less than Platt's, he saw their skepticism as well. "It's fine ... neither of you are one hundred percent convinced either. I get that." He smiled at his mother's uncomfortable expression. "Look ... we've taken all this into account. Of course, no one will easily believe the kind of things I'm saying ... what at first will be perceived as the rantings of a crazy person. That and perhaps a somewhat entertaining sideshow carnival act."

Scotty glanced at the digital clock readout on the DVD player, positioned on a shelf just below the TV set. It was closing in on 3:00 p.m. By this time, his Vallic-Human counterparts aboard the spacecraft should have made themselves known to the crew of the International Space Station. He remembered back to his own childhood abduction and shook his head. Now would come the hard part.

"Mom . . . would it be okay to turn on your TV? To a full-time news channel?"

chapter 44

"Sir...we, the ISS, have been taken aboard another ship. One you do not have the technology yet to detect. We are well above Earth's orbit. The *vehicle* is pretty much in one piece; stored within the confines of this...um...alien ship."

"Did he just say alien ship?" Borkner asked, staring up at Mannford.

Ignoring the acting NASA Administrator, Flight Director Paul Mannford unconsciously took a step forward and then another, as if getting a closer view would somehow make better sense of what he was seeing. He stared at each of the three familiar faces, now on display on the six large MCC screens at the front of the room. Commander Jack Landon, astronaut Greg Fischer, and cosmonaut Peter Mirkin appeared to be in relatively good health, although they clearly were nervous. But it was what was directly behind the three men that completely captivated Mannford's attention: technology clearly distinct from anything within on the ISS vehicle. He also caught a sudden movement behind the three men that he almost missed.

Beings—clearly not Human—bluish in color; so faint physically they were a mere whisper of form. Mannford couldn't really tell just *what* they were.

The control center, typically filled with a combination of sounds—talking, fingers tapping at keyboards, the shuffling of papers—all the general sounds of people hard at work, was instead very quiet. All eyes were glued on the front displays.

CapCom's Margaret Haskell, now at Mannford's side said, "Sir . . . seems this definitely is not ISS-based communications. Synchronization and checksum protocols are all wrong. I've never seen anything like it. Can't explain how we're even communicating with them."

Mannford nodded, without looking at her. Clearing his throat, he said, "Commander Landon—Paul—how about providing us a rundown on your current situation. Over."

Landon exchanged a quick glance with Fischer and Mirkin before speaking. "We're okay, for now. But let me be clear, the ISS vehicle is no longer operational or inhabitable. We presently are guests onboard an alien vessel. But I want to stress we have not been harmed in any way. Over."

"Just tell us—what do they want from us, Landon?" Borkner interjected.

"To help us, sir. They're here to . . . well, save us. Over."

Borkner *brusquely* spun on his heels and scurried off. Mannford caught sight of the NASA Administrator on his way out, putting a cellphone up to his ear.

Commander Landon, speaking again, said, "Sir, the beings here . . . the aliens—God, that sounds so strange to say aloud—have a briefing, an information package, that they would like to transmit down to MCC. Would that be acceptable? Over."

Mannford shook his head. "First, we'll need to make available a dedicated separate coms' channel, as well as a secure firewalled network. It could be a few minutes. Over."

Mannford next heard Marty Kline's voice, his IT supervisor, in his ear, "I'll have that for you in about five minutes, sir. Can you ask him how big a file this will be? Wait, never mind . . . the file just appeared. Strange that they knew where to transmit it to. Boy, it's big. *Very* big," Kline said.

Commander Landon said, "Sir, there's an element of time here; an urgent lack thereof. What you are about to see, which is something we've already viewed several times now, will be a hard pill to swallow. I've been assured it's something we'll be able to verify, once our scientists are provided with all the specific, deep space telemetry numbers. They'll be able to see it coming."

"See what coming exactly?"

"Access the file and watch the display, sir. It will speak for itself. Over."

* * *

Acting NASA Administrator Gordon Borkner stood alone within the second-floor stairwell. Cellphone pressed to one ear, his voice echoed off the surrounding concrete walls. "No, Mr. President, I assure you, every second we spend talking about this, brings our country, hell, Earth, one second closer to total annihilation. I am right here on the front lines, so to speak. I'm your man at ground zero."

Borkner listened as Dale Hardy Granger, President of the United States, responded back in a slow southern drawl. "Now, Mr. Borkner, let's take a brief breather and appreciate this momentous occasion. No one has been killed from what I've been told. Is that correct?"

Gordon Borkner looked up, as if searching the high heavens for someone to save him from the man's dimwittedness. "Sir . . . if I may be so direct, the International Space Station has already been attacked, has sustained heavy damage. It's been captured. Top that off, her crew's been abducted. Sir, if these aren't the acts of hostile beings . . ."

"I have already ordered military readiness to a level of DEFCON one. What else would you have me do?"

Borkner tapped an impatient toe as he listened to the president drone on.

"Make a preemptive strike? Start sending missiles into space? Our boys are up there . . . alive. So that's not going to happen, Gordon. We're not there yet."

"Well, that, of course, is your decision, sir. I just want to go on record—we should have . . ." Borkner suddenly realized the president was still rambling on and hadn't heard a word he'd said. He rolled his eyes and waited.

"I want an update on the half-hour, Gordon. The media has already gotten wind of this and I'll need to address the nation this evening, at the very latest."

"Yes, someone will brief the White House. I need to get back to . . ."

"No! Not someone else! You, Gordon, will update me personally, not the White House, on the half hour. Right now, I have other things to deal with. I will talk to you within the hour, Gordon." The president ended the conversation without saying goodbye.

Borkner continued to stare at his phone. *Idiot.*

chapter 45

Present Day: Nantucket Island, Brianna Sullivan's Apartment

"Yeah, Wolf, the unfolding story here is ... well ... beyond anything I, and I suspect anyone else, has ever reported before. Let me break it down for you, what is known at present. Just hours ago, leaked reports coming out of NAS, were quite dire. News that the International Space Station had, in all likelihood, burned up in Earth's upper atmosphere. Also, that the three-man crew aboard—a crew consisting of two Americans and one Russian had been lost. No one ever anticipated that today, instead, would be the day so many science fiction enthusiasts have waited for: actual contact made with an alien race. If these reports are true— and there are multiple, inside, reliable NASA sources saying that they are—then not only is the ISS still in one piece, but our heroic ISS crew is also alive and has been taken aboard an alien vessel of *some kind. To top that off, the ISS crew is currently in contact with Houston's Mission Control Center."*

"What a crock! Totally fake news . . . this is nothing more than a ratings stunt," Officer Platt said.

Scotty had listened to the CNN news report, covering the latest events in space, but he'd done so while watching the three faces of those in his mother's apartment. Now seated on the couch next to his mother, she had her hand resting on his shoulder. Knowing now he really was her son, *her Scotty*, she couldn't stop touching him, gazing at him. It warmed his heart that they were back in each other's lives, even if only for a short while.

Scotty made brief eye contact with Alison and wondered what she was thinking. He wondered if the ones sitting here were a close cross-section of the present mindset within the rest of the country—the world. Would the public believe what they were learning now? And, even more importantly, what was to come next?

Platt, keeper of the TV remote, flipped through channels, finally settling on the FOX News channel.

"Dana, this has gone well-beyond speculation. Well-beyond hyperbole. FOX News, as well as other major networks, has been instructed to clear airtime for a presidential address to the nation in thirty-five minutes. The leaders of other nations will be doing the same thing at the top of the hour."

Scotty watched what seemed to be looped, stock footage—televised from inside Mission Control Center in

Texas—transmitted along with multiple, older video clips of the ISS, the International Space Station, in orbit.

"You know what the president's going to say, don't you? You're part of this?" Alison asked, her tone somewhat accusatory.

Scotty nodded. "Yes, I am a part of this. I am the *living* example."

"Example of what?" Platt sneered. "You're going to jail . . . that's hardly an example of anyone of much importance."

"Shut up, Platt. If anyone's going to jail, it's you, for obstructing an FBI Agent in the course of her duties," Alison said.

Even now, with the momentous news about aliens and saved astronauts—the two were back bickering; both avoiding the implications of what news stations across the world were urgently reporting. At that moment, Scotty had serious doubts the people on Earth would be able to handle what was soon to follow.

"Scotty, your father, Kyle, and Sara need to know you're alive. That you're back." Briana Sullivan looked at him, her eyes filled with doubt.

"I won't be staying, Mom. Soon, very soon, everything will change. It's why I'm here." Briana, studying him, nodded back.

"It's like the Apollo landing," Platt said, sitting on the floor, his legs outstretched like an overgrown child's.

"What does that even mean?" Alison asked.

"Moon landing back in the late seventies . . . it was all bull-shit. Nothing more than a Hollywood movie-set stunt. Aliens? Come on, spare me!"

Alison, rolling her eyes, turned to Scotty. "What is the president going to say?"

"He's going to speak to the American public; hopefully convey a sense of calm, prepare them for what is coming."

"That cataclysmic cosmic event thing, you spoke about?" Alison asked.

"In sixteen months, Earth will be destroyed by a tremendous, interstellar, gamma ray. It'll shoot through this solar system in the blink of an eye and nothing will remain in its wake."

Officer Platt snickered as Larry, wedged between the couch and the coffee table, angled his head, left then right, as Scotty scratched behind his floppy ears.

"Mom, sorry to do this, but you'll need to come with me. You too, Alison . . . if you will?"

"Come with you where, hon?" his mother asked.

"Washington, D.C."

Platt pulled his eyes away from the TV. "Ahh, and you don't want me to come with you, too? I'm crestfallen."

Scotty chose that exact moment to transform into his Vallic, energetic, state. His mother, inhaling abruptly, jerked her hand away. He smiled, not taking it personally. He knew this was way beyond weird for them as he stood and proceeded to *walk right through* both his dog and the coffee table. Standing before Platt, his hazy form barely blocked the TV set behind him.

"Are you really that certain this is magic?" he asked Platt, who continued to watch the only slightly obscured FOX report.

"What would convince you otherwise?" Scotty asked, fairly certain Platt was already convinced. Probably a little scared too. "The truth is, I could use your help."

Platt didn't say anything, but he didn't snicker, or make a face back either.

"If you could do what I'm doing now, this type of magic, as you put it . . . would you be interested in that?"

That brought a smile to Platt's fleshy face. "Sure . . . it'd be a riot. I'd join the circus."

Both Alison and Scotty's mother Briana laughed at that.

"It took years of physical therapy to do the kinds of things you witnessed me doing today. It was also incredibly painful. My flesh burned so bad I wanted to die . . . either that or cut it away. I was nine when I went through the procedure. It's called Dyad-Geneses: A process that involved my Human DNA merging with alien Vallic DNA. I am no longer 100% Human, Officer Platt. I am a Human-Vallic."

"Yeah . . . so?"

"Anyone who wants to survive—live out a full life—will have to go through a form of what I went through. Not as painful, and not as long, time-wise, to recuperate."

Platt's eyes were searching Scotty's featureless face. "You're serious?"

"I am."

"You want me to become . . . whatever *thing* you've become?"

"Only if you want that. But you may be too scared."

"You're serious?" Platt asked again.

"If you want to live, you'll do it. And you'll say goodbye to everything you've ever known while living on Earth. You'll travel to another world, a new home, called Hope."

"Can't I just go there without the whole Human-Vallic mumbo-jumbo?"

"No. The radiation on Hope would eventually kill you."

Platt didn't say anything back for a long minute. Finally, he said, "I guess."

Scotty changed back into his Human form then sat down by the obese police officer to reconsider things. *Perhaps there was some hope, after all.*

Hearing heavy boots storming up the outside stairs, all eyes went to the apartment's curtained window. *They were coming for him*, just like Scotty knew they would.

chapter 46

Exhausted, astronaut Commander Landon sat beside Fischer and Mirkin; both had their heads tilted back and were fast asleep. The three men sat in a row on what he assumed was intended to be a kind of bench seat. Strange, how the aliens never seemed to sit down themselves. Perhaps, little more than glowing energy forms, they had no need to ever do so.

Landon ran his hand along the seat's smooth surface. The bench-like protrusion was actually part of the bulkhead. A bulkhead that was warm to the touch and laced with multiple, somewhat translucent, layers of what looked to be an intricate vascular system. Nerves and nerve bundles, and even a type of skeletal support system that he could now make out, set deep within the flesh-like material. In essence, the walls were *alive*—he figured the whole damn ship was alive.

Landon briefly tried to make sense of this strange kind of technology; one that could be grown, instead of built. To some degree, it made sense. It certainly sparked his interest, wanting to learn more about it. He contemplated upon how involved it was to manufacture a simple panel of steel—all the time and energy it took to mine the ore—have it melted down and refined, then roll it out into sheets, etc. And then it had to be delivered—the whole complicated freight, distribution aspect. And if it should get damaged, then someone had to go and fix it. All that for just one aspect: a steel panel. Virtually thousands, perhaps millions, of parts went into the construction of a spacecraft. So why bother, Landon mused, when one could get something to grow at an exponential rate; even fix itself? This went far beyond Human's current engineering skills—still limited to two-dimensional computer chips, even though it was known they could get a massive increase in transistor density using three dimensions. But they hadn't yet figured out how to remove the heat generated in the chip fast enough. Strange to think that Earth's future might have evolved in this same direction—one day. He thought about that—Earth's potential future. But there would be no future for Earth. He now whole-heartedly believed that. He'd been shown the scientific evidence, had asked all the right questions. No, he was convinced Earth was doomed.

His thoughts then turned to the aliens onboard this huge space vessel. A strange and aloof race of beings, there didn't seem to be that many of them aboard. In fact, Landon had the odd feeling they more or less were a skeleton crew.

They'd been asked to wait on the bench seat. To rest up—that more would be asked of them soon. Over the preceding hours, Landon had spent the most amount of time with the one called Seve. An alien female, she moved noticeably slower than the others—as if she were in pain, or perhaps just getting older. She'd provided them the fundamentals of what was happening; the direction the aliens wanted things to move. She had specified what was to be conveyed to Earth's various high-government officials, including the President of the United States. Astronauts Landon and Fischer had been communicating, for the most part, with NASA's MCC, while Mirkin had spoken with their Russian counterpart—RKA Mission Control Center, in Korolyov, Russia. A lot of information had been disseminated. The three astronauts had earlier agreed among themselves that they would make sure that those they had contact with on Earth understood that they were merely the conduits of information provided by the aliens.

Of course, NASA higher ups and government official's initial outright skepticism had been anticipated. Seve, taking that in stride, responded by saying that verifiable science would speak for itself. With that said, the aliens were asked to provide what had seemed an endless amount of technical data. Data that clearly confirmed what was coming—a gamma ray of inexplicable destructive force, zooming along at nearly the speed of light headed directly for the Solar System—for Earth.

"How are you feeling, Commander Landon? Can I get you anything . . . some water perhaps?"

Landon hadn't noticed Seve's ghost-like form approach. "Um, no, thank you. This is just . . . a lot to take in."

"Yes, I apologize for putting you in this position."

"It just seems so much will need to happen, and in such a relatively short span of time. Basically, moving off all of Earth's Humankind. It sounds impossible."

"We will do what we can. Please remember, we have done this already, a number of times."

Landon sensed she had smiled, but wasn't sure of it. "I have to tell you, if it could, you know, be done, God how I'd love to visit another world. As an astronaut, I'm probably more predisposed to thinking that way." He looked at his sleeping compatriots. "We're explorers by nature. But I have a question for you: What about the very young, like tiny infants, or, on the flip side, the very old? Will this even be a possibility for those Humans?"

"Certainly, Commander. The young and old, if they so choose, can make the transition, as well as certain animals. The procedure, the recovery times, have greatly improved. In addition to our own people, there are premier Human-Vallic scientists now living on Hope. Taken from Earth years ago, they have dedicated their lives to make this procedure work . . ." Seve hesitated, seeming to need time to collect herself.

"Are you all right?" Landon asked.

"No, unfortunately, I am not. You see, Commander, I am dying. We all, the original Vallic-Humans that is, are dying."

"I don't understand. What do you mean you are dying? How . . . ?"

"I spoke to you about the Dyad-Geneses treatments . . . procedures, yes? That all Humans will need to undergo this process, prior to living on Hope."

"You told us about that, about the thousands of Humans, many of them children, who have already made this transition successfully. Some of them are back on Earth now," Landon said.

"Well ... the Vallic, the ones who chose to be part of this endeavor, elected to go through a very similar Dyad-Geneses. Only our intention was to join Human DNA to our existing Vallic DNA. To become Vallic-Human."

"That makes sense, Seve. It seems, then, that you, all the original Vallic and all the original Humans you brought to Hope, would now be identical ... the same kind of, um, being. Is that not the case?"

Seve shook her head. "No, it did not turn out that way. I do not wish to be insulting ... what I'm about to tell you. The Vallic ancestry on our world of Lorimar, are predisposed to both kindness and gentleness. That is our heritage, Commander. Can you say the same for your own heritage, even centuries back, not to mention millennia? Our newly acquired Human DNA is having adverse, negative effects on us emotionally and physically."

Landon studied Seve, her slightly hunched shoulders, the pain she seemed to be barely tolerating. He asked, "And the early Dyad-Geneses Human subjects? Are they exhibiting the same negative affects?"

"On the contrary, just the opposite. Those subjects are physically, emotionally, even mentally thriving," Seve said.

"I'm sorry. I truly am. Here you are, undergoing all this hardship for Humankind, and how are you repaid? The Vallic people, having to go through such a terrible turn of events, doesn't seem fair," Landon said.

"Perhaps it's perfectly fair. We, the Vallic, don't forget, were the ones who originally set these events into motion. Starting with an unimaginable, cataclysmic, fusion reaction on a far distant world, many light years away."

"But that was unintentional, Seve. I can see something similar happening from future Humans. And I'm not so sure we would be as forthcoming about fixing things as you have been." Landon held his next question until two Vallic-Humans passed by them and left the area. "So this leaves me with one more question . . . will you, any of you, survive long enough to bring this spatial endeavor to fruition?"

"We will see . . . I hope so," she said.

"Maybe one of your scientists will find a cure for what you have," Landon added. Seve silently left him the way she'd come.

Over the next few hours, Landon spoke at length to the President of the United States twice more. Peter Mirkin did the same with the Russian president. It had been decided early on by government officials that the media should not be granted access to any more than the barest minimum of what was actually transpiring. Yes, the ISS was intact. The crew was alive and well. And yes, an alien contact had transpired. But nothing yet would be forthcoming about Earth's impending fate. The last thing anyone wanted was to ignite worldwide mass hysteria. But Landon had little faith that mass hysteria was avoidable. Within days, maybe hours, virtually all lives on Earth would be forever altered. Seve had spoken of the impending timeframe. Landon shook his head. He couldn't reconcile what needed to be accomplished in such a short period of time.

chapter 47

A t least they had the courtesy of pounding on the front door twice before breaching it with a heavy entry ram. *BOOM!* The door flew open and six men dressed in black, wearing tactical gear and brandishing automatic assault rifles, stormed through the opening. They yelled for everyone to get down on the floor, hands clasped behind their heads. Brianna Sullivan let out a scream and Larry barked once before scurrying beneath the coffee table.

"Hold on . . . I'm an FBI agent!" Alison yelled, already feeling strong hands driving her face down hard onto the carpet. She glanced over at Scotty and found him back in his Human form. When the stock of a rifle smashed down on the back of his head without warning, his body slumped forward—he was out cold. *Again.* Two ops guys each grabbed an arm and roughly pinned his arms behind him.

"Who are you . . . what is this all about?" Alison asked with as much authority as she could muster, with her head pressed low and her ass up in the air.

"Come on, I'm a local cop here . . . you have no reason to handcuff me, man," Officer Platt whined.

Alison watched as the man closest to her—undoubtedly the team leader— withdrew her creds wallet from her inside jacket pocket. Glancing at it, he tossed it onto the floor as though it was just a piece of trash.

"How about telling me, at least, who you're with—what agency?" she asked, straining hard to look over her shoulder to get some indication from their clothing. The FBI, ATF, US Marshals, and other agencies, were required to have clearly identifiable insignias printed on their jackets. These guys had nothing of the sort. Then the man closest to Alison, the apparent leader of the group, spoke again but in a normal tone, his accent heavy Bostonian. These men were asshole thugs, but at least they were American asshole thugs.

"Do not try to follow us."

With that, Scotty was lifted off the floor by two of the team. As quickly as they'd arrived, they left, dragging Scotty along in the center of the pack.

"Oh my God . . . they took him! How could they just take him like that?" Brianna cried out.

* * *

Since it was the weekend and unable to reach him on his cell-phone, Alison was forced to call Supervising Agent Donald Price on his home phone number. She had a strong suspicion that he, along with the rest of his family—like just about every-one else in the world at that moment with the events in space taking place—were planted in front of their family room television set. Clearly, he had noticed her Caller ID.

"Agent McGuire ... in what universe do you think you have permission to bother me at home on the weekend?"

"You watching the news, sir?"

"Yeah ... that's some crazy shit going down. Not sure how much of it I believe. Hah ... aliens?"

"That's what I'm calling about."

"You're calling me about the aliens?"

"Sir, ten minutes ago, the front door into Brianna Sullivan's apartment was literally ripped off its hinges when a government black ops team stormed in, rousted those of us inside, then left with a now unconscious Scotty Sullivan, his hands handcuffed behind his back. I and a local law officer were within the premises."

"You're talking about your case, the one with the missing kid. Um ... Scotty Sullivan, who was swept out to sea over a decade-and-a-half ago."

"That's the case ... but not what happened."

"All you had to do is close the damn file and be back in the office Monday morning. But what ... now you're now bringing aliens into the mix? Is that what I'm hearing?"

"Sixteen years ago, Scotty Sullivan wasn't washed out to sea, he was abducted. Abducted by the same aliens that have taken our astronauts. As unbelievable as all that sounds, there's still more. Scotty Sullivan now has dual sets of DNA. He is both Human and Vallic, that's what the aliens call themselves. I've personally witnessed him transition between both ... ah ...

physiologies." Alison waited for her supervisor to mutter something glib. As *dead air* on the line became uncomfortable, she anticipated Price demanding that she first undergo a psych evaluation before returning to work.

"You've actually seen this?"

"I have." Alison let the dead air on the line speak for itself, before adding. "Ops guy in charge spoke with a heavy Boston accent."

Supervising Agent Price said, "Hang tight. Let me do a little inter-agency checking on this. How is . . ." she heard Price flipping through some file pages, "How is Mrs. Sullivan doing with all this? Was she injured in any way?"

"No, sir. But Scotty was hit fairly hard in the head prior to being dragged out of here, and he is still suffering from an earlier concussion. They didn't need to hit him, he wasn't resisting."

"I'll get back to you as soon as I have something," Price said, and the line went dead.

Alison took a seat on the couch next to Briana, who was wiping fresh tears off her cheeks. When Larry's head poked up between them, Alison scratched him behind his ears.

"What are we supposed to do? I can't just sit here and do nothing while my son is . . ."

Alison interrupted her, "I have no intention of doing nothing, Brianna. My supervisor will probably get back to me as soon as he knows something definitive. In the meantime, I think we should contact NASA. Beyond doubt, they'll be immensely interested in what we have to say. They'll surely want to know just who it is that's been visiting here . . . and that Scotty is actually one of them."

Brianna gave her a pained expression. Hearing that her son was, at least partially, an alien was difficult for her. "I don't want you to get in any trouble. I know you need to follow orders. The FBI, I'm sure, has procedures you must follow."

"More than you can possibly imagine," Alison replied. "But this is so much bigger than my job. This is the most important thing to happen to . . . well . . . to the entire world like never before, right? The world's populace is clueless about what's coming . . . or what's up there orbiting Earth. But I do know . . . we do. Right now, I have some calls to make. I just hope the people I talk to will believe what I have to say."

Brianna offered back a lopsided smile. "You're going to sound like a lunatic."

Officer Pratt had remained quiet up to this point. He was rubbing one of his wrists where he'd been roughly manhandled. He then noticed that his gun was missing from its holster at his hip.

"What about you?" Alison asked.

The big man didn't make eye contact with her, but he did nod his oversized head. "I'm in."

chapter 48

Taking a red-eye flight from Washington, DC, the former acting NASA Administrator, Gordon Borkner, hurried across the nearly filled parking lot, heading in the direction of Building 5D at the Johnson Control Center in Houston, Texas to take command in his new position. Taking the long way around was necessary in order to avoid the large contingent of no less than twenty network news media trucks, along with their respective reporters, waiting with microphones in hand.

The morning wind had picked up and Borkner's loosened necktie flapped and fluttered over his right shoulder, like it was frantically attempting to make an escape behind him. The exertion from the quarter-mile hike had only aggravated his rosacea, and he inwardly cursed his parents for passing the errant gene of this dreadful facial skin condition down to him. For God's sakes, he was supposed to be on camera sometime later today. *Fuck! I'll look like a goddamn painted harlequin!*

Borkner noticed four olive-green US Army armored personnel carrier trucks rumble by on Avenue D, then make a slow turn onto 2nd Street. All five of the US armed services were now on high alert because of his recommendation to the President. Borkner's presidential appointment couldn't have come at a more opportune time. One he'd lobbied for—made a compelling case for. A case chock-full of dire predictions if the right man wasn't selected and put in place immediately. No, Borkner would have been very surprised if he hadn't gotten the cabinet-level promotion. He watched as more military trucks turned into the lot. But their assembly was far bigger than mere preparation for utilizing military force. He'd had little time, only mere days, in fact, to quickly rally support from the national heads of multiple government agencies, including Homeland Security and the Justice Department, as well as both the FBI and CIA. Alone, he never could have wielded the kind of clout necessary to make any kind of demand on them. Hell, nearly half of those respective government agency chieftains had never even heard of him and didn't realize he'd once been the acting NASA administrator. What Borkner did have, with everything now going on in space, was actual decision-making power. Something Borkner had always craved. That and, *surprisingly*, the President's full backing.

Around the world, NASA was front and center in the news for the miraculous events currently happening in space. The attention of every worldwide news and media organization was focused now right here. To date, very few details had been released for the public's general consumption—only that the International Space Station crew had, miraculously, reestablished contact with Mission Control. Yet even that news was insignificant compared to the astounding latest reports that extra-terrestrial beings had indeed arrived in local space via some kind of immense spaceship. The general public, both in America and around the world, was desperate for any new information. *Why were they here? What did they want? Was an invasion imminent? Was mankind destined to become some kind of interstellar alien slaves?*

All of his earlier agitations concerning the expensive ISS program were now gone. Borkner could not have imagined a better personal scenario—one in which his once-meandering career path would be so exponentially accelerated. He turned sideways, shimming between two parked, side-by-side behemoths — government Yukon vehicles. He purposely avoided glancing at his reflection in the tinted windows. A ten-foot-high, recently erected, chain-link fence surrounded Building 5D in its entirety. *His new, repurposed, building.* He slightly changed course and headed for the front gate. Two-armed MPs stood at attention as he approached. Borkner, wrangling his tie back into position, did his best to look calm, cool, and collected. As both guards saluted him, he gave them a cursory salute back, inwardly reveling in his own newly found importance.

One of another pair of two nearly identical-looking MP's opened a glass door at the front of the building and greeted him with, "Good morning, sir."

Borkner ignored the comment as he strode within the front lobby of the building's voluminous interior where white marble-clad floors and walls gleamed. No less than forty men and women—some in business-suit attire and others in military uniforms—turned as his loud footfalls resounded off the flooring, making his presence known. They were all awaiting him. Waiting to greet the newly formed agency head. Actually, the new agency moniker wasn't his idea. It was, in fact, a previous president's coined term—*Space Force*. At that time, it was immediately ridiculed. But that was then and this was now. Since Borkner hadn't technically served in any military branch himself, he had lobbied to make Space Force an agency instead of just another military branch. Of course, it would have the same military effectiveness of the other current branches, but it would also possess equal government standing and influence as, say, Homeland Security, and the FBI. It also allowed Borkner to personally fill a newly formed presidential cabinet position, enlarging the cabinet from fifteen seats to sixteen.

As the murmured conversations within Building 5D's lobby became muted, Borkner addressed the men and women, his team, who'd formed a semi-circle around him. He scanned their faces and soon found the one person he was looking for. His eyes locked onto Paul Mannford—NASA's senior flight director. He didn't especially like the man, but then that held true for most people. But due to Mannford's ongoing interactions with the ISS crew, as well as with several of the alien visitors themselves, he was the preeminent expert on everything extra- terrestrial.

"So . . . is he here?" Borkner asked.

"The young man is in custody, sub-level four, sir," Mannford said. "But I don't believe we need this tight level of security. He's a willing, open participant in these proceedings."

Borkner scoffed, "Who's been living, supposedly, on an alien world for the past sixteen years. No one knows where his true loyalties lie. No! We'll maintain the highest-level of security possible until we know more. Understood?"

"Sir . . . the conference room is ready for you," a tall, waifish-thin woman, wearing a tight bun atop her head, announced. "This way, sir."

Borkner feigned annoyance at the interruption. "Fine . . . lead on, Miss . . ."

"Wentworth, sir, Amy Wentworth."

* * *

Paul Mannford merged with the others, moving into the oversized conference room. A gargantuan-sized coffin-shaped table sat on its centerline. Within several minutes everyone was seated and looking toward the head of the table—toward Borkner, the newly appointed head of Space Force. Mannford fought to keep all signs of incredulity from his expression. He simply could not imagine a more unsuitable candidate to hold this new position. But with the advice and help from others, many in this room right now, perhaps Borkner could rise to the occasion. Maybe he *could* become the leader necessary to pull off what seemed to be an all but impossible task: One that would save Humanity.

Borkner's brows furrowed tightly together as he stared at Amy Wentworth, now closing the outer door and leaning against it. "I'm assuming everyone in this room maintains the necessary level of high-security clearance to hear what I have to say?"

Amy nodded. "Of course, sir. It's your selected team."

Borkner refocused his attention on the serious faces now situated around the table. "Let me start by saying welcome. Welcome to what we've tagged as the Earth-to-Hope Migration Directive. The science behind the aliens' gamma ray revelations has been verified, unfortunately. In approximately sixteen months, the Solar System will indeed be struck by radiation levels so intense that Earth's oceans will become instantly heated ... will boil and evaporate into the atmosphere. All surface life will be eradicated. It is expected that all planets within our solar system will also lose their structural integrity, becoming little more than spacial dust within a short span of time."

One of the uniformed men, one with glimmering gold stars upon each shoulder, asked, "So I take it we can immediately get moving on some prescribed courses of action? The steps Commander Landon, as their intermediary, laid out for us?"

"General Cole. Let me first ask you a question. If this were, let's say, the Russians who'd inadvertently caused our world's imminent total annihilation, what would you, as the US Army's highest-ranking officer, be most concerned with? Would you simply take their word that their actions were innocent, unintentional? Or would you first ensure their intentions were indeed what they claimed them to be?"

The general shook his head. "Well ... they're not the Russians. And, if the incoming onslaught has been scientifically verified, that the gamma ray is inbound as described, do we have time to . . ."

"This is not a discussion, General. We have been attacked. We are under attack by extra-terrestrials. The Vallic are not our friends, they are our enemy. For those of you within this room, that decision needs to be perfectly understood. But then again, what we voice once outside this room will be a different story. I've been told we have little choice but to do as the Vallic have suggested. But that doesn't mean we won't maintain our own hidden, albeit clear, agenda. There will be hell to pay for the destruction of our home world. It may take years, decades even . . . but certain retribution will be ours. We must quickly learn their technology. We must determine their weaknesses and, in time, exploit them."

Mannford let out a long, frustrated breath. *Borkner was so much worse than he'd even thought.* "Back to the young man, sir, Mr. Sullivan. He's the one, apparently, who has the knowledge, the wherewithal, to guide and build the technology infrastructure here on Earth that will enable our mass exodus. Shouldn't we be engaging with him now? Get the proverbial ball rolling, instead of holding him below ground in a prison cell?"

Borkner swung around to face Mannford, his face twisted in a near-rage snarl, "Don't you dare undermine my authority on this. I will not warn you again. Until the prisoner has been deemed harmless; that he has our best interests at heart, not those of the Vallic, he remains in chains."

Mannford made a bewildered expression. "How will you do that? How will you ensure he has our best interests at heart?"

Borkner turned his gaze toward a suited gentleman seated at the far end of the table. "For those of you who do not know him, I'd like you all to meet Carl Ransen, the head of the CIA."

Ransen was a man about sixty. His perfectly groomed dyed wavy hair was a color that matched the mahogany table. His dark eyes, cold and lifeless, had puffy bags beneath them, giving him a tired, hound dog, appearance. In a smoker's gravelly voice, he said, "At this very moment, several of my associates are speaking with Mr. Sullivan. Most assuredly, it will be an unpleasant experience for him, yet one that must be undertaken to ensure his motivations are in alignment with our own."

Borkner looked pleased with Ransen's update. "Excellent."

"So, are we then to understand that Mr. Sullivan is being tortured? Seriously?" Mannford asked.

Before the new head of Star Force could answer, Amy Wentworth leaned in close. "Sir, the other three are here and have been taken into custody."

"They are below ground?" he asked.

"Yes, sir . . . and the dog."

chapter 49

S cotty was lying flat on his back atop some kind of padded examination table that had his arms positioned straight out, perpendicular to the rest of his body. He was prepared for this possibility. It was just one of the scenarios he'd trained for within a smart dunking simulation.

There were three men in the room, wearing identical dark-grey business suits and matching crew cuts. They introduced themselves as Steve, Bob, and Mike. Mike was in the process of strapping Scotty's right arm down onto the extended arm support.

"You know that I'm here to help," Scotty said.

Mike continued to fiddle, inserting one end of the thick leather strap into its adjoining buckle.

"Best not to speak unless spoken to, Mr. Sullivan," Bob said, taking ahold of his left arm, beginning the process of securing it.

Steve, standing by Scotty's feet, began securing his ankles with two attached straps.

"I'm just letting you know, before you invest too much time in all this rigmarole, that I won't allow you to do whatever it is you're planning on doing to me."

"Is that right?" Mike asked, his face exhibiting an *I've heard all that before* expression.

Scotty was neither annoyed nor angry, he'd prepared for this, though he'd hoped it could be avoided. He waited for his four limbs to be secured to the table, "Is that it? You done?" he asked Mike.

Mike nodded.

Steve had momentarily left the room, but he was back now, maneuvering a waist-high metal tray on rollers into the room. Atop it was an assortment of sharp-looking metal instruments. It was high time to dispense with this colossal waste of energy. Scotty would enjoy watching their expressions as he transformed into his energetic state.

Ouch! What the hell . . . like a bee sting. Scotty wanted to rub the burring spot on the side of his neck, but his arms were too tightly secured. He turned his head to see who was standing just out of his field of view. *It was Bob.* He was smiling, holding up a hypodermic needle for him to see.

"Sorry, stung a little, huh?"

Scotty tried to answer him. Tried to convey back some glib verbal response, but the simple task of properly repositioning his tongue, activating his vocal cords, moving his lips—automatic sensory responses that normally came so readily to him—were now anything but easy. A slurred jumble of words escaped his mouth—sounds of total gibberish.

Bob, Mike, and Steve laughed out loud.

"Never gets old," Mike said.

Scotty waited for his mind to grow hazy, for his eyelids to feel heavy and sleep overtake consciousness. But that wasn't happening. In fact, his mental acuity was only getting sharper. Whatever drug Bob had administered seemed to be affecting his muscular system—also his mind. Feelings of dread, of hopelessness, were quickly infiltrating his psyche, dominating his every thought. He tried transforming into his energetic state again but couldn't.

He watched as Mike studied the various metal instruments laying atop the metal tray. Mike wore an almost whimsical expression—like someone perusing an assortment of chocolates nestled inside one of those bright-red, heart-shaped, candy boxes. He slowly picked up a scalpel, probably the least interesting looking of all the instruments there. Scotty was conscious of his own quickly elevating heart rate as Mike stepped across to his right hand.

Mike said, "I have a few questions for you, my friend. Answer correctly, honestly, and you can avoid tremendous pain. Unfortunately, at this stage of things, you don't really possess what we call a baseline. Something with which to make an accurate comparison. Scotty . . . prepare yourself. This is going to hurt. A lot!"

* * *

Alison was seated on a hard metal chair, one bolted into the concrete floor near her feet. She took in her sparse surroundings. An interrogation room, similar to several others she'd been in during her short career with the FBI. Two empty chairs were across from her on the other side of the metal table. Undoubtedly, the others, Brianna Sullivan and Donald Platt, were in custody nearby, probably seated in rooms just like this one. She glanced up, toward the opposing corner, where a camera with its red light glowing was positioned.

She thought back to the previous seven or eight hours. Alison should not have been surprised when a second team was also deployed to Nantucket Island—to the little apartment directly above the Stillworth's Skiff. But instead of a few men in tactical gear appearing, it was six men and two women from her own agency—the FBI. It made sense her immediate supervisor, Donald Price, stationed in the Chelsea, Massachusetts FBI office, wasn't part of the team. He obviously wasn't aware of the planned raid. She wouldn't be surprised to learn he was brought in for questioning too.

Although Brianna, Officer Platt, and Alison were not handcuffed, they were patted down and it was made clear to them that restraints would quickly be administered if they didn't come willingly—without resistance. The agent in charge, a Ms. Bright, with a square jawline and boyish blond haircut, instructed her team to just leave the dog behind. Let it run loose outside. But Brianna spoke up, telling her the dog arrived with Scotty. Brianna glanced skyward—tilted her head to one side in a dramatic fashion." Do you really want this one particular dog wandering loose in the neighborhood? A dog that has been living with aliens for sixteen years?"

The three, who were now in custody, along with Larry on a short leash, were taken to the nearby Air Station Cape Cod—a Coast Guard base—where they boarded an awaiting C-130 J Super Hercules. Once onboard the ginormous air force plane, Alison saw Scotty, already situated forward. His arms and legs were chained to the bulkhead and decking respectively, as if he were some kind of mass-murderer, and surrounded by the same heavily armed black ops team still outfitted in tactical gear.

Scotty watched the others board and then was guided over to a series of flip-down seats. Alison held his gaze, offering him her most reassuring smile. He smiled back, seeming surprisingly calm considering the situation. *But what could they really do to him?* Alison wondered. *Scotty wasn't normal.* Wasn't even entirely Human. But then Scotty hadn't fared all that well against Platt's big flashlight. Pushing aside her growing concern for the strange man, she recalled his physical reaction to her presence back in the hospital. The way he'd looked at her. And, if she was perfectly honest with herself, she too had felt *something*. She certainly didn't believe in love at first sight— nothing like that. *Of course not!* Little more than a childish concept, anyway—one best left to cheap romance novels. Like those she'd read while vacationing at the beach of Martha's Vineyard last year. But even so, she couldn't deny what she was feeling. And she was surprised, too, at what little concern she felt for other areas in her life that only days earlier held foremost importance—namely, her career as an FBI agent. She'd always been focused, had never let relationships sidetrack her well-thought-out life plan. All those years in college preparing—the prerequisite classes in law enforcement, then the arduous time and energy spent training at Quantico.

Now, sitting alone at the interrogation table, Alison knew that life was going to be very different. *Well*, for her and for everyone else on the planet. Where she once thought that having the career of a lifetime, climbing the corporate ladder, was *everything*, now that seemed almost ludicrous, at least, compared to the simple fact that Earth, along with all its vulnerable inhabitants, was destined to become in a relatively short span of time, totally annihilated. She thought of Scotty again and wondered where he was. Then she heard—somewhere off in the distance—the desperate screams of a grown man.

chapter 50

S cotty had never experienced such god-awful pain in his entire life. These men truly knew what they were doing. And they appeared to enjoy their work. He tried to swallow, but his throat was far too dry for that. Hot tears rolled down both sides of his face, while two rivers of snot dripped from his nose into his gaping, open mouth. His breath expelled in short fast gasps. Now hyperventilating, he felt dizzy and light-headed—sick to his stomach.

Before his return to Earth, Seve reminded him that Humans had a great capacity for both kindness and cruelty. He was experiencing the latter in all its glory. It was during times like this that he wondered, *why bother? Why bother saving a species so intent on being indifferent to another Human's suffering?*

Scotty tried not to look over at what Mike was doing to him. Tried not to listen to his monotone voice, giving him a detailed explanation of what he was doing with a sharp, curlicue-shaped instrument beneath the fingernail on his left hand's little finger.

Again, Scotty screamed in agony as Mike inserted the tip of the instrument a bit farther beneath the nail and began to twist it.

Mike waited for Scotty's shrieks to subside, before saying, "Scotty . . . it is important for you to be perfectly honest with me, with all of us here. Do you agree?"

Scotty tried to nod his head in assent but found it difficult. He slurred the word, "Yeth."

"Good. Now I'm going to ask you again. What are the true intentions of those Vallic aliens in space? What are their ulterior motives down here?" Mike angled his head slightly, focusing his eyes onto Scotty's.

"No . . . ultherior . . . mothives," Scotty replied, slurring his words again.

Mike nodded as he pursed his thin lips. "Did you know that beneath the thumbnail there are far more active nerve endings than there are beneath the pinkie finger's nail?" He then tapped the pointy end of the curlicue instrument onto Scotty's thumb several times—*tap, tap, tap*—to emphasize the point. "What do you say we move onto your thumb? Really get down to business."

On the verge of passing out, Scotty noticed a sudden motion—a blurry movement coming from the direction of the door. *Yet the door hadn't opened.* Typically, when the door opened he would see the florescent light fixture affixed near the hallway ceiling. But all he could see now was that the door was still closed. The blurry motion moved farther into the room: A knee-high, golden-colored, haze. Scotty rapidly blinked the moisture from his eyes. His focus cleared enough to see Larry's goofy face staring up at him, wagging his tail. Again, Scotty's eyes filled with moisture.

"What the fuck! Who let that mutt in here?" Mike yelled, angrily eyeing first Bob, then Steve. "Get it out of here! Then feel free to shoot the damn thing!"

Steve lurched forward with both hands extended out but still missed getting ahold of Larry. Bob lowered down onto his haunches, his arms widespread, ready to catch, or even tackle, the fast-approaching golden retriever. But all Bob managed to get ahold of was empty air as Larry transformed into his energetic state and ran right into and almost all the way through the government agent's body. Then, just as quickly, Larry transformed back into his wonderful *doginess* self. Scotty watched as Larry quickly jiggled his hindquarters off to one side—a fast motion that pulled the end of his waving tail free and clear from inside Bob's upper back. In a dramatic flash of red gore, blood and flesh whipped onto the nearest adjacent wall. Bob's eyes momentarily widened in terror, just before he keeled over into a lifeless heap lying on the concrete floor.

Perhaps it was the emotional, welcoming effect of Larry's sudden appearance within the confined space, or perhaps the drugs in his system had finally begun to sufficiently dissipate, but Scotty knew—even before attempting it—that he was fully capable of transforming himself into his Human-Vallic energetic state. He then proceeded to do just that, which allowed his wrists and ankles to pass through their bindings. Swinging his legs down to the floor, Scotty stepped away from the examination table. Larry, too, transformed—little more than a bluish-glow now, standing next to him, leaning against his side.

Both Steve and Mike froze—disbelieving what they just witnessed. Scotty was tempted to kill them both and considered doing just that. Instead, he said, "If I see you leave this room, I'll kill you both. You won't see it coming. You'll be dead; like that *mess,* lying over there on the floor. Do you want to end up like Bob?"

They both shook their heads.

"Carefully now, hand over your phones, and any weapons you have on you," Scotty demanded. "Put them on the table then take a few steps back."

They both did as told.

Scotty picked up both iPhones and, one at a time, waved a nearly invisible hand through each device. He then tested both iPhones, attempted to power them on. Both were dead; he had used directed magnetic energy to compromise their internal circuitries. Next, he removed the magazines from both semi-automatic handguns. He recognized them—Glock 19's— then checked each to make sure their chambers were clear.

Scotty had excellent familiarity with most weapons, both Vallic and Human, thanks to a portion of his DNA Inculcation Infusion, *dunk learning,* training, back on Hope. He closed his fingers around both magazines. As the two government agents watched, Scotty pushed his fist through the slump-stone wall— as easily as if it were an open window. When he extracted his hand, both magazines were gone—deposited within the wall.

Scotty glanced down at Larry, smiled, and gave him a couple of affectionate pats on his flank. Clearly there were a number things he didn't know about this dog. He probably would never get the full story.

Together, they stepped through the blood-splattered wall and entered into a identically sized room on the other side. This one had a metal table at its center, with three metal chairs placed around it. One of the chairs was occupied by Special Agent Alison McGuire. Scotty's breath caught in his chest. He felt his heart skip a beat. She was staring blankly ahead toward the opposite wall, wearing a faraway, almost wistful, expression on her face. He wondered what she was thinking about at that very moment.

"Alison?" he said softly.

She spun around, but he could tell she didn't immediately see him. Scotty moved closer and she narrowed her eyes. "That's really creepy ... the way you can do that, sneak up on people ... you know?"

"Sorry."

"Was that you? Screaming bloody murder a few minutes ago? Are you all right?"

Scotty held up his left hand, transforming that bit of anatomy into Human physicality. A trickle of blood was still oozing underneath his fingernail.

Alison leaned forward. "Your little pinky? All that screaming over your pinky?"

"Well, you'd be surprised how much pain is involved when a sharp object is jammed underneath one's fingernail," he said defensively.

"How 'bout you make the rest of yourself visible so I can see you?"

"Sure." Scotty transformed himself into his fully Human form and smiled. Alison smiled too. He could tell she was happy to see him.

She stood up. "I guess you're getting what you wanted . . . this is big. Do you know who I've been talking to in this room?"

"Nope."

"The head of NASA. A guy recently put in charge of something called Space Force. I know it's a really stupid name, but this guy, Borkner, reports directly to the President. Scotty, I don't think he's buying anything that you, or your alien friends up in space, are selling. He almost had me second guessing things too—that you really are who you say you are."

"Who else would I be? Why would anyone put themselves through all this?" Scotty asked.

"He thinks this is all part of an alien invasion. A way to manipulate Humanity into surrendering their home planet."

"Oh, come on! The science stands on its own, the fast-approaching gamma ray . . . it's unequivocal. He should listen to his own people, his own scientists."

"I don't think he's much of a science-minded guy. More paranoid than anything else," she added.

"We can't worry about that right now. When will he be back?"

"He stepped out to grab us a cup of coffee, maybe return a few phone calls, so I guess pretty soon. Look, Scotty, I have the feeling this guy wouldn't hesitate making you just disappear."

"I'm not worried about it," Scotty said.

"Yeah, says the man who fell apart while having his little pinkie tortured."

Scotty ignored her comment.

"And your interrogators?" she asked, glancing at the wall he'd entered through.

"One is dead; the other two won't be making any trouble."

"Wait . . . you killed one of them?" she asked, a flash of anger in her eyes. "They'll use that against you. It'll prove you have nefarious intentions! It'll play right into his paranoid theories. Paint you as one of the evil aliens."

Scotty looked down. "It wasn't me. Seems Larry here picked up a few tricks of his own over these past years. He was only trying to protect me, I'm sure."

Only then did Alison notice Larry's glowing form there at Scotty's side. She shook her head, bewildered by it all. "No one's going to believe that dog killed anyone." She let out a breath, maintaining the same addled expression. "So, what now? You know, your mother's in the room next to this one. I saw them lead her inside there."

"That's good to know; that'll be my next stop," Scotty said. "We're all getting out of here. Guess I'll need to find Platt, too."

"Seriously, Scotty . . . where would we even go? And, in case you've forgotten, your mother and I can't exactly walk through walls like you. Hell, Platt can barely walk through a door."

"You won't have to. And we won't be going very far anyway."

Chewing the inside of her lip, Alison was *somewhere* in her head. Then, she nodded, as if coming to some internal decision. She surprised him, taking another hesitant step forward and placing her open palm on his chest. She let it rest there a moment. Locking her eyes onto his, she said, "Listen, um ... I don't know what's going on with me ... why I can't stop thinking about ... certain things. Things I shouldn't be thinking about, especially at a time like this."

She was standing close enough now for Scotty to breathe in the sweet fragrance of her strawberry-scented shampoo. Close enough to see the dusting of small freckles scattered across the bridge of her nose and the pretty flecks of gold within her large brown eyes.

She said, "I just want you to know, I'm here to help you in any way I can. What you're doing here is incredibly important. I really do know that. And I want to be a part of that." Alison rose up on her tippy-toes and gently kissed his cheek.

It was a tender gesture that momentarily stopped his heart—stopped time itself.

In his peripheral vision, Scotty saw a shadow appear beneath the door. The doorknob began to turn ...

chapter 51

Scotty observed the chubby man standing in the doorway, wearing a business suit. His face was round and overly red—perhaps a skin condition? Both Scotty and Larry stood perfectly still, their energetic forms nearly invisible beneath the bright florescent lights.

"Sorry that took me so long, Ms. McGuire." The portly man handed over a lidded cup that Scotty assumed was coffee. "I hope it's still hot enough for you," he added.

"When can I get out of here, Mr. Borkner?" Alison asked flatly.

"I prefer, Secretary of Space Force. Or, simply Secretary will do."

Alison nodded without correcting herself. "I've told you everything I know. I'd like to get back to my duties."

"Have a seat, Alison. Please. May I call you Alison?"

She let out a breath and blinked several times impatiently.

"You have the unique distinction of having personally interfaced with one of them. With Scott Sullivan."

"He goes by Scotty," she volunteered.

"Do not concern yourself about returning to your office in Massachusetts. I've personally spoken to your supervisor and cleared your current case load."

Scotty could practically feel the anger emanating off Alison.

"You have been in close contact with the subject. With this Scotty Sullivan. So, there are quarantine procedures we'll be initiating."

"Seriously?"

Borkner waved her question away. "Now, what do you say we start from the beginning? When you were first assigned the case . . ."

Scotty used this period time to try to connect with Seve. Worried about her, he knew she wasn't doing well. He honestly didn't know how he'd be able to carry on without her involvement—without all the remaining Vallic-Humans' involvement. They'd each paid, both individually and collectively, the ultimate price for their own world's one colossal mistake. The few original Vallic, now Vallic-Humans, who were still alive had mere weeks, perhaps only days, to live. *What then?* Did Scotty and the others have enough root knowledge to complete the task? A monumental task—one encompassing Humanity's very survival? He half-listened to Alison recount her involvement with himself. He could detect her frustration, the growing fear in her voice.

He then directed his thoughts to his Orand-Pall, conveying his happiness to be speaking with it again as well. Once again, Scotty felt the small creature's bliss—its contentment at being a part of his physiology. *I need to speak with Seve. Can you contact her Orand-Pall . . . quickly now, please.* He waited while the tiny creature established communications.

Organism's Communications: Protocols Initiated . . .

Absolute Command: Searching Broad Spectrum Spatial Coordinates . . .
Absolute Command: Intermediary Base Ship Identified . . .
Absolute Command: Intermediary Specific Organism Identified . . .
Absolute Command: Synchronizing To Intermediary Orand-Pall 012333 . . .
Absolute Command: Initiating Direct Contact With Host . . .
Absolute Command: Communications Established . . .

Scotty was instantly relieved to learn Seve's Orand-Pall was still receiving. *She was alive.* In that moment, he missed her terribly. Although she had never presented herself as such— she had been as much a mother to him as his own biological mother now sitting in the next room over mere feet away.

Scotty's Orand-Pall mentally conveyed that it was ready to convey any message he wished.

Seve ... how are you doing?

It took another moment for the two Orand-Palls, both his and Seve's, to better synchronize their back and forth thoughts and feelings. From prior experience, he knew the exchange would become more normalized, faster, over time.

Seve: The same, Scotty. Thank you for asking. More importantly ... how goes the mission? I have been waiting for an update from you. I assume you have made contact with Hank ... through his Orand-Pall?"

Scotty inwardly cringed. He'd had multiple communication requests from his professor/teacher whom he assumed was still back on Hope. He needed to connect with him. Find out what is, or was, so damn important.

Scotty: I apologize. I will speak with Hank. There have been complications. But I'm where I need to be right now. I am at NASA headquarters in Houston, Texas. There are those in government here that want to hinder, perhaps even stop completely, our directives.

Seve: You know that was anticipated, Scotty. You must remember what is at stake. Not one person, or any group of persons, can be allowed to derail what must happen. What must be done today ... right now. I suggest you locate the person named Paul Mannford there. He is the flight director of the International Space Station program. We have determined he is sufficiently convinced regarding Earth's imminent peril.

Scotty was still half listening to the exchange going on between the man called Borkner and Alison.

"... you do realize that Earth will soon be completely annihilated ... do you understand, Secretary? That we have very little time to do what needs to be done in order for any of us to survive?" Alison pleaded.

"We need to take a little extra time now, just to verify all the facts. To make sure these aliens have our best interests at heart. You can understand that, can't you Alison?"

"How much time are you talking about?"

"Maybe a few weeks; a month or two at most," Borkner said back, stealing a glance at the screen on his constantly vibrating smart phone.

"From what I understand, countless people will possibly die with even the slightest delay."

Borkner answered her comment with a patronizing smile. "Now, now, let's not get overly dramatic. Personally, I don't believe there's any imminent danger at all. Earth has been spinning on its axis for what? Billions of years? It'll keep on spinning for several billion more, I'm sure. What I'm not going to let happen is for our world to be taken over by aliens with hidden, nefarious intentions."

Scotty turned his whole attention back to Seve.

From Scotty: Seve, I do not believe any one person, or group of persons, will make enough of a difference here...not in time. We anticipated that could be the case; we developed alternative actions for just such a scenario.

From Seve: We also determined that the results could be devastating. We never wanted to be perceived as an enemy. Not when the complete opposite is true. You must be careful, Scotty...I fear any deviation from our planned course of action could spawn disastrous consequences. Then all will be for naught.

From Scotty: I still think Humans are good at heart. It's the governments, the ones in power, who will never allow us to fulfill our directives.

From Seve: It is your decision, Scotty. Please be careful. Be mindful that after today, I probably won't be here to help you.

Scotty let that sink in. He wanted to argue with her—tell her she was wrong . . . that she would be fine. But he knew better. He also knew the agents next door would soon be sounding the alarm that one of their own had been killed. After that, all hell would break loose.

From Scotty: I understand. Here is what I need you to do for me...

chapter 52

S ome twenty-four hours had passed since NASA Flight Director Paul Mannford last received communication from the alien vessel. Within that same timespan, he'd watched personnel from other government agencies, namely, he surmised, from the NSA, take up positions within the MCC, not so much supplanting his own people, but certainly observing them—overseeing them. Now there was also a military presence. No less than ten heavily armed soldiers had assumed a position around the room's perimeter. As of early this morning, in and outgoing communications with outside support personnel had been terminated.

Mannford had been working with some of the world's greatest minds, reviewing the immense amount of alien data regarding the impending Gamma Ray strike. The team included such notables as Stuart Church from Georgia Institute of Technology, an expert on space exploration, who also had a background in Astrophysical Cosmic Microwave Cosmology. As well as Mary Moot from the Massachusetts Institute of

Technology, an expert in environmental monitoring from space, planetary exploration, and climate change impacts. And Daryl Conway, 'retired' from NASA's Jet Propulsion Laboratory, and an expert on just about anything related to outer space. Each one had reviewed the complex files that were downloaded from the alien vessel. Individually, they would take advantage of the spacial coordinates provided them. Each had unique access to the recently deployed James Webb Space Telescope. Bar none, there was no instrument better suited for the job.

Decades in the making, the successor to the Hubble Space Telescope was nothing short of miraculous. The size of a three-story home, the Webb telescope was the largest telescope ever deployed into space. It was an amazing one hundred times more powerful than the famed Hubble. The new telescope could not only see things in the far distance, but could also virtually see back in time—how long it had taken light from galaxies far away to reach Earth. This feature would allow the Webb telescope, using infrared wavelengths, to even view the first stars and galaxies formed billions of years ago—even going back to the Big Bang.

Mannford was concerned that he still hadn't heard from any of his independent experts. Hadn't heard back what their individual findings were concerning the fast-approaching Gamma Ray. He suspected that they indeed had verified the findings but maybe had been *persuaded* to keep their findings to themselves. He looked about his MCC, at the lurking agency personnel and the military presence around, and feared not only for his nation, but his own family. It all came down to one man: Borkner, an arrogant, stupid man, but one who just happened to have the president's ear. For the umpteenth time, Mannford tried to figure out what the man's end game was. What would motivate someone to ignore the immense amount of science provided?

CapCom's Margaret Haskell abruptly stood up, excitedly pointing a finger toward the wall of monitors. "You'll want to see this, Paul!"

Mannford stood up straight and stepped away from his typical position of leaning against the back wall. A hush fell over Mission Control as one-by-one the large monitors came to life on the forward wall. Until that very moment, there'd been no visuals taken of the alien craft. Seeing it now for the first time, it truly was immense, like nothing Mannford had seen before. There was nothing conventional about it. Nothing that directly correlated to what one's mental expectations were—what an alien spacecraft should look like. He was already aware of the Vallic's predisposition to utilizing some kind of living, organic technology, but this was far beyond anything his imagination could have ever conjured up. The vessel had soft curves and strange, nonsymmetrical, bulbous areas. Now, as the vessel rotated, sunlight struck a portion of the hull—the color of darkened flesh, arterial vessels could be seen pulsing with life deep within its surface.

Everyone now was up on their feet.

"We've got operational tracking sensors coming back online!" someone yelled out. A myriad of super-imposed data elements appeared on the largest monitor. Spatial coordinates, constantly updating orbital positioning matrices, plus a whole slew of other numeric calculations, were being presented in real time.

Mannford mentally calculated that the alien ship had roughly the same exterior size footprint as one of the US's big Nimitz-class aircraft carriers.

"She's descending, sir," Drake Reinhold announced from the Trajectory workstation three rows up.

* * *

Forty-five seconds after being alerted to the alien ship's visual appearance, now commencing its slow descent to the surface, Gordon Borkner barreled his way through Building 5D's east-side exit, out into the bright Houston sunlight. Buffeted by the wind, almost immediately his tie resumed its frantic attempt to escape over his shoulder. Not quite at a run, Borkner hurriedly strode in the direction of the MCC. *Shit!* He'd forgotten about the horde of network news trucks parked in a neat line outside the entrance. He considered making a U-turn, entering through the MCC's rear entrance instead, but that would take too much time. *No, things were happening now.* He'd just have to ignore them.

There was nothing inconspicuous about the new Secretary of Space Force, Gordon Borkner. Overweight, ruddy-faced, and perspiring heavily in the humid Gulf of Mexico climate, he was spotted forty yards out by a CNN assistant producer. Borkner heard the young woman's alerting voice, "I've got Borkner, coming in fast from the west!"

He saw them, en masse, making frantic preparations—camera operators and sound techs readying their equipment. News correspondents, throwing on suit jackets, with makeup personnel rushing along near their side, dabbing concealer and powder onto overly shiny faces.

"There he is!"

The stampede came toward him like the running of the bulls. All Borkner could do was trudge forward with focused determination. He was well aware that to them he was some kind of newly found celebrity, though very little of the media's attention had been positive thus far. In fact, it was *dismal.* Much of it centered on his almost meteoric rise from a mid-level, temporary, government NASA position to obtaining one of the most influential and important jobs in government—answering directly to the President of the United States. And, of course, all the recently snapped photos of him—and all the live video streams of him—only highlighted his unsightly facial skin condition. *He* was the man who habitually wore a snarky, self-righteous expression and had a *fucking* red balloon of a face.

The reporters drove toward him, their microphones positioned out in front, like a charge of bayonet-wielding soldiers storming toward the approaching enemy. Within seconds, they were all around—engulfing him.

"Are we being attacked by the aliens?"

"Secretary Borkner, what's the President's position on their arrival?"

"When are you going to bring our ISS boys back home?"

"What makes you think you're qualified to run Space Force, sir?

"What's going on with your ... um ... splotchy complexion?"

By the time Borkner reached the MCC entrance, his shirt was completely doused in sweat—his sparse hair plastered onto his pink scalp.

Glaring at the MP opening the door for him as he approached, he snarled, "You couldn't fucking clear a path for me out there?"

* * *

Paul Mannford was in the process of speaking to the on-screen Astronaut Commander Jack Landon, seated next to Fischer and Mirkin. The three looked well—relaxed, even. They appeared to be seated, with only their upper bodies framed in one of the monitors, while the other monitors covered various perspectives of the now rapidly descending spaceship.

"So, you'll be taking up a static position near the MCC, right offshore?" Mannford asked.

"That's right. Hell ... I suppose you'll be able to view the spacecraft right from there, on the rooftop of the MCC," Landon replied.

Heads turned as Gordon Borkner, followed by two MP's, entered the control center. He made an undecipherable gesture, twirling one hand over his head, shouting, "Cut that transmission. Cut that transmission, right now!"

The space center went quiet as Borkner strode toward Mannford. He looked angry. *Hell, he looked crazy.*

Four of the newly arrived men, whom Mannford assumed to be NSA government personnel, were busy setting up sturdy-looking folding tables. Next, a series of big black equipment cases were hefted up onto the table surfaces, then unlatched and swung open. Military hardened devices were powered on—dark computer screens instantly coming to life. Six blue-uniformed Air Force personnel filed in from *somewhere*, taking a position at the tables behind the complex-looking computers. Mannford, ex-military himself, had little trouble recognizing it as a Surface to Air Missile system. All this was the very latest in SAM's deployment, guidance, and control gear, the kind with the cutting-edge, laser-guidance technology.

One of the young Air Force crewmen suddenly spun around toward Borkner. "Bogey is being tracked. We have an active lock on the target. Ready to fire on your command, sir."

chapter 53

S cotty told Larry to stay with Alison. He moved through the cinderblock wall as easily as if it weren't there at all. Once out in the deserted corridor, he listened as he made his way to the next door. He heard a distant television, an excited newscaster's voice, and pictured virtually everyone in the building huddled in front of department TV's, watching the historical event unfold right before their eyes. The Vallic vessel was descending toward Earth as planned. *Good!* From this moment on, things for the Human race would never, *ever,* be the same.

Standing at the door in his Human-Vallic energetic state, Scotty reached a nearly invisible hand through the door's locking mechanism, and then used projected gravity waves—a well-practiced ability—to empower natural forces to manipulate solid matter. The internal latch retracted with an audible *Click.* Scotty opened the door then stepped inside, already transformed again into his Human physical state.

"Hi Mom! Ready to go?"

Like Alison, Brianna was seated on a metal chair in front of a metal table—both were bolted onto the floor. What Scotty didn't expect to see were the two men, garbed in business suits, seated directly across from her. Both glanced up, alarmed expressions on their faces. His mother's eyes were red-rimmed—clearly she'd been crying. Fighting his first impulse to kill the men right where they sat, he simply motioned for his mother to come with him. She stood without looking at her interrogators then walked past them and out the door. Scotty waited for one, or both of them, to reach for a weapon, but neither one did. Instead, the man on the right said, "Do what you have to do. I . . . we . . . have zero doubt about who you are and what you're here to do. Go."

Scotty nodded. "Where can I find the one called Mannford? Paul Mannford?"

"He's the NASA Flight Director here. Outside, look for the biggest building."

Scotty believed them but locked both inside the room just the same. Back in the hallway, his mother stood still waiting for him. Pulling him into a close embrace, she said, "They were not nice men. Their questions . . ."

"Well, whatever you said to them, Mom, they believed you." Brianna pulled away from him and said, "Maybe. I hope so."

"Come on, Alison's just next door." After he got the door open, Alison and Larry hurried out.

"What now?" Alison asked.

"You mean, other than changing life on Earth forever?"

Alison merely rolled her eyes at him.

"Too dramatic?"

"Yeah . . . just a tad," Alison said.

Scotty pointed toward the exit down at the far end of the hall. After three strides he glanced back, realizing Alison and his mother weren't following along behind him. "What is it?"

"What about the cop? We're just going to leave him here?" his mother asked.

Scotty instantly was reminded of the large bump, still-aching at the back of his head. "Fine. Wait here." Jogging back past both doorways, he stopped at the third door, on the other side of the corridor. Unlatching it, he nudged it partially open with his foot. Officer Donald Platt, now alone inside, was leaning his bulk against the opposite wall. It caught Scotty off guard, how surprisingly vulnerable the big cop seemed. Standing quietly, his gun holster empty, he wore an almost child-like expression—one filled with both surprise and anticipation.

"Promise me you won't hit me with your flashlight ever again."

The big man shrugged. "They took my flashlight."

Scotty waited.

"Let me come with you. Let me do this thing too, whatever it is . . ."

* * *

They made their way out of the building unaccosted. The outside parking lot was a flurry of cars speeding by, and excited pedestrians running frantically here and there. Like wildfire, news had spread fast. *The aliens were landing. Were landing right now!*

Scotty eyed the long line of network news vehicles and the multiple hordes of people. Most likely NASA employees, he figured, being interviewed by reporters. More than half of the news vans were in the process of pulling away, one after the other, out of the parking lot. They'd undoubtedly gotten the news of the alien ship's arrival nearby off the coast.

"You're going to want to stay clear of those people," Alison warned.

"Can you get me in front of one of those cameras?" he asked, instead.

Alison stopped. "Really?"

Scotty nodded. "Time to speak directly to the masses."

Brianna said, "They're not going to know you from Adam, Scotty. Getting anyone's attention will be near impossible. You're either too ordinary looking, or you become too invisible to be noticed out here."

"I have an idea at how you can grab their attention," Platt said, with a crooked smile.

Three minutes later, they strode into the media mayhem. What was noticeably different about this particular contingent was twofold: One, Scotty was invisible. Two, the large golden retriever he held in his outstretched arms was anything but invisible. As far as anyone could tell upon first seeing them, there were three people—two women and a policeman—walking together beside what appeared to be, a totally self-propelled flying dog.

It took a few moments. Although no one could actually see his expression, Scotty was smiling ear to ear.

It was one of the many camera operators who commented: "What the . . . ?"

"Look!" exclaimed another man being interviewed.

"Oh, my God . . ." exclaimed a pretty reporter, holding up an MSNBC microphone.

"This isn't possible! That just can't be real . . ." another reporter said.

"Move it! Get over there! Stop them!"

It didn't take long for the interviewing news organizations to wave away their far less interesting interviewees, and scurry over to them. Invisible Scotty, along with Larry in his arms, spun around, finding they were completely surrounded.

"Hey, how are you making that dog do that?"

"Is that some kind of trick . . . like a magic act of some sort?"

"Does the dog talk or do other tricks?"

Scotty laughed out loud, raising Larry higher up. He swooped him quickly left, then right, then high in the air again.

"Now you're just being annoying," Alison said, scolding him dryly. The contingent of reporters, jostling around them, was quickly getting out of control.

"I think I heard the dog laugh . . . did you hear that?"

"Yeah, I heard it too . . ."

Scotty said, "You need to listen to me very carefully. I am not a talking dog . . . even though it may appear that way." All eyes stayed focused on Larry.

Scotty chose that moment to transform back into a visible Human state. Now everyone there could see him, holding Larry in his arms. Putting the dog down on the ground, he stared into a camera lens, then another, and then another one. "Hello, my name is Scotty Sullivan and . . . well, I guess you can say I am an alien, of sorts . . ."

* * *

Paul Mannford watched in horror as things quickly turned from bad to worse. He tore his eyes away from the busy uniformed men—stationed at the now fully operational mobile SAM command center—and over to the now pacing back-and-forth Secretary of Space Force, Donald Borkner. He had his cell phone up to one ear, "Yes, Mr. President . . . I assure you, it is now or never . . . Yes . . . yes, sir . . . of course, sir . . . thank you Mr. President, I'll be in contact when it's done.

Even before Borkner's phone was returned to his inside jacket, Mannford was confronting him. "There is no danger here! What you're doing . . . what you are about to do here is absolute madness!" he yelled, meeting the Secretary in the mist of his back-and-forth pacing.

"Don't even think about hindering this military operation, Director," Borkner ordered, not taking his eyes off the largest display monitor. "In time, you'll understand. In time, you'll realize my expedient actions today—this quick military response—just may have saved mankind."

Mannford stared back at Borkner in amazed frustration. "Did you even look at the reports? Listen to any of our own scientists? Or listen to all the independents scientists world-wide, concerning the incoming Gamma Ray? Well, it's real! The destruction it will yield on our Solar System will be absolute."

Borkner momentarily glanced his way and smirked, before turning his attention back to the wall of monitors. He said, "That alien ship coming down from space, getting this close, that's a red line that shouldn't have been crossed. Now best you take a seat, Director, before I have you escorted out of the building."

Mannford stared at the multiple view perspectives of the enormous alien craft now hovering just above the sparkling, calm blue waters of the Gulf of Mexico.

Mannford pleaded with him one more time. "Secretary, let's open a channel to Commander Landon again. Let's get his take on things before you take any further action. Those three astronauts onboard don't know what's happening here. They have families . . . Sir, we owe it to them . . ."

Mannford's pleas ceased, hearing new orders leave Borkner's lips: "Fire . . fire everything you've got!"

Everyone within NASA's Mission Control Center went silent. Mannford then heard a collective moan escape from several of his equally shocked coworkers. No less than ten separate missiles had simultaneously been launched. White exhaust plumes trailed behind them as they rose from different, land-based, deployment trucks. The plumes rose higher and higher above the still-stationary, hovering, alien vessel.

"Come on! Do something!" someone yelled at the display—at the alien ship.

But no amazing, super high-tech anti-missile defense system had been deployed. *Not yet*. Now the collective white plumes, reaching the apex of their upward ascent, were making a slow arch, in unison, in a downward descent.

Both hands balled into fists, Mannford shook his head. "No, no, no, this isn't fucking happening," he said out loud.

The missiles hit their target all at once. A combined series of immense, white-hot explosions took place, which, a moment later, made the floor beneath their feet shake and the walls of the MCC rumble. The alien ship burst outward into great swaths of scarlet. Blood, mixed with ragged, car-sized chunks of gore, filled the sky. A full minute passed before the air had cleared enough to see the full damage that occurred. A decimated, half sunken carcass bobbing up and down on the Gulf's now-discolored sea surface.

chapter 54

One hour and ten minutes earlier...

It had been days since Commander Landon had spoken to, or even seen, the alien female, called Seve, who obviously was ailing from some kind of progressively worsening malady. Thus, their subsequent time onboard the alien ship had been spent with others—those who were Vallic-Humans. On a near- consistent basis, Landon, Fischer, and Mirkin, had been learning not only what was to come, but what was transpiring on a distant exoplanet, one called *Hope*, some six light years distance from Earth.

Glancing up, Fischer was the first to notice Seve's slow approach.

Seeing her now, in her bluish ghostly form, Landon noted she was being supported by another alien walking beside her. The three ISS crewmembers rose to their feet.

Her voice was weak. In her current Vallic form, she seemed slight—a mere whisper of energy that the slightest breeze might easily dissipate. "It is time for you to leave here. We must hurry now."

"Leave? Where are we going?" Fischer asked.

"Abandoning this craft."

The three men exchanged surprised looks.

"You're returning us to Earth?" Landon asked, sounding hopeful.

"Eventually . . . perhaps later today. But first you will be transferred to one of the other vessels." Seve motioned for her escort to let her be—let her stand on her own. Standing up, appearing somewhat taller, she studied the three Humans.

"What other vessels?" Mirkin asked.

Seve nodded to the other energetic form, standing next to her. "Show them, please."

The Vallic-Human stepped over to the nearest living bulkhead. Swiping her hand across a large section of the bulkhead, it immediately became just as blue, as ghostly transparent, as the aliens were themselves. But *something* out in space—beyond the inner confines of the ship—had captured their full attention. It took a moment for Landon to determine exactly what it was he was looking at. They were higher up, in an elevated section of the vessel, looking back toward the stern. No less than ten small objects were moving about in space. The closest one was rotating on its axis.

"It's another ship . . . like this one. But tiny," Fischer said.

"I think they're all ships," Landon said.

A burst of *something* sprayed outward from somewhere below and aft. Landon felt the slightest shudder beneath his feat. Thinking about it, he realized he'd experienced the same exact occurrence pretty much continuously in the last few hours. Another burst then occurred, but this time something other than a misty-liquid goo emerged. It was another of the tiny ship-like objects.

Landon glanced over to Seve. "This ship ... it's ..."

Fischer finished his sentence for him, "The ship's giving birth?"

"That is correct," Seve said. "Remember, there is no *manufacturing* process with Vallic technology. Once you have migrated to Hope, you will discover our technology there supplants the antiquated ... the inefficient methods you Humans are so accustomed to."

Landon watched as the tiny individual living crafts continued to grow in size, en masse, and at an astounding rate. The closest one looked almost as large as the vessel they were on now. And the other crafts weren't far behind.

"So why must we leave this ship?" Landon asked.

"This organism has fulfilled its purpose. We have other plans for it."

"Like what?" Fischer asked.

"It will be, well ... most probably, destroyed."

"I'm sorry to hear that, though I am curious. You don't seem to be upset by that prospect," Landon said.

"That is because this is merely a spacecraft. It is replaceable. Purposely, this craft doesn't possess any kind of real self-awareness. No consciousness, so to speak. There is no associative spirit, no life-force connection. We take care not to think of ships as living beings. We do not name our vessels."

The three Earthlings continued watching as a new infant spacecraft emerged from the lower aft section of the alien craft.

"That will be the last of them," Seve said. "Now we must go greet the newly arrived Human-Vallics coming in from Hope."

Landon almost missed it: Not Vallic-Humans, but Human-Vallics. And then a blindingly bright ray of light streaked across local space right before them.

"Mother of God!" Fischer exclaimed, as the three stared.

"There's something else out there," Mirkin said, pointing. He then gave a disgusted grimace. "It's another object, not a ship. Something that looks like a big bug-like thing ... more like a maggot."

"What you see out there is called a Porthwamp," Seve said. "Come, now we really must go. I will introduce you to the new arrivals, others of your own kind."

It took Seve another ten minutes, even with the help of her assistant, for them to make their way aft to the ship's version of a flight bay. The first thing Landon noticed was a brightly glowing, circular membrane along the ship's port side. A membrane not much different from others he'd noticed internal to the ship. But this one was larger, easily by a factor of one hundred. Parked within the cavernous flight bay area was a collection of what Seve had referred to as Rompers. In neat rows, they were like parked cars in designated spaces like what one would find in front of any supermarket back on Earth.

For the first time, Landon encountered the entirety of the alien crew. Seventy-five to one hundred Vallic-Humans were hurrying to board small, clear-sided, almost bubble-like, transport vessels.

Landon, Fischer, and Mirkin were guided toward the nearest of the Rompers. One by one, they stepped into the small craft. They then quickly shuffled out of the way when three Vallic-Human crewmembers boarded right behind them.

Seve did not come onboard, instead just standing outside by the clear surface of the Romper. With what seemed like an enormous amount of effort, she transformed into her physical Human state. Only then did Landon see how ravaged her body had become. Her skin was cracked and gray, and clumps of hair had fallen out. But her eyes were still bright. Surprisingly, she was smiling up at him. He had to lean closer to hear her faint words.

"You will be so very important in the coming days ... weeks ... even years. Think of this as the great adventure that it truly is. Soon it will be time for you to make *Hope* your new home." Seve swallowed hard. A tear rolled down her cheek. "Please tell Scotty I said goodbye. Tell him how proud I am of him and that ... I love him dearly. Will you do that for me, Mr. Landon?"

Landon had always hated goodbyes, and this was no different. Unable to speak, he nodded reassuringly instead. Seve took a frail step backward as the Romper began to rise into the air. She gave a gentle wave goodbye from below, and then, in a dazzling flash—a glittering kaleidoscope of colors—she was gone.

Almost inaudibly, Fischer said, "Now that's how I want to go . . . in a blaze of light and color."

The small craft, falling in behind another identical-looking Romper, passed through the membrane that separated the spaceship's flight bay from open space beyond. Landon saw a reflection of light against the sheer blackness of space. There, in the not too far distance, another ginormous living spacecraft could be seen moving closer to them.

Glancing back at the spaceship they'd so recently departed from, he saw it moving away, traveling now in the opposite direction. It then turned and began a steady descent into Earth's upper atmosphere.

chapter 55

Present day ... present time ...

Scotty looked out into the crowd of network reporters, along with their two or three-man camera crews, and found they easily topped one hundred people. He watched as they pushed and jostled for better positioning of their cameras and microphones. When he began to speak, his commentary was immediately drowned out by a barrage of yelled-out questions.

Officer Platt barreled forward—moved his bulk in front of the growing media frenzy. Raising his beefy hands high over his head, he ordered, "Quiet down! ... Just let the man speak!" Even without his sidearm or flashlight, Platt was an imposing figure. His forceful presence worked and order was restored. He eyed them angrily for good measure then returned to his previous position behind Scotty.

Scotty stole a glance over his other shoulder, toward his mother and then to Alison. Both conveyed their full support of him through their eyes. Alison shrugged and said, "Go on ... now is as good a time as any."

He started again. "My name is Scotty Sullivan ..."

Scotty spoke forty-five minutes straight. He spoke first of his abduction when only a child, some sixteen years prior; then of his time spent onboard a living, alien, space vessel where he met other children who had also been singled out and subsequently abducted. He spoke of an alien race called the Vallic—of the horrendous mistake made by them earlier when an experiment went terribly wrong. Scotty next described the fusion reaction that shattered a distant planet and associate planetary system, and the subsequent bi-directional Gamma ray that was currently causing cataclysmic destruction along their dual trajectories deep within their galaxy—the Milky Way. And that this same Gamma ray was now headed toward Earth and soon, mere months from now, our solar system— and Earth itself—would be ravaged by radiation levels high enough to turn everything in its path to dust. Scotty hesitated long enough to let that sink in.

Heated questions came fast. First, there was total disbelief. Someone used the term crackpot. Eventually he noted fearful realization, even acceptance, upon most faces. And Scotty knew the populace watching at home, or at work, was experiencing the same emotions—the same fear. He did not answer their questions, instead continued on with his story. He spoke of being placed into individual pods, along with the other abducted children, and transformed into a form of light energy prior to being shot light-years away across the cosmos toward another planetary system, to a wonderful exoplanet called Hope, a world not all that different from Earth. The crowd settled down and began to listen.

Scotty then spoke of a dangerous medical procedure called Dyad-Geneses that changed his, and would change other Human beings, genetic makeup. THis procedure was necessary to survive long term on an alien world that had higher levels of radiation, radiation levels not suitable for long-term Human habitation—but was perfectly fine for the Vallic, who were mostly comprised of *energetic* matter. He spoke of what life was presently like since he was no longer completely Human.

As Scotty spoke, he occasionally, and dramatically, altered his appearance. He thought of Tori, back on Hope, in the hospital where he'd seen her after her own Dyad-Geneses procedure. He then altered his appearance so only half his face was visible. Next, he switched things up a little, allowing only the upper half of his body to be visible. His words were important, but they needed to be believable too. That was absolutely essential. He wanted zero doubt to exist in anyone's mind that he was, in fact, an alien, as well as Human, on another level. That he was still one of them.

A youngish, mousey-looking, woman reporter asked, "Scotty, can you tell us more what it is like there on Hope?" A chorus of other, similar, questions came fast from others in the crowd—they wanted to know more specifics about the distant world.

Unconsciously, a smile formed on Scotty's lips as he thought about his second home. Suddenly, he missed being there. "Well . . . for one thing, there are two Sun-like stars called Spar and Lore, one is a red dwarf and the other is a farther away blue giant. When they cross paths in the sky, something amazing happens. An atmospheric condition. The Human-Vallics there call it a halo spectrum effect. Imagine a high-intensity rainbow of colors fanning out across the sky. It's a truly heavenly part of the day there that lasts twenty to thirty minutes, depending on the time of year." Scotty saw wonderment on their faces and kept going. "Most birds there on Hope have two sets of stubby wings as well as dual sets of tail feathers. And the birds there are far more colorful . . . imagine the bright colors of a South American macaw, present on virtually all bird classifications."

A neighborhood teenager, balancing on a skateboard, called out, "What about the oceans?"

"Well, for one thing, the oceans are warm and pristine, and the beaches are comprised mostly of geodescent gravel. With such an abundance of crystalline geo rock within the ocean seabeds, the result is a shoreline that sparkles and glimmers — some beaches are more violet, others are aquamarine blue and match the color of the surf."

Suddenly, an enormous series of explosions came from the south—from the Gulf of Mexico. It rocked the ground beneath their feet. Rising in the distant sky was a great, black and billowing, smoke cloud. Camera operators swiveled their cameras, while news correspondents excitedly spoke into their microphones, describing the dramatic scene taking place.

* * *

Several hundred yards away, deep within the concrete walls of NASA's Mission Control Center, all eyes were glued on the forward monitors. Everyone stared in shocked silence and disbelief. The repercussions from such an attack were a visual affront to the senses. Long-lasting effects of what had occurred, what was occurring now, were sure to be profound.

But Secretary of Space Force Gordon Borkner didn't see it that way. He threw an exalted punch into the air. "Yes! We got them, we got those motherfuckers!"

Flight Director Paul Mannford felt sick. He was beyond angry. He was beyond wanting to physically pummel the Secretary's fat red face for what he had ordered his men to do. Instead, he just felt nauseous. Embarrassed, too, at how badly the Human race had handled their first contact with intelligent beings from another world. But other than Borkner's outburst, no cheers were heard. There were no congratulatory pats on the back. Silence was the new norm. Even the uniformed men and women, seated in front of their mobile launch control station, looked disheartened. Mannford saw it on their faces—guilt. Guilt at taking down a clearly unarmed, massive, alien craft. It had been done violently—blasted out of the sky without so much as a *Hello, or Welcome to Earth, or Do you come in peace?* Now, all that remained was a torn-apart carcass of some sort— floating on the shallow shores of the Gulf's northernmost coast.

Suddenly two, then three, then all six forward monitors switched over to a different video feed where a live broadcast was in progress. Banners with CNN, NBC, ABC, CBS, and

FOX News indicated the network affiliations. A tall man in his mid-twenties, with sandy-colored hair, was speaking to a fairly large crowd.

Mannford didn't notice at first that half of the young man's face was gone—invisible—just not there. Then it was there, but the lower part of his body had suddenly disappeared ... though not completely. NASA's super-high definition monitors picked up a slight bluish outline showing his waist, hips and legs. Mannford listened intently to what he was saying. He quietly murmured, "Oh boy ..." as sudden realization set in. What he was witnessing was the same as, undoubtedly, what the entire world's populace was also witnessing—that of Earth's not so distant untimely fate. Listening, he heard the man speak of a distant world called Hope. But was there really any hope for mankind? He turned his attention to Borkner, who was back on his cell phone.

"Well ... I apologize, sir. Certainly not, Mr. President! I had no idea the aliens would just take it up the ass like that. No! I don't mean to make light of anything! Again, I'm sorry. Yes ... I suppose this incident could have been handled far better. I'm watching the same broadcast you are, sir. A Mr. Scotty Sullivan is on. Believable? Well, I have no idea if he's telling the truth, or not ... but he's certainly putting on a good show. I still believe we had no choice. Shooting down that alien vessel ... well ... no ... of course ... again, I'm very sorry, sir. I most certainly am the right man for the job! One minor setback ... Yes, in retrospect, perhaps we did act somewhat impulsively. I'm leaving now, sir; should be on my way to DC within the hour. Good bye, sir." "Shit! Shit! Shit!"

Mannford almost felt sorry for the man. *Almost.*

chapter 56

Scotty had patiently waited for the reporters to refocus their attention back in his direction. But now, only renewed fear and confusion stared back at him, reflected off a thousand faces. And, beyond all doubt, the same emotions were being mirrored on millions, perhaps billions, of faces watching this broadcast around the world.

Suddenly distracted, there was a tingling on his forearm— more of a highly agitated twitching of movement. Raising his palm to the awaiting crowd, Scotty gestured that he just needed a moment. He closed his eyes and made inner contact with his Orand-Pall. *Tell me . . . what is it that has you so unsettled?* He could tell the small, embedded, emotional creature—one far more a part of his physiology than not—was more than just unsettled, it was despondent. Scotty thought it might be in reaction to Hank's Orand-Pall's repeated contact requests over the last few days. He felt ashamed—not even inquiring what was so important—but this was different. Scotty had ignored Orand-Pall messages before.

...trying to make contact... need to make contact! Seve's Orand-Pall... not responding. Why is Seve's Orand-Pall not responding? Seve's Orand-Pall always responds...

Scotty was fully aware that all Orand-Palls constantly checked-up on each other. They were little busybodies; not so much directly communicating but checking to see who was in relative close proximity, and who was light-years away. They kept tabs on one another, not so different from what Human family members did. Scotty suspected his own Orand-Pall also knew exactly where Seve's Orand-Pall was at any given time. But if a host passes on, then so does their Orand-Pall. Even though he'd anticipated this moment, it still hit Scotty hard. To the point he inwardly moaned—inwardly folded. Not unlike that day, years ago, when Tori was taken so abruptly from him. Now, standing in front of this sea of concerned faces, all he wanted to do was run away—to hide and grieve. To be left alone with his memories of Seve. He pondered whether his heart might actually break in two. As his eyes filled with moisture and his throat constricted, he desperately turned to the two women behind him.

Confused, Alison hurried forward and leaned close to him. Gazing into his eyes with concern, she asked, "What is it, Scotty? What has happened?"

His voice cracked as he spoke, "I've only now learned of... the loss of a special friend. No... she was more than a friend. Can you..."

Alison squeezed his arm. Nodding, she moved in front of him. His mother then positioned herself beside her. Standing together, Alison addressed the awaiting crowd.

"Hello . . . I am FBI Special Agent Alison McGuire. I work out of the Chelsea, Massachusetts, bureau office. Next to me here, is Brianna McGuire, Scotty's mother. Over there, is Police Officer Donald Platt, stationed at the Nantucket Island police department.

"And the dog?" someone at the back of the crowd queried.

"That's Larry, who at one time was the Sullivan's family pet." Alison then turned to Brianna to provide further explanation.

Brianna, her voice quavering some, sounded far less sure of herself. "Yes . . . Larry went missing along with my son. That was sixteen years ago. One moment they were playing together on the beach down by the shore, and the next minute they were gone. I saw them again for the first time only two days ago."

A woman reporter, standing out front, yelled out, "How do you know it's him? That he really is your long lost son?"

Brianna glanced over to Scotty, then back to the reporter. "Besides the fact he has an identical birthmark to the one my little boy had on his foot, I assure you, a mother knows her son . . . no matter how many years have passed."

One of the major cable news network reporters raised a hand. "So, you're telling us the world is coming to an end? We're all going to be killed off by this approaching gamma ray? What are we supposed to do with this kind of information?"

Scotty had regained his emotional balance and he inwardly chastised himself for leaving out this last, most crucial, aspect.

He stepped forward, standing alongside Alison and his mother. "There is still time. But we need to act, and to act soon. Sure, many will not believe the end is coming. Many will not want to leave their homes here on Earth. No one will be forced to do anything they do not want to do. But for those who decide this is what they must do, we need to prepare those people . . . prepare them for what will be, in essence, a worldwide migration from planet Earth to the exoplanet Hope."

Officer Platt resumed his crowd management activities as the nearly riotous masses became unsettled—there was pushing and shoving and their excited voices became both angry and loud. Scotty had a hard time discerning new questions being asked. He envisioned what must be going on in living rooms across the world. *Did they believe him?* Perhaps not at this moment, but eventually they'd have to. Over the course of the past hour, he'd watched additional network news vans pull up into the parking lot. The crowd had tripled in size: more NASA employees, more reporters and crews, and more everyday people—some wearing shorts, two more kids balancing on skateboards, and moms supporting toddlers on hips.

Scotty waited as Officer Platt continued in his position as both bodyguard and crowd controller. Then he felt the familiar tingling and twitching within the confines of his right forearm. Inwardly, he listened as his Orand-Pall, now overwhelmed with happiness, conveyed to him several connections coming closer. Scotty smiled, even though the news was bittersweet in light of his loss of Seve.

"Look!"

"What is that?"

"God . . . it's huge!"

Scotty glanced up to see an immense spacecraft slowly descend from high above them in the sky. Alison leaned in again. "Geez, another one? That ship doesn't honestly think there's room for it to land here, does it?"

"It'll take up a position several hundred feet above us," he said.

"Is that smart? I mean, won't it just be destroyed by more missiles . . . like the first one?"

Scotty shook his head. "I don't believe so. Unfortunately, that attack was somewhat expected. Meant to be an example. A demonstration how nonthreatening, even vulnerable, the arriving Vallic fleet of ships will be. At this stage, it will be important to convey how self-defeating all acts of violence, as with the previously destroyed Vallic vessel, would be for Humanity."

It wasn't long before the Vallic spaceship eased into a hovering position several hundred feet, almost directly, overhead. Alison's words could hardly be heard above the roar of the crowd. She gestured upward, "So there are more ships like this one?"

Scotty smiled. "Yeah, at this moment they're descending all over the world."

A combination of military and news helicopters, like disturbed bees around a hive, were circling high above in the sky. Officer Platt moved, placing himself between Scotty, Alison, and Brianna, and the still growing crowd—now in the multiple hundreds. Police and military personnel, patrolling amongst them, were having little affect, neither controlling nor dissipating the masses.

Scotty's mother tapped his shoulder as she stared upward. Scotty, following her line of sight, watched as a small Romper craft emerged from the spaceship, quickly descending toward the ground. The crowd quickly scurried back out of its way. Murmurs filled the air as the odd-looking Romper craft settled onto the parking lot pavement.

"This is an unbelievable, crazy mess," Alison exclaimed, shaking her head.

A hatch door slid open on the Romper. Perhaps it was the fear of the unknown—*like the sudden appearance of three-headed aliens emerging*—or for any number of reasons, the throngs of people backed even farther away and quieted down. At this point, the police and military personnel had pretty much given up with their crowd control directives and had become a part of the crowd instead.

Scotty let out a long breath. *This is finally happening.* He took several steps into the clearing then stopped and looked back, "Mom, . . . Alison . . . you too, Donald, please come with me. There are people, friends, I want you to meet."

They did as asked and stood at his side. Scotty took in the Romper craft and wished he'd been able to arrive here this way himself. Days earlier, Projected Transport—*miserable and uncomfortable*—had been his means of energetic transit, just as it had been when he had first arrived on Hope. He preferred this more traditional means by far. He saw movement within the Romper.

The first one to jump down from the craft onto the pavement below was a tall, slim, black man. Scotty returned Ernesto's wave and smile. As if remembering where he was and what he was doing here, Ernesto turned to offer a helping hand to the next person ready to exit the craft. "Come on ... let's go, girl! People to see, things to do!"

Tiffany slapped his hand away and athletically jumped down to the pavement on her own. She looked beyond exuberant at being back on planet Earth. Her red hair, of course, was pulled back into a tight ponytail. On seeing Scotty, she ran full throttle across the clearing and into his open arms—nearly knocking him over in the process. But her cheerful laughter was short-lived. Almost immediately, he felt her shoulders shake, felt deep sobbing against his chest. A moment later Ernesto stood beside them, his arms encircled them, making it a three-way embrace. They stayed like that as the masses—both present and around the world—looked on.

Eventually, Tiffany stood upright. Regaining her composure, she sniffed then wiped her eyes and cheeks. "Is this really happening? Are we finally doing this?"

Both Tiffany and Ernesto looked over to Scotty for an answer.

"It's already started. Here, and in twenty other locations around the globe," he said.

"Is it true?" Tiffany asked, her expression one of full contempt. "They *fucking* blew-up our Vallic ship?"

Scotty nodded, almost apologetically. "It was just the one. We talked about this . . . an example was necessary."

"Do we really want to bring this kind of mentality to planet Hope? I'm tempted to just say screw them all . . ."

Scotty and Ernesto exchanged a look.

"Your parents, and you have a brother, are you going to leave them here too?" Ernesto asked. Tiffany simply shook her head.

Off to the side, Officer Platt cleared his throat. Scotty said, "I want you to meet my mother . . . and some new friends."

chapter 57

Alison watched the emotional reunion between Scotty and his newly arrived spacefaring friends. Obviously, she personally had no claim on Scotty. *Hell, I barely know the guy,* Alison reasoned. But seeing the three of them together, especially the redheaded, athletic-looking woman with *those* endless legs—she couldn't deny she did feel a little jealous. And, oddly, a bit left out. She noticed Brianna looking on too, her facial expression mixed.

Scotty said, "Ernesto, Tiffany, this is my mom." They all exchanged hugs.

"The big guy there is police officer Donald Platt. When he's not bashing me with his flashlight, I think he's actually helping us."

Platt raised his chin to both of them—the full extent of his greeting.

"And this here is Alison McGuire. She's . . ."

"I'm an FBI agent," Alison interjected, "and also a friend. I wanted to help. I still do."

Ernesto and then Tiffany shook her hand. Tiffany, holding on to it, said, "You do know Scotty is our leader, right? That much of the responsibility of what will ensue—the planet's migration to planet Hope—rests on his big shoulders?"

Alison nodded then shook her head. "No, wait, there are other ships . . . other teams like yours, right?"

"Sure . . . and they all answer to Scotty Sullivan. We all do. Over the past sixteen years there were hundreds of snotty-nosed kids just like us. We were all vying to become *the primary*. It turned out that Scotty was most suited for the position. Though I still think I would have been a far better choice," Tiffany said, leering at Scotty with a crooked smile.

"I don't disagree," Scotty said, sounding like he meant it.

Alison turned to Scotty. "So, what does that mean? The *primary?*"

"I think it's best thought of one being the liaison." He gestured to the remarkably subdued crowd looking on. "I'm the designated representative from planet Hope. More like the Human-Vallic welcome wagon guy."

Alison, glancing down, noticed Tiffany still holding her hand.

Tiffany continued, her voice just above a whisper, "All I'm saying is that nothing can come between Scotty and his mission here. The last thing he needs is some distraction. I'm sure you can understand that."

"As I said, I just want to help out any way I can," Alison said flatly. "Having someone assist, one who actually works within the government, can be an asset I assure you."

The crowd surrounding them was again on the move—shuffling now even farther backwards. Noticing that their faces were all raised toward the sky, Alison glanced up too. Two Rompers were circling downward from the spacecraft above. She then noticed Tiffany, now several paces away, seemed to be talking to herself. Not to herself, exactly, but to two others in their nearly invisible energetic forms. They must have landed in the same Romper with Ernesto and Tiffany.

As the two crafts maneuvered overhead in final descent, the crowd suddenly separated—like Moses parting the Red Sea. Only now, no less than ten armed Marines preceded the newly appointed Secretary of Space Force Gordon Borkner, as he approached. Alison briefly wondered how he would react, finding they had escaped from their respective interrogation rooms. And since he previously had no qualms at all about shooting a spaceship out of the sky—would they be dealt with in a similar manner? *Hell, maybe he'd have them shot right where they stood?*

The Marines looked formidable as they assumed positions around the clearing. Coming up now behind a disheveled, sweaty-looking Borkner, was another man in shirtsleeves. She recognized NASA Flight Director Paul Mannford.

Alison meant what she'd said to Tiffany. She truly did want to help; to be some part of all this. As the two men rapidly approached, she said, "Let me handle this," then moved ahead to greet them.

"Secretary Borkner, we meet again. Flight Director Mannford . . . I'm Special FBI Agent Alison McGuire."

Borkner's eyes were focused on Scotty. Throwing a quick glance at Alison, he looked annoyed at being deterred. "I'm in a hurry, um, Miss, so please step aside."

"I told you before, when you had me forcibly locked into that small room, that I am Special Agent Alison McGuire of the FBI. I insist you tell your men to point their weapons somewhere beside Mr. Sullivan's center mass." Alison wasn't even sure herself what she was doing now. Why she was ordering the military to adjust their aim to somewhere else. But then again, in light of what had happened to that alien spacecraft, her instincts were guiding her to make a stand. They also told her something else—where, and with whom, her loyalties now truly resided, a potentially irreversible and dangerous career move.

Her comment caught Borkner's attention. "You know who I am then. That I work directly for . . ."

"Perhaps I can be of assistance here," Flight Director Paul Mannford cut in. He then extended a hand out for Alison to shake, which she accepted. She did her best to maintain some composure, although both men were the superstars of government agencies—Mannford was the George Clooney of NASA, although certainly not in looks.

Mannford said, "It is important that we speak with Mr. Sullivan, Agent McGuire. I'm sure, in light of everything that's going on here, you can understand that."

"Sir, what I do understand, as the rest of the world now looks on, is that America's first response to a friendly alien encounter was to totally annihilate their spaceship . . . even before exchanging any real dialogue." Alison had no idea if that was actually true, but suspecting that it was, she went with it. "So, no, you will talk to me first for now. I officially request that you and Mr. Borkner have the muzzles of those M4's held by those Marines pointed elsewhere." Her eyes were on Borkner. She knew that Mannford, the flight director, had nothing to do with the Marines' presence there.

When Gordon Borkner moved closer to her, a waft of sour body odor assaulted her nostrils—the kind of BO that often results under intense stress. Bringing up a hand, perhaps to point a finger in her face, she heard four words come from someone nearby.

"Back the fuck off."

Alison wasn't sure just when Officer Pratt moved to her side. She didn't need protection from the red-faced blowhard, but she appreciated Pratt's intentions all the same.

Scotty broke the tension by speaking calmly—even friendly. "Secretary Borkner, I am glad to meet you. Do you mind if I call you Gordon?"

"Well, I would prefer—"

"And I prefer you call me Scotty. Everyone calls me Scotty. First of all, I want to enlighten you some . . . it will expedite matters immeasurably. I'm sure that's what you want too. It will dissuade attitudes of *them versus us*. Because, Gordon, I'm sure you truly believe you're simply doing your job. Keeping our citizens safe—protecting America, along with the rest of the world, from potentially dangerous alien beings. Perhaps even from an alien invasion. Am I correct in my assumption?"

Borkner glanced at the ever-growing crowd now encircling them. His eyes not focused on the myriad of citizen faces out there, but on the multiple network news camera lenses now pointed in his direction. "That's right ... that is exactly what we are doing here. Why the President of the United States and I spoke just a short while ago ..."

Scotty continued, "But that's the thing, Gordon; there is no *them*. There are no aliens here to speak of. Not really. You see we're from Earth." Scotty gestured toward Ernesto and Tiffany and, as if on cue, two other people suddenly transitioned from their energetic state into Human forms. "We're not aliens, we're all Humans. My mother is standing right over there. I was born in Massachusetts. Tiffany was born in ..."

"Castle Rock, Colorado," Tiffany offered.

Ernesto volunteered, "Thousand Oaks, California."

"The aliens, the small team that there was, have, for the most part, died off—have literally given their lives to save mankind. There are twenty other Vallic spacecraft, identical to the one above us, positioned above population centers all around the world. Soon there will be more. Manning each of those crafts are Humans, or, more accurately, Human-Vallics; beings dedicating their lives to saving Humanity. Because what is coming, coming soon to this Solar System, is total annihilation."

"He's exactly right," a distant voice said.

All eyes then turned toward the procession of six men, exiting from two recently landed Romper crafts. Alison recognized the two men out in front immediately—Astronauts Jack Landon and Greg Fischer—and she briefly wondered where

Russian cosmonaut Peter Mirkin was. It then occurred to her that he very well might be in Russia where another alien ship, like the one now stationed above them, had assumed a similar position.

The crowd gave them leeway as the astronauts strode closer. While Fischer and the others slowed as they approached, Jack Landon did not. His haymaker punch slammed into Gordon Borkner's jaw hard enough to spin the big man around, sending him off-balance to the pavement. He landed on his ass—looking dumbfounded.

Alison automatically moved to get between the two but quickly realized one punch was all Landon intended to throw. What surprised her most was the eruption of loud cheers and applause coming from the encircling crowd, which had easily increased to thousands. *When . . . how . . . did all these people arrive here?*

Commander Landon stared down at the Secretary, his hand still balled into a tight fist. "You never even asked us, never considered that I, or Greg, or Peter, might have insight into who these aliens actually were; if their intentions were, in fact, beneficial to mankind. Instead, you fired upon a spacecraft sent to our Solar System to save us. To save us all!"

Alison, surprised, watched Scotty help Borkner up onto his feet. The government official's suit coat had split in back, making him seem even more pathetic than before.

Alison glanced over at Scotty and asked, "So what now? How's this all going to work? How do you get over seven billion people off a doomed planet?"

Scotty looked back at her, into her eyes, and held her gaze for several long beats. "We don't. We can't."

Commander Landon, nodding his head, said, "He's speaking the truth. Something I learned, too, when speaking with Hank. We'll be lucky to save half the world's population, and that's if we start right now. Today . . ."

chapter 58

Scotty interrupted the astronaut, "Wait... did you say Hank? Like in Professor Hank Stiles?"

Commander Landon momentarily appeared confused, then looked off to the side—toward Tiffany. She was having a heated conversation with one of the Human-Vallic's who'd only recently become visible. Scotty's eyes went to the man's ridiculous-looking *boy bun* then into his pale blue eyes. "Hank?"

Although Hank's hair had turned completely white, the man unmistakably was his mentor, the professor. Hank briefly smiled back, nervously noting everyone's attention was focused solely on him.

Hank quickly approached, his smile replaced with a look of concern, perhaps even fear. "Scotty... I've been trying to reach you. Didn't you get my messages? Is your Orand-Pall no longer operational?"

"No... it's fine. It's me. I just haven't had time to check. What is it? What's up?"

"The Vallic were wrong. Having never gotten this far ahead in front of the gamma ray . . . their calculations . . . it's not going to hit here in sixteen months. Well, not all at one time. Sure, that's when the brunt of it will be most destructive. But it's a gradual build-up of force . . . a build-up that's already started heading our way, making its way into our Solar System . . . right now!"

Scotty stared into the old professor's eyes, seeking to find some morsel of hope there, but saw none. He spoke softly, quietly, trying to keep all signs of tension free from his voice. "Come on, Hank . . . what we are trying to do here—the migration of Earth's population to planet Hope—was already problematic. Nearly impossible, in fact."

Hank glanced at him apologetically, then turned toward the mostly well-behaved mass of onlookers. Scotty barely made out the words Hank said next.

"I fear most of the populous won't make it off Earth, Scotty. Not with what we've recently learned. It would take a miracle to save any more than a fraction of Human kind . . ."

The End

Thank you for reading Boy Gone, Book 1. *The adventure has only just begun—stay tuned for* Boy Gone, Book 2, *to be released within the next few months.*

If you enjoyed this book, PLEASE leave a review on Amazon. com—it really helps!

To be notified the moment all future books are released—please join my mailing list. I hate spam and will never, ever, share your information. Jump to this link to sign up:

http://eepurl.com/bs7M9r

acknowledgments

First and foremost, I am grateful to the fans of my writing and the ongoing support of all my books. I'd like to thank my wife, Kim. She's my rock and is a crucial, loving component of my publishing business. I'd like to thank my mother, Lura Genz, for her tireless work as my first-phase creative editor and a staunch cheerleader of my writing. I'd also like to thank Kimberly Peticolas for her detailed line editing work, and Ra Inta for his science and technical guidance. Others who provided fantastic support include Lura and James Fischer, Stuart Church, and Eric Sundius.

Made in the USA
Las Vegas, NV
13 April 2024

88608923R00207